THE SECRET

OF THE EARTH

CHARLES WILLING BEALE

ARNO PRESS
A New York Times Company
New York — 1975

828
B3662s

Reprint Edition 1974 by Arno Press Inc.

Reprinted from a copy in The Library
of the University of California, Riverside

SCIENCE FICTION
ISBN for complete set: 0-405-06270-2
See last pages of this volume for titles.

Manufactured in the United States of America

---◆---

Library of Congress Cataloging in Publication Data
Beale, Charles Willing, 1845-1932.
   The secret of the earth.

   (Science fiction)
   Reprint of the 1899 ed. published by F. T. Neely,
New York.
   I. Title. II. Series.
PZ3.B366Se6 [PS3503.E1173]   813'.4   74-15950
ISBN 0-405-06276-1

79-3551

Library of
Davidson College

SCIENCE FICTION

This is a volume in the
Arno Press collection

SCIENCE FICTION

ADVISORY EDITORS

R. Reginald

Douglas Menville

See last pages of this volume
for a complete list of titles

THE SECRET

OF THE EARTH.

BY

CHARLES WILLING BEALE.

Author of "The Ghost of Guir House."

F. TENNYSON NEELY,
PUBLISHER,
LONDON. NEW YORK.

Copyrighted, 1899,
in the
United States
and
Great Britain,
by
F. TENNYSON NEELY.

(All Rights Reserved.)

THE SECRET OF THE EARTH.

PROLOGUE.

WHEN Dirk Waaijen, master of the Voorne, was five days out from the island of Celebes, a strange thing happened. For nearly a week the Dutchman had idled along with a cargo of cocoa, jaggaree, trepang, some Manado coffee, a few bags of nutmegs and other products of the Archipelago, but without an incident worth logging; when suddenly, an odd looking cask, with mast and streamer, was seen floating in the waters ahead, and all hands became alive with excitement. A couple of burly fellows hauled the barrel upon the deck, with the expectation of a prize, but were discomfited on finding that it contained only some cotton cloth, carefully wrapped about a dirty water-stained document, written in a language which no one could understand. Even Captain Waaijen himself was unable to read a word of it, despite his wise look, and the volumes of smoke which he blew from time to time over the packet. Had he confided in me, his only English speaking passenger, I might at least have made him comprehend the importance of the paper, even if unable to render a literal translation; but the captain was surly, and took the bundle to his room. It is even possible that he was ignorant of the fact that it was written in the English language. However this may have been, I was surprised on reaching Gravenhage, the end of our voyage, to have the paper thrust into my hands by Waaijen himself, and without a word of explanation. Believing it to be merely the record of some unfortunate craft foundered in the South Sea, I laid the packet aside, not even unrolling it for weeks. When I did so, I was amazed at the contents, and immediately sought the master of the Voorne; but he had left upon another of those endless voyages, the length of which even the company was unable to decide. Assured that no claim will ever be made upon the document, and overwhelmed with the profundity of its contents, I offer it to the public, convinced that in the history of our planet, there is nothing half so astounding as the revelation it contains.

It is to be regretted that the paper cannot be given in its entirety; the omissions, indicated by asterisks, being the result of damage caused by salt water to the MS., which has made it undecipherable in those places; the total thus lost amounting to more than a hundred pages.

The following is an exact rendering of the decipherable parts of the Attlebridge papers, handed me by the captain of the Voorne.

I.

I AM to write roughly of the past—more carefully of the present. Of the past that our identity may be established by reference to certain events which many will remember, should we be lost. Of the present, for reasons that will be obvious as I proceed.

On the morning of the 16th of November, 1894, I awoke to find myself the occupant of a narrow iron bedstead, in a small, poorly furnished room. The wall paper was mildewed, and the ceiling discolored with smoke. I was unable to remember where I was, and called aloud:

"Torrence!"

A sleepy answer recalled the situation, and assured me that all was well. Torrence, who was my twin brother, occupied the mate to my bed, on the opposite side of the room. Not wishing to disturb him, I lay quietly watching the approach of dawn through a small window with Venetian blinds, crank-sided and broken. Later, I was myself aroused by a curse coming from the other bed. The curse was launched broadly against the town, and concentrated into a deeper venom as it reached its objective climax—the room. I smiled and turned over.

"Glad you're awake at last," I ventured, observing that he was looking around the place with a disgust equal to my own. It was our first experience of London. We were Americans, and had just landed. Torrence yawned and declared that he had been awake all night, despite my assurance that he had been snoring shamefully.

"I wonder when the old lady will want her pay for all this finery," he said, feeling the quality of the sheets, and looking up at the ceiling dismally. Indeed we had a right to feel blue, having but little money, and no friends, in a strange land.

"She wants it as soon as she can get it," I replied, having consulted our landlady on the subject the previous evening. "In fact, she told me on our way up the stairs last night, that she generally required her lodgings to be paid for in advance; but that as we were Americans she would not insist, although she trusted that we would be able to settle in a day or two."

"She's too trustful by a jugful. We may not be able to pay her at all!" yawned Torrence.

"Don't talk that way; you scare me!" I exclaimed.

The truth is, I was never so daring as Torrence, who resembled me only in looks, and when he alluded to our impoverished condition, and its possible consequences, I shuddered. Instinctively I glanced at the two modest trunks against the wall, and reflected that they contained the bulk of our possessions. I knew there was not enough value in both to pay our passage back to New York, when the little money we had brought with us should be spent. Moreover we had burned the bridges, and must look ahead.

We had come to England for the same reason that Englishmen sometimes go to America, to ply our crafts, and earn a living, and now that we were there, I heartily wished we were back. My eyes rested in a kind of reverie on the ends of the trunks where our names were painted in large, white letters—Torrence and Guthrie Attlebridge, respectively. Then I began to wonder if the

Attlebridges would ever distinguish themselves, and if either of us would ever carve a fortune out of the Babylon we had adopted as a home. Torrence was an inventor, while I was a writer; and strangely enough, with proclivities so widely divergent, we had managed with twin-like harmony to quarrel with our patrons, and our bread and butter simultaneously and irrevocably. Torrence decided at once to accept the rather dubious offer of an Englishman, with whom he had corresponded, to aid him in the development of his air ship, and I—well I decided to go with Torrence. Accordingly we scraped together what little cash we could, and bade farewell to Gotham. We took passage in a cattle boat, and were nearly three weeks upon the water, having reached London on the afternoon previous to the opening of this record. A search for cheap lodgings in a moderately respectable part of town, had landed us in the cheerless apartment described.

Torrence was again stretching himself, preparatory to rising; but this time his invectives were hurled against the ship that had brought us over, and the bellowing beasts that had loaded it. Not heeding my brother's unhappy reminiscences of the Galtic, and being anxious for the future, I inquired how much money he had left. His answer was not cheering.

"About twenty pounds in those white paper things; three of those little gold pieces, and a couple of dollars' worth of silver. That is from my recollection of last night; but I must get up and count it."

We jumped out of bed at the same instant, and began emptying our pockets. We were not expert in estimating English money, but concluded that we had a little over two hundred dollars between us, and that being in a strange land, with no positive assurance of work, it behooved us to be up and stirring. We determined to part with nothing we could help until one or the other of us had found employment. At Torry's suggestion I had requested our landlady to remit her usual rule of advance payment, but reflection now made us doubt the wisdom of such a course.

"She may think we have less than we really have," I remarked.

"How much time did you say she would give us?" asked Torrence in reply.

I saw that he was anxious, and when my brother was anxious, I was generally more so. In fact, although twins, I had always leaned upon him, due, I suppose, to a tacit acknowledgment of his superior powers, and the fellow had powers superior to most men. Answering his question, I said:

"She didn't mention any particular day, but only remarked that gentlemen usually paid in advance, but that as we were Americans——"

"I see, as we were not gentlemen, but Americans, she'd wait till she got it. What do you think under the circumstances we'd better do? Remember that a couple of hundred dollars for two men to live upon until they find work in a city like this, isn't exactly wealth. Remember also the saying about a fool and his money. Now what shall we do about the landlady?"

"Pay her," I said without hesitation.

"But when?"

"Now! Give her a couple of weeks in advance, and then if we want a couple more on credit, it will be easier to get it."

We decided that Torrence should take what funds we had, and in his off-hand, plausible manner, make the payment agreed upon. He had a wonderful way of impressing people with the idea that money was of no importance to him. When the settlement was made, I was glad he had done it, it being evident that Mrs. Twiteham was impressed. I make a note of these trivial circumstances to show our actual condition, as well as for future reference should it ever be needed.

This little transaction disposed of, we sauntered out into the street to look after breakfast, which we found in a neighboring restaurant. The voyage had sharpened our appetites, and we ate a dollar's worth of food in an alarmingly short space of time, an extravagance we agreed should not be repeated. After breakfast, however, we felt that having started the day so liberally, it would hardly be fair to "clip off the corners of a square meal," as Torry declared, by slighting its proper ending, and so we bought a couple of large cigars, and then climbed on top of one of those great omnibuses with three horses, to seek our fortunes.

It is singular how indifferent men will sometimes be to expenses with the narrowest margin separating them from starvation, and yet how parsimonious they often become with untold wealth at their disposal; and in each instance their better judgment will condemn the course pursued.

My brother's air ship had been for years upon the verge of success. A fortune had been already spent upon it, and his friends had grown distrustful. It was always a trifle that was needed to perfect the mechanism, which was doubtless a triumph of inventive genius. It is not my purpose to describe the machine, in fact it would be impossible for me to do so, being neither a mechanic nor a scientist, but I will simply say that it was built of aluminum; shaped like an exaggerated cartridge sharpened at both ends and supported in the air by the application of an extraordinary discovery which neutralized the attraction of gravitation, and propelled by a horizontal screw beneath, which could be made to revolve at such enormous speed that the effect of the most violent hurricane was practically inoperative. As yet, only models had been made of the machine, the design being too intricate and costly to admit of a full sized apparatus until every detail had been mastered; but his last model had flown, and come so near perfection, that an English gentleman had written to him about it, offering assistance under certain conditions. This offer might never have been considered, were it not for the disaffection of his patrons about that time, but as it was, we left America at once.

The business firm that we were seeking was that of Wetherbee & Hart, No. 3 Kirby Street. As the omnibus carried us through the crowded thoroughfares, it was plain that Torrence was growing uneasy. Things had looked promising in the distance, but as the time approached for an interview, we began to realize the consequences of a failure to elicit Wetherbee's interest. Should he refuse to aid us we could see nothing but the poorhouse ahead.

On leaving the 'bus, we had a short distance to walk, and it is safe to say that we were lost in less than five minutes. The multiplicity of ways and their labyrinthic character, was confusing to our rectangular conception of a town, and after a number of fruitless efforts we found ourselves back at the corner from which we had started. But perseverance finally conquered, and we stood facing a doorplate which read: "Wetherbee & Hart, Inventors and Solicitors of Patents." At that moment I was so oppressed by the thought of the pending interview that I wished we were lost again.

Walking up a narrow flight of stairs, we stood before a glass door with a blue paper shade screening the interior. There was no mistake; we were there at last, for the firm's name was painted in sprawling letters over the panel. The outward appearance was not indicative of wealth, and our hearts sank. There was an old-fashioned bell pull, in the absence of electricity, and I rang. A boy came to the door with many brass buttons sewed on to a dirty coat, and Torrence inquired if Mr. Wetherbee was in.

"No, sir, but Mr. Hart is here," answered the boy.

It was a disappointment, no letters having ever passed between my brother and the gentleman named. We decided to go in, however, and having given our cards to the boy, passed in to an ante-room.

The place was scant of furniture, and had a poverty-stricken look. Two large tables were covered with models, while the walls were whitewashed and hung with mechanical drawings. As there were no chairs, we stood, and as we had not finished our cigars, continued to smoke. The sound of a deep, pompous voice proceeded from an inner chamber, presumably the sanctum of the proprietors. Presently the owner of the voice entered. He was a man with bushy eyebrows and a square chin.

"Well, gentlemen, what can I do for you?" he asked magnificently.

We were so taken aback that neither of us knew exactly what he could do. I believe Torry thought of asking him if he could turn a handspring in a half-bushel measure, a feat he had once seen performed at a circus, but something in my manner must have stopped him. I waited for Torrence to answer respectfully, the man evidently being accustomed to inspire not only respect but awe. My brother, however, took his time, and after a couple of pulls on his cigar, he said, without moving from the place where he stood:

"Mr. Hart, I presume!"

"Yes, I am Mr. Hart. Do you wish to see me?"

"Well, rather!" answered Torrence. "I've come all the way from America to see you; or I should say your partner, Mr. Wetherbee."

Hart coughed, and waved his hand a couple of times at an imaginary cloud of smoke.

"I must ask you to stop smoking. It is contrary to our rules," he observed querulously.

"Certainly!" answered Torrence, throwing his cigar stump upon the tiled floor and stepping on it. There was no receptacle provided for such things, and the floor looking as dirty as the street, I followed his example.

Hart called for the buttons, and directed him to pick up the stumps and throw them in the grate in the next room. The boy did as he was bid, and passed back into the sanctum.

"It was a matter of business," I began, observing that things looked squally, and dreading the consequences of an unfavorable impression at the very beginning of our interview. "It was in relation to my brother's air ship that we came, and——"

"And what, pray, do you mean by an air ship?" demanded Hart, with a look of supercilious superiority that was more exasperating than withering.

"I supposed you must have heard of it," I ventured to observe.

"Heard of an air ship! The idea is preposterous!" he exclaimed.

"And yet," said Torrence, "I have one, which your partner, Mr. Wetherbee, is anxious to investigate, and perhaps to purchase, as I have been led to believe."

"That is impossible!" cried Hart, holding his chin higher, and adding to his general offensiveness. "Wetherbee is a man of sense—and—the thing is absurd!"

He turned half around on his heel as if about to leave us, but my brother's quiet, well-possessed manner deterred him.

"I beg your pardon. I have Mr. Wetherbee's letters, which are sufficient evidence. We need capital to put the scheme into practical shape, and give it commercial value, and I have come to London to seek it."

"The old story. The one desideratum with you fellows always. You have nothing to risk yourselves, and everything to gain. If you can delude some fool into pushing your crazy schemes you are satisfied. But this, of all the absurdities, is the most preposterous—the most utter——"

"And has Mr. Wetherbee never spoken to you of my invention?" demanded Torrence, growing pale.

"Never! nor is he likely to do so. Mr. Wetherbee is a sensible and practical man."

"Perhaps it may have been his good sense and practicability that led him to take so much interest in my patent, and I can only express surprise that he has never mentioned it to you. But I do not wish to intrude, Mr. Hart, and as you are doubtless a busy man, I am merely going to ask you to tell me where I can find your partner, my business being with him."

"Mr. Wetherbee has neither the time nor the inclination to talk about such balderdash as you propose, and as my time is valuable, I must bid you good-morning."

"Stop!" cried Torrence, as the man was about to go, "when I came here I expected to find a gentleman, but now acknowledge my mistake, and yet I am going to honor you with a bet, if you have the nerve to take it, which I doubt; but I now and here offer to wager you a thousand pounds against a hundred that I will carry you to Paris in my air ship within a month!"

It was an absurd boast considering we had not fifty pounds in the world, and that the ship was not built, and that we depended on Wetherbee & Hart for the money to build it. But the speech had its effect, for Hart relaxed a trifle from his haughty bearing, and said, with a manner approaching civility:

"No, gentlemen, you will never carry me in your air ship anywhere, nor will I bet with you; but if you are determined to find Mr. Wetherbee, his address is The Bungalow, Gravesend. He seldom comes to this office, and you can reach him by either boat or train."

Torrence took down the address and we bid Hart good-morning; thoroughly disappointed, but rather pleased that the interview had not terminated in a fight.

In the street I observed that my brother looked more anxious than I had yet seen him. What was to become of us if we failed to interest Wetherbee?

II.

The Bungalow was a quaint, old-fashioned place in neither town nor country. The house stood in a garden, and beyond the garden were some fields belonging to the premises; and in the distance scattered groups of buildings like an abortive effort to start a village. There was a barn in one of the fields, and from the look of his surroundings, we should have said that Mr. Wetherbee had been a farmer whose domain had been encroached upon by the vanguard of suburban residences.

We went through an iron gate with the words "The Bungalow" blocked in brass letters between the bars, and walked down a cemented path bordered with boxwood, to a green door opening directly into the house. There was no porch, and the entrance was only a step above the path. We were shown into a musty parlor, which felt damp and cold, although a small fire was burning in the grate. The windows were low and opened upon the garden, but the trees were bare and the flowers dead. There were pictures on the walls, and jars upon the tables and mantel, where bunches of withered grasses were displayed as relics of the summer. The carpet and furniture were old and faded. It did not look like the abode of wealth, and we saw no ground for hope. Observing the dejected look on Torry's face, I tried to comfort him with the reflection that some of the wealthiest of the English live with the least ostentation.

"I know it," he answered looking up. "The man may be worth a million, but I doubt it."

There was a cough in the hall, and the sound of some one approaching with a walking stick. In a minute the door was opened, and an old man bent nearly double, and supporting himself with a cane, entered the room.

"Two of you! I didn't expect to see but one," he muttered, hobbling across the carpet without further salute, and then, as he hooked the handle of his stick into the leg of a chair, and pulled it up to the fire for himself, added:

"Have seats."

"My brother came with me, as we have always lived together," said Torrence, by way of explanation, "although I only sent my individual card, as it is you and I who have corresponded. I hope we find you well, Mr. Wetherbee, and that this damp weather doesn't disagree with you."

Wetherbee grunted, and poked the fire.

"Nothing disagrees with me," he said after a minute. "I've been hardened to this climate for eighty years. It has done its best to kill me, and failed." Then with a grim smile, he added:

"My figure isn't quite as good as it used to be; but I'm not vain, Mr. Attlebridge; I'm not vain."

"I suppose you've been a sufferer from rheumatism?" I suggested, by way of talk.

Evidently he did not hear me, as he was raking cinders from the bottom of the grate. When he had finished, he said:

"Did you come over from America in your air ship?"

Torrence laughed.

"Not this time, Mr. Wetherbee, but I expect to go back in it," he answered.

"Great confidence! Great confidence!" exclaimed Wetherbee; "Well, I'm glad of it; nothing is ever accomplished without it."

The old man leaned his head upon his hands, while his elbows rested on his knees. It was impossible for him to sit upright. His hair was white, and his face wrinkled; he looked his age. Certainly he was a different person from what Torrence had expected.

"I suppose you have brought a model with you," continued Wetherbee; "you Yankees are so handy with such things." This was evidently intended as a compliment.

"No," said Torrence, "I did not suppose it was necessary. The transportation would have been costly, and I knew that if you insisted, it could be shipped after me. My last effort was deficient in some minor details, which would have necessitated a thorough overhauling of the parts, with readjustment. My position now is that of absolute mastery of the subject, and I thought, with your assistance, that I might build a full-sized vessel at once. There is no longer any need to waste money on models, as the next machine will fly, full size."

Mr. Wetherbee lifted his head a little.

"How can you be sure of it?" he asked.

"Because my last model did," answered Torrence.

"And yet you admit there was an error."

"There was a slight error of calculation, which impaired the power I hoped to evolve; but I know where the mistake lay and can remedy it. All my plans and formulas are with me. There is no vital principle at stake. The thing is assured beyond a doubt."

"And what would be the size of the vessel you propose to build?" asked Wetherbee.

"My idea is to construct a ship for practical aerial navigation, capable of carrying half a dozen passengers, with their luggage. Such a vessel would be about sixty feet long, with ten feet beam; while her greatest depth would be about eleven feet."

"And how long a time would it take to construct such a craft?"

"With everything at our hand, and all necessary funds forthcoming, I should say it would require about six weeks."

The old man's figure was growing wonderfully erect. His eyes shone with vivid intensity. I could see that my brother was making an impression, and hoped for a successful turn in affairs.

"And what did you say would be the probable cost of such a machine?" inquired Wetherbee, his back still unrelaxed.

"I did not say," answered Torrence; "but from the best of my knowledge—provided labor and material are no dearer over here than at home—I should estimate that the thing could be turned out ready for service, at an expense of—say, twenty thousand dollars."

Wetherbee's eyes were fixed intently upon the fire. He looked even more interested than our most sanguine expectations could have pictured.

"That is—let me see!" he muttered.

"About four thousand pounds," I answered.

"And you will guarantee the result?"

"Mr. Wetherbee," said Torrence, drawing his chair a little nearer the invalid's, "I have not the means to make a legal guaranty; but this much I will say—so absolutely certain am I of success, that I will expend the few pounds I have with me, in a working model, provided I have your promise, in the event of my demonstrating satisfactorily the principle, to place the necessary means at my disposal for building and equipping a ship of the dimensions named. But let me repeat my assurance that such a model would be a waste of time and money. I have a large batch of evidence to prove all that I say."

Here Wetherbee left his chair and hobbled about the room without his cane. He seemed to have forgotten it. Suddenly he stopped, and supporting himself by the table, while he trembled visibly, said:

"What if it should fail?"

"Why, in that event I should be the only loser!" answered Torrence. "But it *cannot fail.* I have not the slightest fear of it."

The old man's excitement was contageous. Here at last was an outcome for our difficulties; a balm for every disappointment. I pictured the airship soaring over land and sea, the wonder of the age, and my brother eulogized as the genius of the century. I could hear his name upon the lips of future generations, and I imagined the skies already filled with glittering fleets from horizon to horizon. Beyond all this I saw untold wealth, and a new era of prosperity for all men. My flight of imagination was interrupted by a long drawn sigh from Wetherbee, as he murmured:

"Four thousand pounds! Ah! if I could only get it!"

The dream of bliss was cut short by a rude awakening. I was dismayed. What did the man mean?

"If I could only get it!" he repeated with a sigh which seemed to come from the bottom of his soul. Then he hobbled back to the fire and resumed his seat. I watched Torrence, from whose face all joy had fled. He was more solemn than ever before.

Again Wetherbee stared into the coals. He had forgotten his surroundings. Neither Torrence nor I spoke, in the hope that he was considering the best manner of raising the money. The silence was ominous. A clock in a corner was forever ticking out the words—"*Four—thous—and—pounds.*" I listened until it sounded as if gifted with human intelligence. Each minute was like an hour while waiting for our host to speak, feeling that our doom hung irrevocably upon his words. Suddenly we were startled by a sharp voice in the hall:

"*Mr. Wetherbee, your soup is ready!*"

The old man pulled himself together, as if aroused from a dream; picked up his cane and tottered toward the door. At its portal he stopped, and turning half around, said:

"Gentlemen, I will consider your proposition, and if I can see my way to the investment—well, I have your address—and will communicate with you. Meanwhile there is a barn in one of my fields, which is sound and roomy. It is at your disposal, and I heartily hope you will be able to raise the money for your enterprise. The barn you shall have at a nominal rent, and you will find the swamps about here to be the best locality anywhere near London for your experiments. I wish you well. Should you conclude to use the barn, let me know, and I will turn the key over to you immediately. Meanwhile I wish you luck!"

He went out without another word, leaving us alone with the talkative clock, and the dead grasses of the previous summer. I glanced at Torrence, who was pale, but with an indomitable look of courage in his eyes. I had seen it before

It was impossible to say from Wetherbee's manner of departure, whether he intended to return or not. We could scarcely consider the interview ended, when we had made no movement toward going ourselves, and while deliberating what was best to do, there was a light step in the hall, and the door again opened, admitting a middle aged woman who approached us with a frown. We bowed.

"May I inquire the nature of your errand?" she began, without addressing either one of us in particular; but Torrence, stepping forward, answered:

"Our visit is hardly in the way of an errand, madam. We are here upon an important business engagement with Mr. Wetherbee, who I trust will soon return to give us an opportunity to continue our conversation."

"I was afraid so!" she replied with a look of regret. She sat down in the same chair that Wetherbee had occupied, and asked us to resume our seats. There was something odd in her manner, which betrayed deep concern in our visit. Putting her hand in her pocket she drew out a spectacle case, and placed the glasses upon her nose. Then she looked at us each in turn with growing interest.

"You need not conceal your business from me, gentlemen," she continued, "Mr Wetherbee is my father. As you are aware, he is a very old man, and I am acting in the double capacity of nurse and guardian for him. He does nothing without my knowledge."

Her manner was thoroughly earnest, and the expression of her face that of deep concern. Torrence replied after a moment's hestitation as follows:

"While not for a moment doubting your statement, madam, would it not be a little more regular to ask Mr. Wetherbee's consent before speaking of a matter in which he is equally interested with ourselves? If he says so, I shall be more than willing to explain to you all that we have been talking about. Meanwhile I can only say that our business was upon a matter of great importance, which I should hardly feel at liberty to divulge without the agreement of all parties concerned."

She did not answer for several minutes, during which time the hard look in her eyes softened; I even thought they were dimmed with tears. For a moment she averted her face and taking off her glasses polished them thoroughly, returning them to her pocket. Then she stared into the fire as if thinking how to proceed, and then without removing her eyes, said:

"I shall not ask your business, gentlemen, but I will tell you something of mine. Mr. Wetherbee, my father, is, I am pained to confess, a monomaniac on the subject of inventions. His fortune, which once was ample, has been squandered in all manner of mechanical foolery, for I can call it by no other name. An inventor who could once gain his eye through the medium of print, or his ear, through that of speech, could wring whatever money out of him he chose. Finding that our means were becoming scattered, and our credit going, and my good father unable to see that he was imposed upon, I applied to the courts for his guardianship, on the ground of mental disability. He has no money whatever that he can call his own; the little that is left between us being at my disposal. Should you have plans requiring pecuniary aid, I must tell you frankly now, that it will be impossible to obtain it here."

She stopped, and Torrence and I stared at each other aghast.

"But, madam!" I exclaimed, unable to contain myself, "We have come all the way from America, and at great personal inconvenience and expense, in response to your father's letters, and should he refuse to aid us now we are ruined."

"It is impossible—quite impossible, I assure you, my dear sirs, to keep track of my father's correspondence. He answers everything he finds in the papers relating to patents. It is unfortunate, deeply unfortunate, but cannot be helped. The public has repeatedly been warned against him through the newspapers, and we can do no more."

"It is indeed most unfortunate," said Torrence; "but let me ask you, madam, if in the event of my being able to demonstrate, to your entire satisfaction, the inestimable value of my air ship, you could be induced to aid in its construction?"

"Alas, my dear sir, I have not the means!"

There was a painful silence, in which, to me, the end of all things was in sight. Mentally I ran over the account of our cash, and roughly estimated how long it would last. Much as we had abused Mrs. Twitcham's lodging, I foresaw that we should have to leave it for a worse one.

"Is there, then, nothing that could induce you to take an interest in our scheme? Remember it is the invention of the century. All the railways, all the telegraphs in existence will be counted trifling by comparison when it shall be built and given commercial value. Remember also, that the insignificant sum required, will be repaid ten times over within sixty days. Remember, my dear madam, that in refusing to aid us, you are throwing away the greatest material blessing that man can possibly acquire. It is the dream of the ages—the culmination of every hope. Think well before you refuse!"

I was so wrought up that I spoke more earnestly than ever before, realizing that if we failed with Wetherbee & Hart, we were outcasts. But all my enthusiasm, and all my brother's eloquence were futile.

"It is not that I *will not*, it is that *I cannot*," repeated the lady, who really did not appear lacking in sympathy, or a due comprehension of the situation.

"Then have you no friends," I persisted, "who might be induced to take a share in the invention, I should say discovery, for it is indeed more of a discovery than otherwise?"

"Most of our friends have already lost money through my father's infatuation, or weakness, and I dare not mention the subject to any of them."

We got up to go, thanking the lady for her explanation, and the interest she had shown. At the door, Torrence stopped.

"I was about to forget," he said; "your father told us of a barn which he would place at our disposal, should we need it for a workshop. Is the offer still open?"

The lady smiled, and said she could not refuse so simple a thing, especially when we had come so far, and had a right to expect so much. We thanked her, bade her farewell and departed.

We passed again down the cemented path between the boxwood bushes, and through the iron gate. When out once more upon the open highway, Torrence turned toward me, and with an air of surprising indifference, said:

"It looks as though we were checkmated, old man, but we're not. These people have only stirred up the mettle in me, and I shall build the air ship despite all of them."

As I have said before, my brother was an extraordinary man; possessed of a fertile mind, an indomitable will, and withal a secretiveness which even showed itself occasionally to me. We walked on in silence; the future looked black and disheartening, I had not the courage to discuss it. It was dark when we reached the river, and the small Thames boat wended its way through innumerable lights, reflected across the water in long, trembling lines. The minutest object claimed my attention, and I fell to speculating on the mental condition of a fellow-passenger who was whistling a familiar tune at my elbow. I looked over the taffrail into the black water beneath, and wondered how it felt to drown, and how many people had tried it in these waters. I pictured their corpses still lying at the bottom, and made a rough calculation of how many years it would take to disintegrate a man's skeleton, after the fishes had eaten all the flesh off his bones. Then in the dim light I saw Torrence walking past the man who held the tiller. He did not speak, and I did not disturb him. Possibly he did not see me, at all events we walked on opposite sides of the deck, each absorbed in his own thoughts. At last we met, as if by accident, although I had purposely wandered over to his side.

"Well, old man! What's the matter?" he cried with a heartiness that startled me.

"Nothing," I answered; "I was only going to ask why you made that inquiry about the barn."

"Because I thought it might be useful," he answered.

"And for what, pray?"

"Why, to build the air ship in, to be sure. Did you think I wanted it for a billiard room?"

"And how can you build the air ship without Wetherbee & Hart?" I inquired.

"I am not quite prepared to answer your question. But I have overcome difficulties before, and I shall overcome this one. Don't fret, Gurt! the air ship will be built."

His manner was confident, and showed such indifference to the gravity of our situation, that I looked at him in amazement. There was nothing more to say, and we wandered apart again.

Once more I began an exhaustive study of my surroundings—the river—the lights—the boat itself, and finally of my fellow-passengers. Thus occupied I allowed several landings to pass unheeded, when suddenly I became interested in a low but animated conversation between two men who were opposite me, the one standing, the other sitting. It was nearly dark in that part of the deck where we were, but presently the man who was sitting, shifted his position slightly to make room for the other, when they both came in range of a dimly burning lantern, and I was surprised to see that one of the men was my brother. The stranger was a rough, dirty looking sailor, and the pair, as I say, were deeply absorbed in conversation, in which they had evidently been engaged for some time.

"Yes, stranger," said the sailor, "you may believe me or not as you please, but I have proof enough of what I tell you; and three times I've been locked up with lunatics for stickin' to the truth, and not lyin'."

"And you say you can prove this?" inquired my brother in a low tone.

"Ay, and *will do it!*"

"It is too marvelous. You astound me! I cannot comprehend it!" said Torrence in a voice that was scarcely audible, and which I observed was purposely subdued.

"And indeed you may well be all o' that, an' more too. I was good crazy for a spell when I first found it out, leastways I was nigh it, but I don't talk about it no more since they locked me up, but when I heerd you fellers a gassin' about a air ship, I 'lowed you was the kind, if ever there was any, as it wouldn't hurt to tell. For my part, it don't matter—I can't live long no way—and I hate to have *that secret* die with me. I'm a stoppin' down the river on the Kangaroo, she's a boat as is fitted up as a 'orspital for crippled seamen and the like. I'm tullable comfortable thar, and doubt as I'll ever anchor to any other craft for a home this side o' Davy Jones'."

"But surely you'll let me see you again," said Torrence, as the man made a move to leave the boat at the landing we were approaching.

"Course'n I will. I won't forgit ye," tapping his breast as if referring to a memorandum which I supposed Torrence had given him. "And I'll keep my word, too, and prove every breath I've done breathed to you to-night. Ta-ta!"

The man left the boat hurriedly, and the next landing was our own.

III.

It was snowing, and the ground was already white when we reached our humble lodgings. All the way from Gravesend I had been struck with my brother's capricious manner, at one moment buoyant, the next meditative and despondent. Upon my inquiring after the singular acquaintance he had made upon the boat, he simply laughed, and said, "*crank*," entirely ignoring the scraps of conversation I had overheard between them. This being his mood, I decided to let him alone, feeling sure that if there were anything worth hearing, I should hear it.

We made a hasty inspection of our property, to take care that nothing was disturbed in our absence, and then, with renewed confidence in the landlady, walked again into the storm in search of food. We had eaten nothing since early morning, and were nearly famished. Our restaurant was not hard to find, and the light and warmth within cheered even my dismal soul into hopefulness.

Seating ourselves in an alcove by an appetizing table, Torrence pushed the bill of fare toward me, but I begged him to choose the dinner himself, and to select the cheapest and bulkiest dishes.

"Rubbish!" he answered; "I'm hungry and am going to have another square feed. If we are to go to the devil, what difference can it possibly make whether we get there on Monday or Saturday?"

I could never argue with Torrence; he had his own way in everything, and yet we never quarreled.

An elaborate meal was placed before us, with a large jug of beer; the dinner costing more than the breakfast.

"I don't know how it is," said Torrence in the midst of a huge chop, "but something tells me that I was never born to be starved!"

After dinner we lighted cigars, and continued to sit smoking over our coffee, having drawn the curtains of our alcove. We had been puffing away for some minutes when Torrence, putting his hand in his pocket drew out the money I had given him in the morning, together with his own, and placing the pile upon the table, said:

"Now listen! We will divide this money into two equal parts, and each take our part. There is no telling what may become of us, and it is better to seek our fortunes separately than together. If we travel the same path, we will meet the some difficulties, but if we divide, there will be double the chance for luck, and whoever hits it first can help the other. It will cost no more than to live under the same roof, with the exception of having paid in advance for our beds, but other considerations will more than compensate for that loss, which may not be a loss after all. We may see a very tough time before we get through, but we will get through in the end, never fear. Now don't starve yourself, old man, and don't get down in the mouth, but dig—dig—dig. Push your manuscript—push a hand car—jump into anything you see, but don't be discouraged, and above all things, write regularly and keep me posted."

My heart was in my mouth, for I could not bear the thought of leaving Torrence. He had been the leading spirit in everything, and from my early childhood I had always believed that what Torrence could not do, could not be done. I had brought some manuscripts with me for which I hoped to find a publisher, but now the thought of it was abhorrent. I could not answer, and so Torrence continued:

"To-morrow morning, after breakfast, I shall leave you. Don't ask what I am going to do, because I don't know; but I am off in search of luck, and shall rely largely on my Yankee brains to bring me out on top of the game. Don't expect me 'till you see me, but I shall either write or return when there is anything to tell."

"Are you going back to Gravesend?" I asked.

"Probably; but don't hamper me with questions. In the first place it won't help you to know what I am doing; and in the second place, it won't help me to have you know. You can picture me as building the air ship, or running a haberdashery, or anything you please; but remember that whenever I run my nose up against luck you'll be sure to know it ; and I only ask that you will do the same by me."

I gave him my hand, and then we ordered two portions of brandy and a bottle of Apollinaris.

While we were disposing of this, and still smoking our cigars, the *portières* of our alcove were pulled suddenly apart, and a rough, unshaved face thrust in at the aperture, and as quickly withdrawn. Although it was for only an instant, I recognized the face as that of the sailor I had seen on the Thames boat. Torrence frowned, but did not look surprised.

When we got up to go, Torrence insisted on paying the bill out of his portion, which he did; and then, just as we were about to pass out into the stormy street, the same rough, dirty looking sailor approached us from one of the alcoves.

"Another word with you, stranger," said the man, advancing and touching his hat to Torrence.

THE SECRET OF THE EARTH. 31

"Certainly," as if he had never seen the fellow before, and then turning to me, Torrence added:

"Would you mind waiting a minute, Gurt, while I speak to this man?" and without another word, the twain entered one of the alcoves. I amused myself looking at some fish in an aquarium that stood near the entrance, and in watching the great flakes of snow falling against the glass panel of the door. How long I remained thus occupied is difficult to guess, but it seemed interminable. The sailor had taken the precaution to draw the curtains after him, so it was impossible to hear anything they said, and even the sound of their voices was drowned by the clatter of dishes, the tramping of waiters, and the noise of arriving and departing guests. At last the interview was ended, and my brother came out with rather a singular expression, as I thought, and we started for home.

"And what does he want?" I asked as we trudged along the sidewalk.

Torrence laughed; and then, as if thinking of how to reply, said:

"Oh, he's a lunatic! Wants the loan of twenty pounds on a house and lot he says he owns down in Deptford. Sailors are generally cranky, you know, and I thought I would talk with him a little just to get his ideas, and see if it would be worth our while to risk the venture, with the possibility of becoming the owner of his property. But I'm convinced the fellow's a fraud."

"If he's a lunatic I think you must be a greater one!" I exclaimed, and then feeling sure that he was putting me off with nonsense to avoid questioning, I turned the subject, and commenced talking about the weather. We did not allude to the sailor again, and I concluded that Torrence had simply run across some poor fellow who he thought might be useful to him, although how, I could not imagine.

The next morning we separated, and I waved Torrence a farewell as he took his seat on an omnibus, with Gladstone bag and umbrella. I stood watching him until the 'bus had turned a corner, and then directed my steps toward Paternoster row, with a bundle of MSS. under my arm.

I do not propose to harrow myself with a recital of the bitter disappointments I underwent in that quarter of the city, nor is it important for the identification of the Attlebridges as the real participants in the marvels about to be recounted, that I should do more than allude to the fact that the firm of Crumb & Crumpet, after much haggling as to terms, long and tedious discussion regarding merit and character, finally refused my book, as well as all shorter papers submitted to them; a fact which those gentlemen will doubtless remember, should their attention be called to it.

Our lodgings were dreary enough at best, but now that I was alone they seemed unbearable. Beyond my own gloomy feelings, I was made to participate in those of my landlady, who constantly annoyed me with accounts of her financial difficulties; her inability to pay her rent, and the dread that she would be evicted. Greatly against my better judgment, she succeeded in coaxing me into the loan of a pound, a thing I could not afford, but which I did, partly out of sympathy, and partly to get rid of her importunities.

I now occupied myself in preparing a paper on the psychological evolution of the ape, which I hoped to be able to place with another publisher, and which, had it ever been finished, I cannot doubt would have succeeded; but circumstances intervened before the completion of the last pages, which compelled me to relinquish my work, and so the world must suffer. I continued my labor steadily for more than a week, and then began looking anxiously for my brother's return, and took several long walks in the direction from which I believed he would be coming; but I did not meet him, and returned home, each time a little disheartened. During these evenings I retired early, having no one for company, and not being able to afford outside amusement. At the end of ten days I had been so economical that I was quite satisfied with the standing of my finances, and felt lighter-hearted than at any time since arriving. Still I had found nothing to do but write, and the future was uncertain.

Sunday morning was dark and gloomy, and it having been nearly two weeks since Torrence had left, I began to wonder with increased anxiety what had become of him. I had a right to expect him by now, but had neither seen nor heard a word from him since his departure. Could anything have happened? I did not believe it, and knowing how averse he was to letter writing, set it down to the fact that he was busy; and I sincerely hoped profitably so. Still I passed the day in gloomy forebodings, and resolved to go to Gravesend the following morning. That night, however, as I was going to my room, the servant handed me a letter, and I did not realize until I had read it, how anxious I was becoming. The letter ran as follows:

"20 NARROW LANE, GRAVESEND.
Sunday Morning.
"DEAR GURT: Sorry, but can't get over to-day as I expected. Will try and come before next Lord's day. How's the book? Keep your mouth straight, and don't get discouraged. Yours,
"TORRY."

It wasn't much of a letter, but it was better than nothing, and I was thankful for it. I put it in my pocket, and gave up all thought of Gravesend for the present. Evidently Torrence had found something to occupy him, and I didn't believe he was a man to work long for nothing, but felt provoked that he had not told me what it was. True, I had never written to him, which he had told me to do in Wetherbee's care, should there be anything to write about; but as there wasn't I felt justified in my silence. However, I should now see him soon, and comforted myself with the thought that all was well.

During the ensuing week, I answered several advertisements, in the hope of finding employment, for despite the satisfaction felt in my ability to economize, there were moments when the reflection that I was making absolutely nothing would come upon me with such force, that I grew despondent, and would gladly have welcomed anything offering even the smallest return. But every effort to find work was unavailing; evidently London was overcrowded.

Another week passed without Torrence, and when the following Sunday came and went without bringing him, I became not only impatient but provoked. Why could he not run up to see me? It certainly seemed strange. Had he not been so emphatic in requesting me to let him alone, I should have gone to Gravesend long before. But here was I scarcely daring to leave the house, fearing that he would come and go in my absence.

A few days after this an incident occurred which placed me in a most unfortunate predicament. My landlady came to me with tears in her eyes, saying she would be dispossessed immediately if unable to raise ten pounds. She assured me that if I would advance her a part of the money she would—but why go into details—

I was swindled out of much more than I could afford to lose; I had lost a friend, and injured my chances of success, and not only was the landlady dispossessed, but all her lodgers as well. I was obliged at once to find new quarters, and with greatly reduced means. Things now locked very squally, and I firmly believed the poorhouse was in the next block, and that I might stumble upon it any day, without warning. I wrote at once to Torrence to tell him of the change in my situation and circumstances, and urging him to come immediately for a consultation. By return mail, I got the following answer:

"20 NARROW LANE, GRAVESEND.

"DEAR GURT: Sorry to hear of your bad luck, but don't fret about a trifle. A handful of gold more or less isn't worth a thought. A begger can pick it up on London Bridge without being much the better for it, and as I told you before, a day or two sooner or later at his majesty's hothouse won't count much in eternity. I shall be with you in a day or two, and hunt you up in your new quarters. Now be thankful you got off so cheap, and don't worry. I have been awfully busy.

"Hastily Yours, T."

My brother always took things easily, but in this letter he had quite eclipsed himself. I could not doubt that he had found some employment.

Again I had been obliged to pay in advance for my new lodgings, and my stock of cash had dwindled alarmingly. If Torrence did not come soon, I should be arrested as a vagrant.

About three days after this, just as I was about to start for Gravesend, having seen nothing of my brother since his letter, a hansom was driven to the door and Torrence alighted.

"Well, old boy!" he said as cheery as possible; "glad to find you at last. But what made you move to such a place as this?"

He looked with disfavor upon the dirty, sad-visaged house I had chosen for a residence. I explained everything as we went up the steps, even telling him to a penny the amount of money I had left. Instead of being dismayed, he only laughed, and turning to the cabby, tossed him his fare, with a liberal surplus, and then we went on into the house. My brother's extravagance had always surprised me, but in our present circumstances, his indifference to money seemed unpardonable.

Torrence looked around my little room with disgust.

"I don't like this place," he said. "We must move out of it."

"When?" I asked in amazement.

"Now!" he answered.

"It's the cheapest I could find."

"I should think so!" he replied.

"But even if you are making a little money, wouldn't it be unwise to spend it? Remember I am doing nothing."

Torrence smiled and said:

"Now, Gurt, don't undertake to lecture me, but order a four wheeler instead—perhaps we had better say a couple—for I want to carry all our traps at once, before they become too strongly impregnated with these quarters, and— Do you owe anything?"

I explained that I had already paid in advance, that we had lost money once in that way, and that I hoped he would not consent to a further frittering of our funds; but Torrence was determined; and in less than an hour we found ourselves seated in a comfortable cab, with our luggage on top. As the driver was about to close the door, he stood for a moment to receive the order, when I heard my brother say, quite distinctly:

"*Hotel Mustapha!*"

IV.

Now, the Mustapha is among the very swellest hotels of London; indeed I doubt if there is any place of public entertainment in the whole of Europe, which is more magnificent, or whose rates are more exorbitant; and when I found myself standing in one of its superb corridors, I naturally wondered why we had come.

In a few moments we were shown an apartment consisting of three large communicating rooms; two bedchambers with a *salon* between and all furnished palatially.

"Do you think it will do?" inquired Torrence, looking around with a critical air of indifference.

"For what?" I inquired.

"For us."

"The devil!" I exclaimed.

"No, not for the devil but for you and me."

I looked at him in dumb amazement, and then without another word, my brother dismissed the attendant, saying that he thought the rooms would answer the purpose, and ordered our luggage sent up immediately. Was the fellow losing his head? I feared he had already lost it.

When left alone, we stood for a moment taking in the grandeur that surrounded us, from the gorgeous frescoes on the ceiling, to the sumptuous carpets beneath our feet; and then unable to contain myself, I asked Torrence if he were really going mad. The earnestness of my manner, and the dead serious look upon my face, made him laugh until he rolled over upon one of the Turkish divans.

"Yes! can't you see it?" he cried, "why don't you send for a doctor? But no, you couldn't afford the expense, and this is better than any asylum I'm sure. Don't fret, old boy; if I am mad there's a method in it, and a devilish good one too. Now you make yourself at ease, for your brother's madness will never hurt you. But it *is* rather neat, isn't it?" he added, getting up and looking around the room. You know I searched all over London before I could find apartments to suit me exactly; and I'm glad you admire my taste!"

"Well!" I answered, drawing a long breath, "you certainly must be making a fortune, and rapidly, too; but all the same I don't approve of your extravagance. But tell me, have you paid for all this? and how much is it to cost us?"

"*Us!* I admire *that*, when you are my guest. Why it is to cost you nothing, of course! But wait here a few minutes, as it seems to worry you, I will satisfy your mind on the money question. I am going to the office, and will be back immediately."

While he was gone I interested myself in a further inspection of the rooms. The more thoroughly I went into their equipment, the more amazed I became at the lavish disregard for money displayed upon every hand. The beds were regal; the chairs and other furniture of the most costly type imaginable, and even the walls were adorned with paintings, which I saw at once were of a very high order of merit. The bathrooms, of which there were two, were on a scale of princely magnificence, and everywhere were mirrors, bronzes, and decorations which appeared to me quite too costly for a public house; indeed there could be few palaces more splendid.

Presently I heard Torrence returning, and as he entered the room he held a paper toward me.

"There now read this, and make yourself easy!" he cried.

It was a receipt in full for the rent of the rooms for two entire months in advance, three hundred pounds.

"Well!" I exclaimed, looking first at the paper, then at my brother, "wherever you got this money, I can't guess, but I will say, that although my fears for the immediate future are relieved, I consider it a wicked waste for people in our circumstances to throw away their means as you have done."

I was provoked and showed it.

"Wait, old man, until you know what you're talking about," was his only rejoinder.

"I suppose you've sold some interest in your air ship," I suggested doggedly.

"How absurd! I haven't even thought of such a thing."

He seemed to enjoy my perplexity, and walked about the room whistling.

"You have sold the invention out and out, then?" I persisted.

"Guess again, dear boy, for I shall never part with the air ship to any human being!"

"And will it ever be built?"

"Rather! I am working on it now. What did you suppose I'd been doing at Gravesend all this time? Courting old man Wetherbee's daughter, eh? Well, you're mistaken, for I've been doing nothing of the kind; but the air ship is begun."

I might as well have pumped the clerk in the office for information, and so decided to ask no more questions. But my resolution was short-lived, for in the next breath I inquired how long it would probably take to complete it; to which Torrence answered that he thought six weeks would probably suffice, and had therefore only taken our rooms for two months, but that the time required for such delicate workmanship as would be necessary on the air ship, was difficult to estimate, and he had therefore stipulated for the refusal of our apartments, should we need them longer, at the expiration of the term, as he did not wish to go in search of lodgings again. He rattled on about contracts he had signed for work upon the air ship, involving such large sums of money that I could only stand with my mouth open and gasp.

At 8 o'clock we sat down in our *salon* to such a dinner as could hardly be surpassed by the royal board itself. The table was loaded with flowers and silver, and lighted with candles. Two men were in attendance; one behind each of us. The wines were of the choicest; each course being accompanied by its appropriate beverage. Such Burgundies and Tokays, such champagnes and liquers, and all dispensed with the utmost prodigality, bottles being opened, merely tasted and set aside for a better vintage. I sat and ate and drank like one in a dream, and earnestly prayed that the money would not give out before we had settled this bill. For our credit, I will say that neither of us drank too much. Indeed the glory undermined my appetite, and I perceived that although there was quite an array of bottles and decanters, mere wasted material, Torrence was also extremely moderate.

After dinner the attendants were dismissed, while we continued to sit around the table, smoking and talking. Our cigars were of the finest, and our conversation consisted mainly of questions upon my part; some answers, and many evasions on Torrence's.

"And where have you located your workshop?" I inquired.

"The air ship is building in Wetherbee's barn; at least the parts, when completed, will be put together there under my supervision," answered Torrence.

"Do you expect to go to Gravesend every day to superintend the work? It strikes me as rather a long journey. Won't it take up a lot of your time?"

"It would under ordinary circumstances," he answered; "but you see I shall travel by private conveyance. In fact I have purchased a steam launch; she is very fast, so that I can run up and down without trouble."

"Oh!" I ejaculated, unable entirely to conceal my surprise even at this minor, and perhaps more reasonable extravagance.

"I suppose you will keep a crew on board then?"

"Oh, yes."

"And the thing will always be waiting for you?"

"Exactly!"

"Couldn't we have saved a lot of money by sleeping on her?" I asked.

"Probably; but I don't think it would have been so comfortable. Surely, Gurt, you're not dissatisfied with our quarters already?"

"Dissatisfied! Heaven forbid! I was only thinking of your purse."

"That, my dear boy, can take care of itself. By the by, do you know we ought to have more clothes, and a couple of men—*valets*, I mean; for whoever heard of people in our position, dressing themselves? I think I shall put an 'ad' in the *Times* to-morrow."

"I hope not," I answered; "for my part I should feel like a fool to have a fellow tinkering about me, holding my trousers while I stepped into them, and washing my face—why I understand that even the Prince of Wales puts on his own clothes!"

"That ought to settle it then," said Torrence; "but a greater variety of wearing apparel is necessary; for the servants that wait on us are better clad than we are."

I didn't offer any objection to the clothes, feeling that they were a tangible asset, which in the event of failure might be turned to some account. But the *valets* were quite superfluous, a money sink, as well as an affectation which I swore to eschew.

The transition from poverty to opulence had been so sudden, that it might have been unnerving were it not for my brother's extraordinary influence. I had always regarded him with unswerving confidence, and even now the relief from monetary anxiety quite outweighed any misgiving I might have felt concerning the manner of this suddenly acquired wealth. As it was, while my wonder was stimulated, my curiosity partook more of the nature of a child's toward a parent's resources, and my efforts to unravel the mystery being so successfully thwarted, I soon became, in a measure, satisfied to receive and ask no questions. I say, in a measure, for of course it was impossible at times to help thinking how this sudden change in our circumstances had been achieved.

After dinner I went down into the lower corridor of the hotel, and admired its superb finish, and elegant appointments, as well as the gay throng that constantly gathered there. Thence wandering into the reading room, I indited a number of letters to friends at home, feeling a peculiar satisfaction in using the gorgeous note paper with the words, Hotel Mustapha, engraved upon the top of each sheet. While I was writing Torrence amused himself in the billiard room, where he had already made acquaintances. When through with my letters, I joined the party, a bevy of fashionable men, who evidently looked up to Torrence as their leader. They were playing pool for stakes, and when the game was over, my brother, putting his hand in his pocket, pulled out a huge bundle of bank bills, and settled the score. The amount lost could not have been large, as he received several gold pieces and some silver back in change, out of a single bill. I marked this fact with interest, as it tended to show that Torrence was not gambling to any excess. He introduced me to the men as his twin brother; and then we went into the smoking room and drank some hot Scotches, and smoked very expensive cigars, my brother again paying the bill.

We soon became looked upon as the Yankee millionaires, no distinction being made between us, and being well supplied with funds myself, I was always able to appear as a gentleman.

A few days after our arrival, I was informed that one of the best boxes at a neighboring theater was reserved for us. Torrence had taken it for the season. "Not that I expect to go there every night," he said, "but it is pleasant to have one's own corner to drop in upon, when one happens in the mood. To-night, for instance, I think it would be nice to take a peep at the ballet; don't you?"

I agreed that it would, and after our usual sumptuous dinner, we entered a very handsome closed carriage, and were driven away. There were two men upon the box in livery, and as we rolled noiselessly on upon rubber tires, I remarked that it was quite the swellest public rig I had ever seen. My observation was received with scorn.

"Public rig be blowed!" said Torrence; "surely you know better than to take this for a hackney coach!"

"What then?" I inquired.

"Private, of course. I bought the entire outfit, horses and all this morning. This is my maiden trip with them; and they—I mean the animals—are a pair of spankers, I can tell you!"

"And how much did the whole outfit cost?" I inquired, unable to restrain my curiosity on the money question.

"Eight fifty!" said Torrence, in an easy off-hand way, as if four thousand two hundred and fifty dollars were the merest bagatelle. I would have been stunned had I not been growing gradually accustomed to that sort of thing. As it was, I simply remarked that I couldn't see how he was going to find time to exercise his purchase.

"Oh, I'll leave that to you," he answered, "I don't want you to go about town in a manner unbefitting the *rôle;* savey?"

We were ushered into the theater with all the deference that could have been heaped upon her majesty, so I thought; and I half expected the audience to rise as we entered our box.

The play was one of those dazzling effects of lights and legs, as Torrence expressed it, with little or nothing beside, and I soon observed that a pretty little soubrette was the principal attraction. Before the second act was over, an attendant was summoned and despatched with a five pound bill, and an order for the prettiest basket of flowers to be bought, which at the first opportunity found its way upon the stage. At times it made me sick to see the money my brother wasted, but I was a mere puppet in his keeping, and could do nothing to deter him. I fully expected he would be going to the green room after the performance for an introduction, but to my amazement he did nothing of the kind, and instead we got into our carriage, and driving to a fashionable restaurant, had supper.

"And why did you throw away your money on those flowers?" I asked him, lingering over a bottle of Pomard.

"Do you call that throwing money away? Why the poor little thing looked as if she needed all the encouragement she could get. I think of leaving an order with the florist to-morrow to send her half a dozen every night. Take them in from different parts of the auditorium, you know, so that she will never suspect they came from the same person."

"And you won't send your card?"

"Decidedly not!"

"And you don't want her to know it is you?"

"Decidedly not!"

"Have you taken leave of your senses?"

"Decidedly not! Why, Gurt, don't you know it would give her a lot more pleasure to think she was a general favorite than a special one?"

"Decidedly not!" I answered, taking up his cue, "any girl would rather—but no, on further consideration, I believe you're right." And it seemed to me that Torrence was always right.

Later we got into our carriage and were driven to the hotel. The night was wet and cold, and I was glad to find myself once more in the cheerful Mustapha. We had a game of billiards, followed by some hot Scotch and a cigar, and then went to our rooms, and to bed.

Once in the dark and alone I kept revolving in my mind the events of the day, and of the time since our change of fortune; and naturally fell to speculating as to the most probable manner in which all this wealth had been acquired. Nothing I could think of was satisfactory, and one idea after another was set aside as equally improbable. I suppose I must have fallen asleep when I began to wonder if the receipt he had shown me were genuine. It was an unreasonable doubt, and at variance with my faith in Torrence, and yet it took hold of me as sleeping thoughts some times will. Had I not seen his money? Why should he not have used it for hotels as well as anything else? And yet the thought annoyed me, so that I could not dismiss it; and finally I found myself sitting up in bed, brooding over it. Lighting my candle I walked quietly across the room and entered the *salon.* Listening at my brother's door for a moment, and making sure that he was asleep, I returned to my own room and dressed. The lights were still burning brightly all over the house, and looking at my watch, I saw that it was only a little past midnight. There could be nothing extraordinary in going to the hotel office and inquiring in a casual way if the rooms had been paid for. It would set my mind at rest to have the verbal assurance of the proprietor that they were. I could not help feeling that it was an underhanded advantage to take of my sleeping relative; but I was driven by a great fear, and after a moment's hesitation, I sped down the stairway into the lobby below. I sauntered into the billiard room, not so much to see if there were any players left, as to assume an appearance of merely lounging about the premises without definite purpose. Half a dozen men were still plying their cues, and I recognized the one to whom Torrence had introduced me. I was invited to join the game, but dread of being led into a carouse deterred me, and after looking on for a few minutes, I said good-night and wandered back toward the office. I walked up and down a couple of times with an unlighted cigarette between my teeth, as if merely seeking diversion, and then going up to the desk, asked some irrelevant questions about the arrivals during the day. My question answered, I turned carelessly as if about to depart, and then as though the thought had suddenly presented itself, looked back, and said:

"Oh! by the by; did I understand correctly that my brother, Mr. Torrence Attlebridge, had settled for our apartments?"

The clerk did not have to refer to his books, but answered promptly with a pleased smile:

"Oh, yes, sir. Everything is settled for in full. Your brother has paid in advance for two months. He has our receipt for the amount—three hundred pounds. They are our very best aparments, sir; decorated by Le Brune, and furnished by Haltzeimer entirely regardless—I hope Mr. Attlebridge finds everything satisfactory!"

I assured him that everything was just as we desired and went away comforted, with the exception of wishing that I had the money instead of the rooms. But such thoughts were idle; I was in Torrence's hands.

After loitering about the smoking room for a few minutes, I returned to my room, and to bed.

V.

WHEN I got up in the morning Torrence had gone. He had left without disturbing me, as he said he should, the journey to Gravesend requiring an early start.

I determined to put in the day writing, having evolved some ideas which I thought might suit a certain American journal; but it is astonishing when the necessity for work has been removed, how indifferent we become to it. Every effort seemed absolutely futile, and after an hour, I put away my writing materials and went out for a drive in the park. I could see that my brother's new outfit was greatly admired, and I leaned back upon the satin cushions, conscious that I was looked upon as an important person—possibly a duke. I lunched at a fashionable restaurant near the marble arch, and then, after a drive along Edgeware road, returned to the hotel.

The mail was just in, and there was a large batch of letters and papers for Torrence. Some of these were unsealed; presumably advertisements, and as such I examined them. But the examination was disappointing, only serving to whet my interest, and enhance my wonder. For what was here? Unaccountable scribbling—such extraordinary charts and figures—such attempts at drawing of birds and unknown animals—such efforts at natural scenery—and withal such crude and childish explanations, in such outlandish chirography, that it was quite impossible to say whether the work was that of a madman or not. Indeed I was by no means sure what any one of the designs was really intended to mean. I pored over these papers for more than an hour, in the very ecstasy of wonder, and then without having reached a single conclusion, put them back in the envelopes to await the owner's arrival.

I tried to believe that the drawings referred to some of the more intricate parts of the air ship; although it was impossible to help feeling that this was absurd.

About an hour before dinner Torrence arrived, cheery as ever. I gave him his mail, and then seating myself near the window, watched him open it. It is not always easy to interpret the emotions by the expression of the face, but on my brother's countenance I was sure that a comprehensive wonder, a wonder that grasped the meaning of what he saw, was clearly depicted. At one moment he would smile with infatuation; a paroxysm of delight; at the next he would frown, and look frightened at the paper before him, and once he passed his arm roughly across his eyes, as if wiping away a tear. If the papers themselves were mysterious, Torrence's behavior was even more so. When through, he put them carefully together and carried them into his own room.

"Anything important?" I inquired, with an assumed indifference, when he returned to the *salon*.

"Nothing," he answered, glancing at me, as I thought, with a slight look of suspicion, "nothing only a lot of detailed drawings about the work going on at Gravesend."

I did not answer, but felt sure that he had not told me the truth. Then he went on to speak of various contracts, which he hoped would soon be under way, and which were to be delivered at Gravesend within a month, and of others that would take longer to complete, and all of which were to be put together at Wetherbee's barn as soon as possible. He was afraid the vessel would be longer building than he had at first been led to believe, but concluded that it would not matter very much after all, as the season was not propitious for a trial.

"No," I answered, "I should imagine that warm weather would be better, but then your expenses here would be running on fearfully!"

Torrence sneered at the suggestion. Expense was always the thing he seemed to think of last.

We dined sumptuously again, and after dinner drove to a music hall. Here the usual extravagance was repeated, indeed it exceeded all bounds. Not only did he buy flowers in vast heaps, which he distributed upon the stage; but later went into the green room, and disbursed considerable money among the actresses. His prodigality was so absurd and unmeaning that I finally left him in disgust, returning to the hotel alone. It was quite late when he came in, and I met him in rather angry mood:

"Well, you have made a fool of yourself!" I exclaimed, as he threw himself upon a large Persian *musnud* to finish his cigar before retiring.

"How?" he asked, quite innocently.

"By throwing away your money among a lot of sharpies, who wouldn't lend you a copper to save your soul!"

Torrence roared, as if he thought it the best joke imaginable.

"Now, look here, old boy," he said in another minute, "don't lose your temper, because it doesn't pay. What's the use of money if not to give pleasure? That's my way of enjoying myself, and I don't either ask or expect any favors in return. As you see, it takes a lot of money to buy my pleasure, but I can afford it!"

"If you have such an income that you can't spend it," I replied, "suppose you give a little of it to me. You might be glad some day if you found that I had saved a few pounds for you!"

The speech would have been contemptible, considering the amount of money Torrence had already given me, were it not for the fact that I intended it for his good as well as my own, hoping to save at least a part of a fortune, which was being squandered so shamefully under my eyes.

"Why, certainly," he answered good naturedly, and half-rising from the lounge, "how much do you want?"

"Anything you have to spare!"

Without another word he got up, and going to the writing table, signed a blank check and handed it to me.

"There! fill it out for yourself!" he exclaimed.

"For how much?"

"Anything you please," he replied, with a look of utter indifference.

"But you must say," I persisted.

"Really, I don't care, Gurt," he answered, striking a match to relight his cigar. "My bankers will pay anything you put on it, I fancy."

"Have you as much as a thousand pounds with these people?"

He laughed outright.

"I should hope so!" he shouted; "but if that is all you want, I have probably as much about me, for you must remember that I am a business man now, and am conducting costly experiments in connection with the air ship, which I intend shall be the most perfect thing on earth!"

"I suppose then it will cost you more than the twenty thousand dollars you thought?"

"Well, rather! If I get off with as many pounds I shall be lucky!"

I gasped but said nothing.

"Why don't you fill out your check?" he continued, observing that I was standing idly by the table, my mouth open in astonishment.

"Shall I put down a thousand?" I asked, not knowing what to say.

"Yes, and two of them, if you wish. I really don't care."

I filled out the check for an even thousand, not being able to overcome my horror at the thought of a larger figure, for notwithstanding all the evidence to the contrary, I was unable to overcome a certain fear that the check might be refused. I showed it to Torrence, whose only remark was that he couldn't see why I had not doubled it. I was determined to save this much for a rainy day, and resolved to go at once to the banker's when my brother had gone back to Gravesend and cash it. I also determined to find out, if possible something about his affairs, as the mystery of all this sudden wealth was preying on my mind. I had quite relinquished the hope of learning anything from Torrence himself, and should now apply to other sources.

That night we retired early, as my brother said he was fatigued with the work of the day, and not knowing what else to do, I followed his example, fully resolved to cash my check and investigate matters on the morrow.

After a couple of hours of restlessness, and finding it impossible to sleep, I got up to go into the adjoining room for a glass of water. I did not take a light, knowing exactly where to find it, but imagine my surprise, when half-way across the floor of our *salon*, at seeing that the light in my brother's room was still burning brightly and shining through the keyhole and under the bottom of the door. Scarcely had I observed this, when I caught the sound of low voices issuing from the room, as of two people talking in an undertone. I stepped noiselessly up to the door and listened.

"There is no danger; he is asleep!" said one of the voices, which I thought was Torry's; and then some whispering followed, impossible to understand. At this moment a horrid thought flashed upon me. Had Torrence embarked in any crime, which he was trying to conceal? The mere suspicion sickened me. I could not believe it.

"It's for you to say," remarked the other; "for my part, I don't care a damn who knows it, provided the news don't come from me. Now look at this."

I could hear the rustling of papers.

"And this; and this. The society shan't never see one of 'em again—I'll let 'em rot first."

Then came Torry's voice.

"Of course if it's so, my brother Gurthrie will know all about it before long. Only I don't want to tell him yet. It isn't that I distrust you, Merrick, but naturally you can see for yourself what a laughing stock I should become if there should prove to be any mistake."

"Don't I know it? and without there bein' any mistake," answered the other.

"Precisely; and that being the case, I prefer to wait until the thing is proved to my own senses before announcing this most stupendous fact of history to anyone."

I was relieved. There was something in both the tone and words that convinced me there could be nothing criminal under consideration. And yet the mystery was deeper than ever. Here was no explanation of how the money had come; which was an assured fact, but dark innuendoes of problems yet unsolved. I continued to listen, absorbed with interest.

"Now, as to the matter o' beasts and birds, bein' no scholar, I can't prove nothin'. Thim you'll hev to study for your own self, and make your own deductions regardin' em. Nayther can I explain the how and wherefore of the light—but it's thar all the same, and you'll see it. I could a' give my notions to the society, but the cussed fools wouldn't listen to nothin', and they can go see for theirselves if they wants to, afore I'll tell 'em another word. Now, don't let that slip your mind, 'cause you're the only man, 'fore God a' mighty!"

"Now, about this belt," said Torrence, "how wide did you say it was?"

By the sound I imagined him to be tapping on the table with a pencil; but the words that followed were impossible to hear; and then the men had evidently got their heads together in poring over some document or paper which I could not see. Suddenly it occurred to me to stoop down and peep through the keyhole. Undoubtedly it was contemptible, but was it any more so than listening? "An eavesdropper is bad enough, but a peeper is worse," I thought, and yet my curiosity was so aroused it was impossible to help it, and I excused myself partly on the ground that it was right to be forearmed if I was not to be led blindly as an accomplice into a possible crime. And so I succumbed, and placing my eye against the opening, obtained a circumscribed view of my brother's apartment. To my amazement I immediately recognized the stranger as the man we had met upon the Thames boat, and afterward in the restaurant. He was the same dirty, unshaved sailor; at least his appearance indicated that he had followed the sea for a living, and I could not doubt that he had. The men were sitting on opposite sides of a table, upon which a pile of papers was heaped in confusion; and so far as I could judge some of these were the same that had come in the afternoon's mail.

"Give him as much time as he wants!" said the sailor, speaking again. "He won't believe it at first, and it ain't reasonable as how he should; but it 'ill come over him by degrees like. He's bound to believe it ef he studies on it—there ain't no other chance."

"No, not if it's so," answered Torrence, "and he won't be as hard to convince as you might suppose; perhaps no harder than I was, for I've half believed it myself, and talked about it before. You found me an apt scholar, didn't you?"

"The only one with any sense I ever had," snarled the man. "But I don't care now," he continued, "I haven't long to live nohow; but I did hate to die with *that* secret, 'case another million years might pass afore it was found out. I'm satisfied so long as you 'uns knows it, 'case the world's bound to get it. But as for them cussed fools——!"

The man rapped on the table with his clinched fist.

"Hush!" said Torrence, "you might wake him up!"

The sailor grinned and scratched his head.

"No harm done, I reckon ef I did," he replied.

"No, but I told you my reasons for keeping mum!"

"Precisely; I mind your word. And the proofs, you found them all correct?"

"Quite so; but tell me don't you want any yourself?"

"Hell, no. I'll send you up a trunk full to-morrow. I've got all the swag I want—a good bed, plenty o' company, and a place to die in; for I tell you I can't last long. It's taken the stuffin' out o' me—but the secret— the secret—Well, thank God, I shan't die with it, and that's all I wanted."

Of course, this talk might almost as well have been in

Hindoostanee, for aught I could make out of it. At one moment my fear of evil was aroused to a terrible pitch, at the next, I felt nothing but idle curiosity. I was, however, surprised to find so little that was intelligible in what I heard. Presently the men began turning over bundles of papers, and Torry having moved his chair, it was impossible to see what these were, and this fact may have helped arouse the awful suspicion that suddenly seized me; a thought which I am sure would never have presented itself under any but the bewildering circumstances in which I had been so blindly plunged. Could it be possible that the money which my brother had thrown about so freely, was counterfeit? A moment's reflection convinced me that it was not possible, and yet a terrible distrust had taken hold of me. For a moment I hesitated. My first impulse was to call out and ask what was the matter. It would have been the frank and natural thing to do, had my suspicions not been aroused, but as they were, I felt that such a procedure would be silly and fruitless. A burning desire to know consumed me, and I walked about the room in an agony of unrest. Again I looked through the keyhole, and was relieved to see no plates, stamps, dies or machinery of any kind. I drew a long breath. Then I recall d that there had been nothing in the conversation to indicate any such business; and I drew another breath. Finally, unable to gain the slightest clew to the mystery, I returned to my room, and went to bed in a very uncomfortable frame of mind.

VI.

THE next morning I awoke early, and resolved to go at once to Torrence's room and ask him to lend me a five pound note. It was my intention to have it examined by a banker in the city for its genuineness, hoping to relieve the anxiety which had so tortured me during the night. While my judgment was opposed to the counterfeiting theory as improbable, yet it was difficult to overcome the thought that it might be the correct one. The truth is, I was impelled to discover some plausible explanation of the mystery. I could not rest as the recipient of means which had no visible source, and especially when there appeared to be so much ground for doubting their legitimacy.

Torrence was already up, preparing for an early start, as I sauntered into his room.

"By the by, old fellow," I said, "have you a fiver about you? I think I might use one to advantage until I can get down to the bank with your check."

He took a roll of bills out of his pocket, and instead of one five, tossed me a couple of tens.

"Let it go for luck!" he called, as he hurriedly left the room on the way to his business.

We rarely breakfasted together, Torry being so full of enthusiasm about his work, that he would brook no chance of delay, and so it was understood that we should not meet until after his return from Gravesend. On this occasion, when he had left me, and after breakfasting alone, I ordered the carriage, and drove into the city. Taking my check at once to the banker upon whom it was drawn, I inquired if it were all right. The cashier smiled, and simply asked how I would have it. I told him I did not want it at all, but wished to place it to my credit.

"Oh!" said the man looking up, "I thought you were Mr. Attlebridge."

"So I am," I answered, "but not Torrence. I am his twin brother. We look very much alike."

"I see!" he exclaimed, somewhat surprised. He then proceeded to take my signature, and give me a book with credit on it for a thousand pounds. There was no mistake about this. Here was an actual transfer of credit from Torrence to myself. I wanted to ask the man some questions about the amount Torrence held in the bank, but hesitated, fearing it might create a suspicion that I doubted his methods. Presently, while still chatting in a careless way, I took out one of the tens my brother had given me, and asked if it were all right, pretending to have received it at a place I was no quite sure of. The man looked at it carefully, and pronounced it perfectly good, and my doubts were relieved. I was about to say "good-morning," when the teller observed:

"We should be greatly pleased, Mr. Attlebridge, if you and your brother would keep your principal account with us, believing that we can offer special facilities, and——"

It was what I wanted. He had opened the subject.

"Oh!" I interrupted, "can you tell me which is my brother's principal banking house at present?"

"Unfortunately," answered the man, "he has not favored us with the name; although I believe it is one of the larger houses in the city. Mr. Attlebridge's deposits with us are all made through an American firm."

I was about to express surprise, but remembered myself in time, so merely smiled and tried to look as if I had known as much before.

"And why do you suppose that my brother keeps another account in London?" I asked.

"Oh!" said the man, shrugging his shoulders, "merely because I once heard him mentioned as the purchaser of a very large foreign draft from one of our city houses. Nothing else, I assure you."

"And you do not remember the name of the concern?" I asked, growing interested.

"No," answered the teller, "I do not. It is even quite possible that I never heard it. The remark was only one of those incidental scraps of conversation that referred more particularly to business in general, than to that of any special banker."

I had heard enough to give me a clew, although I confess, a slight one. Torrence evidently had business with another bank, and also had funds in America of which I had never heard, and could not understand. A thought had flashed upon me. I would go into the different banking streets and find out where this other account was kept, if possible, by passing myself off for my brother. Doubtless I should be taken for him as soon as I entered the right establishment, as I had been here. Bidding the teller "good-day," I passed out, fully bent upon my new enterprise. It was a bold scheme, but I was growing desperate to know something about Torry's affairs; moreover, I was conscious of greater [independence with a credit of a thousand pounds in my pocket and a bank book, which I pressed against my finger from time to time when needing encouragement.

As luck would have it, the first place I entered was the right one, and as I had surmised, the clerks recognized me at once as Torrence. I had made up my mind how to act, and what to say while walking along the street, having dismissed the carriage as unnecessary, and was fully prepared on finding myself addressed as Mr. Attlebridge.

"By the by," I began quite carelessly. "What was that last—er—that last——"

I purposely halted to give the teller a chance to help me out. This he did, but I was utterly unprepared for the word. I expected to hear deposit, or check, but when the man came to my assistance with the word cable, I was dumfounded. Was Torrence trying to hang himself? However, my common sense returned, and I replied as if suddenly recalling my errand:

"Oh, yes, that was it. Will you let me see it again please, if you have a copy of it?"

I had not the slightest idea what the cablegram was about, but knew that copies of important messages were always preserved, and thought I might as well see this one. In a minute a clerk appeared with the copy in question, and the teller glancing at it for a second to make sure it was the right one, passed it over for my inspection, and I read as follows.

"LONDON, December —, 1894.
"To DEADWOOD AND BATES, BANKERS, New York City.
"Place to the credit of Torrence Attlebridge sixty three thousand eight hundred and forty pounds sterling, and charge same to our account.
"WHITEHOUSE, MORSE & PLUNKET."

I almost choked with astonishment. Here was a single deposit of considerably more than three hundred thousand dollars. No wonder he could so easily afford to give me the check for a thousand pounds. I was provoked that I had not asked for ten times as much. But where did all this money come from in the first instance? I continued to look at the message in amazement, not knowing what to say; and then pulling myself together, remarked, still as if trying to refresh my memory:

"And let me see—I gave you for this, a draft on——"

"You forget, Mr. Attlebridge," promptly responded the man, "you merely drew upon your credit with us, reducing your account to that extent!"

"So I did," I answered, apparently quite satisfied. "My memory is so fearfully faulty sometimes, I not only forget amounts, but the manner of payment." Then remembering that Torrence had no doubt a further balance here, I thought I would make another effort to discover what it was before leaving. The question was not nearly so difficult as the others.

"By the by, be kind enough to tell me what my balance is to-day, here with you."

The big books were turned over, and in a minute I was informed that my brother had still more than one hundred thousand pounds with these people, Whitehouse, Morse & Plunket. I was astounded. Instead of solving a mystery I had only sunk deeper in the mire. Here was a credit that was practically boundless. A bank account worthy of a king. I could not show my amazement, and so for a minute turned my back, trying to collect my thoughts. Could I leave the place without one more question? I resolved to risk it, and so added:

"Sorry to trouble you again, but be good enough to tell me how my last deposit with you was made."

"By a large batch of your own drafts, Mr. Attlebridge, on prominent bankers in Paris, Berlin, Vienna, St. Petersburg, Constantinople, Munich, Rome, Naples, New York, Chicago, Boston, Philadelphia and San Francisco, besides others. We have a list of the bankers here if you would like to see it; and, by the by, I forgot to mention that several of the drafts were upon London houses, which you doubtless remember. Beyond this you have not forgotten that several thousand pounds were paid to us in cash!"

"True!" I said, and turning hurriedly, left the place, only too glad to get away. Evidently my brother's drafts had all been honored, or the balance would not be to his credit.

I wandered down the street like one in a dream. I could see no earthly chance of ever solving this problem, except through Torrence himself; but I could not ask him, and if I did, had no reason to expect an answer. No, I must wait for further developments. Something was sure to turn up. To my certain knowledge, then, my brother had nearly a million dollars to his credit in New York and London, and from what I had heard it seemed probable that he had much more elsewhere

VII.

At the expiration of the six weeks the air ship was still far from finished. Contractors had disappointed; orders for material had failed to be filled, and only two courses of the hull were laid. As Torrence took everything good-naturedly, he was not seriously disturbed, although he considered it a duty to push the work forward as fast as possible, hoping to make his trial trip early in the Spring. The plans were difficult of execution, the more delicate parts of the mechanism requiring the labor of the most skillful workmen and my brother's constant supervision. He spent the whole of every day at Gravesend, and sometimes the night; meanwhile our expenses at the Mustapha continued at the same extravagant rate. The apartments had been retaken indefinitely, and the proprietor would have regretted losing us, as we probably spent twice as much money as a score of his best guests. Of course, I was the principal beneficiary of all this luxury, Torrence being at home so little, but this fact did not disturb him in the least.

At the end of two months there was no prospect of completing the vessel for a considerable time to come, as new complications and fresh disappointments had arisen; nevertheless, things were getting well in hand, and the first warm Spring days would probably see her ready for a start.

It is not my purpose to recount our life during this

Winter and the following Spring in the great metropolis. It is sufficient for the purposes hereinbefore named to say that it was a period of extravagance beyond reason, and of somewhat equivocal pleasures when I considered the vast sums these pleasures cost. Wherever we went we were looked upon as the great American millionaires; the men whose pockets had no bottom, and whose bank accounts were exhaustless. My efforts to discover the goose that laid our golden eggs continued fruitless, and if I still doubted the regularity of the methods, so far as I could see, no one else did. As the time wore on, Torrence would occasionally show some irritability at the unavoidable delays; though what he intended to do with the vessel when finished was a myth. The time was when I had looked upon it as a means of wealth, if not fame; but now with a vast fortune at our command, he seemed even more anxious about the machine than ever. More than once I thought seriously of leaving him, fearing some dreadful climax to our affairs in which I might be implicated; but when I alluded to the separation he seemed hurt, and so I remained.

During all this time we were in the swim of fashionable life, both entertaining and being entertained constantly. If Torrence gambled it was never extensively, so that he never either won or lost any considerable amount. Every effort had been made to keep the intention of the air ship a secret, and so thoroughly had the workmen been mystified, that when Spring came it was exceedingly doubtful if any of them knew what it was, and fortunately old Mr. Wetherbee was so laid up with rheumatism that he never left the house. I think the general impression was that it was a new kind of torpedo boat, although some believed it to be a submarine passenger craft. The barn was kept closely shut during working hours, and the outer world had little chance of guessing what it contained.

By the middle of May the thing was nearly completed, and I saw by my brother's increased anxiety that his hopes were soon to be either realized or dashed to the ground. It was an unfortunate remark when I inquired, innocently enough, if he were sure the vessel would rise. He answered with an oath in the affirmative, but became moody and out of sorts immediately after. Upon several different occasions I felt sure that I heard him conversing with the sailor at a late hour, although I never again looked through the keyhole. Once when the conversation was particularly lively, I confess to listening, though only for a few minutes, and with poor result, as I could understand but little that was said. It was in reply to some remark of my brother's that the man answered:

"Don't bother about me. My pay comes in satisfaction! Revenge! Sabe? Now if you'll do as you're told, you'll do more for me than the five continents full o' men, women, and children ever would do. No, pardner, I'm alone in this world, and that stuff's no good to me, as I done told you; couldn't use it nohow; but I'll damn the society, and every one of 'em as turned a cold shoulder on me, through you. Now, I don't expect to live to see it, but I'll die happy, and that's worth more'n money can buy. Now, don't ever let your nerve give out; in fact there ain't no occasion for it, seein' how much better you 'uns is fixed than I was. Promise you won't never turn your back on it."

"I'll do my best; no man can do more!" answered Torrence.

"And you'll never regret it!"

"I've no doubt about my part of the contract," he added, "and can feel but little doubt of all you've told me, after the proofs."

"That's right, you're my man—God bless you, and if ever you——"

Here there was a shuffling of feet, and fearing they might be coming into the *salon*, I beat a hasty retreat to my own room. Of course I could form no conception of what they were talking about, and went to bed trying to put meaning into the maze of words.

Some days after this, while brooding over our absurd and unfettered prodigality, I resolved to ask Torrence for another and larger check. My object was, as before, to save something out of the whirlwind of our extravagances, fearing my brother's improvidence. I pretended that there was an investment which I was anxious to make, that would take quite a large sum. Without a word of inquiry he turned with alacrity and said:

"Why, certainly! How much?"

I began an explanation which partook of the nature of a sermon on the expediency of putting by something for a rainy day, but he cut me short:

"Now, my dear fellow, I can't really stop for the lecture to-day; keep that for to-morrow; but as to the money, why it's yours anyhow, and you might as well take it now as at any other time. How much did you say?"

"Well, I didn't say exactly, but a good deal would be necessary to do what I thought of doing," I replied.

"Since you don't seem to know exactly how much, take this," he said, "and if it isn't enough, let me know!"

Without another word he sat down and dashed off a check for twenty thousand pounds, and handed it to me.

"Here, take it," he said, "it's only a small payment on account at best. Let me know if you want more."

He was off in a second, and left me standing like one

petrified with the paper in my hand. I placed the amount to my credit with Whitehouse, Morse & Plunket, and got a friend to identify me as Gurthrie, instead of Torrence, Attlebridge.

Shortly after this my brother came to me one day with a despatch box in his hand. Opening the box he showed me that it contained a canvas bag, in which was a smaller one of oil silk. These he opened and emptied the contents upon the table. To my amazement I saw that it was a batch of conveyances, or deeds for houses and lands, real estate of great value in America, all in my name. By the values here mentioned alone I was worth more than a million dollars. According to the vouchers before me, this property had all been paid for by myself within the past few months. I felt as if I must unknowingly have come into the possession of Aladdin's lamp. I was dumfounded, but before I could utter a word Torrence went on to say:

"There now, all this is yours!—now, not a word—I have only a moment in which to speak, and wish to say this. Of course all this stuff is properly registered, recorded, and witnessed, and all that sort of thing as you can see; but for your future convenience and perhaps for mine, I must remind you of the importance of keeping this packet in your possession. There are other papers in it which we have not time to examine now, but if ever you should be hurried to move anywhere, don't forget to throw away the box, and shove this wallet in your pocket. It is of the utmost importance!"

I promised without asking a question; and when he was gone I went to a tailor's and had the packet, minus the canvas bag, securely sewed inside the coat I was wearing; seeing to it myself that the job was well done.

As the time wore on Torrence grew more impatient at

the delay in finishing the work. Evidently there was something he was dreading; which I thought might be the possible failure of the machine to rise.

"Suppose she fails," I said one day, "we have plenty to live on, and what does it matter?"

He looked at me with an expression of horror, and walked away without a word.

One day I walked suddenly into his room without knocking, thinking he was away. To my surprise I found him and the sailor, Merrick, talking together. As before they were sitting on opposite sides of the table, upon which was spread a packet of papers; some of them I recognized as having seen before. Torrence immediately got up, and asked if I would mind coming a little later, as he was just going over some important business, and of course I went out immediately. Although only in the room a minute, the strange motley of papers was distinctly seen. The same extraordinary attempts at drawing and chirography—and among these I observed what I had not seen before—a crude representation of a human face, but with so peculiar an expression that I could not forget it. There was also a lengthy, and very illiterate looking document, which appeared as if the signatures at the bottom had been done by children.

I went immediately into the *salon*, where although not really intending to listen, I overheard quite accidentally a remark of the sailor's, which, as nearly as I can remember, was as follows:

"You'll find him thar, jest as I'se told ye, pard, without he's died since; and you'll find the box, and them docyments inside of it, I reckon, if you hunts for 'em whar I tell you. There ain't nothin' to be afeard of in him; he's just plumb gone, don't know nothin' You needn't try to catch him, because you can't do it. Now,

I must be goin'. Reckon I'd better be fixin' to die anyway!"

This was really all; at least all I could understand; and a few minutes later the door was shut and the man evidently gone.

On the 25th of May Torrence came home rather later than usual, and the moment he entered the room I saw that something had happened. The look upon his face was one of unequivocal delight. Striking an attitude in the middle of the floor, he shouted:

"Hooray!"

"Not so loud!" I cried, "you'll disturb people in the house."

"Let them be disturbed. It's time they were disturbed," he replied, pouring himself out a glass of wine at the sideboard. Then holding the bumper aloft, exclaimed:

"Here's to the air ship; God bless her. But where's your glass?"

I joined him in the toast. "Well, what's happened?" I inquired, touching my glass to his.

"She rises; she floats; she steers. She advances and reverses, just as I please. She cuts the teeth of the wind. I tell you, Gurt, it is the triumph of the century —of the ages. A child can handle her. We shall be off in a couple of days!"

"The devil, you say! Have you had a trial trip?"

"Well, rather! but no one knows it. The truth is I took her out in the dark, before day, all alone, and had her back in the barn before any one guessed it. Arranged it all beforehand. Sent all the hands off. She responds like a leaf in a gale. We can sit in her, solid as a rock, one foot above the ground, or ten thousand, just as we please. We can float along four miles an hour, or a mile a minute. We can stand before the wind, or we can run in the teeth of a hurricane. We can right about face, or maneuver her with more ease than you could a wheelbarrow. Her power is exhaustless, and is evolved without steam, electricity or—but what's the use of going into that? You couldn't understand if I did. It would take a course of mathematics to get into the first principles; but some day, when you and I are floating away in the blue sky, above the fogs of London town, I'll take time and explain it all to you."

"At all events she's a success," I answered, finishing my wine.

"She's more than that; she's perfect!" and Torrence drained his glass. Then lighting a cigarette, he added:

"We'll be off in a couple of days, old man, or near about it, as I just now told you."

"And for where?" I asked.

Torrence pulled down the corner of his left eye.

"That's my secret!" he said.

I congratulated him on his success, and told him I was ready to go anywhere away from the fog and gloom of the city. We embraced each other, and despite my warning, sent up three cheers for the air ship. I had never seen Torrence so elated about anything in my life; indeed it was contagious, for I was almost as happy as he was.

"And you are sure there will be no hitch?" I said, fearing the news was amost too good.

"Sure! Haven't I tried her? We have taken out the end of old Wetherbee's barn, and I sailed out over the fields alone. I ran her myself the other night, through the darkness and fog when no one could see. There were then a few slight changes to make for absolute control which have since been completed. Last night I had her out again through the river fogs when every one was asleep below, and, as I have just told you, she is simply perfect! Oh, Gurt, you don't know what it is to float aloft out of reach of everyone. Fortunately the fields were deserted, and the air too thick for a man to see more than fifty yards, even had it been day, otherwise I should have frightened some of those Gravesender's to death. And I had a nice time, too, in finding my way back to the barn, despite the red and green lights I had hung out for signals!"

Torrence danced around the room.

"Suppose she should drop with all aboard!" I suggested.

"Drop! She can't. The thing's impossible so long as the current is—but what's the use of my explaining to you? She can no more drop than you can fly."

"But suppose she did," I persisted.

"Well, such a thing can't possibly happen, unless the current is turned off too suddenly, and if it did, nobody would be hurt, because the pneumatic buffers on her bottom would make the contact with earth scarcely more than perceptible. No, my dear fellow, she can't go up, or she can't come down until I want her to, but when I do, up or down she goes. In short she is under absolute control. When the current is at the neutralizing point it is as natural for the air ship to float in the upper atmosphere as for you to walk on dry land, or a fish to swim. Don't be uneasy. I tell you I have mastered the secret of aerial navigation."

I had to be satisfied, and was really full of confidence in Torry's ability.

"Do you propose to make a long journey to begin with?" I inquired.

"Yes," said Torrence, a very extended one, as you will

see for yourself. I have had her stocked with enough provisions to run this hotel, figuratively speaking, for a year, and all manner of other necessaries; in fact, we shall be supplied with all the luxuries of life. You won't mind going with me, old man, will you, and letting me act as your pilot?"

"To be sure not; but when shall we be off?"

"Very soon. But you must not say a word to any one. Remember our movements are not to be known. Have I your word?"

I promised; but why he demanded this I was at a loss to guess.

Before going to bed that night Torrence told me that he should probably be absent a couple of days attending to the final equipment of the machine; and when I bid him good-night it was with the understanding that we should not meet for a day or two. He would certainly return before the end of the week; and I was to have everything ready for leaving at a moment's notice, as he was anxious there should be no delay. That was on Tuesday. Imagine, therefore, my surprise upon seeing him enter my bedroom at a late hour Wednesday night. I had been in bed long enough to fall asleep, and was aroused by a light shining in my eyes. There was a strange look in Torry's face, and I started up alarmed.

"Hello!" I cried, jumping up. "What's the matter? Has anything happened?"

Torrence put his finger to his lips and said:

"Hush! Be quiet! Don't be scared, but get up at once and do as I tell you without losing a moment's time!"

I did as I was bid; and dressed as hurriedly as possible, not doubting but the climax I had so long dreaded had come at last.

THE SECRET OF THE EARTH. 73

"We must be off immediately," said he, as I was putting the finishing touches to my toilet. There was something too dead earnest in his look and manner to permit of a single question.

"The trunks are quite ready," I observed; my teeth chattering with excitement.

"Damn the trunks! We must leave them behind. Have you the package?"

I showed it to him, sewed in my pocket.

Torrence looked at his watch.

"What o'clock is it?" I inquired.

"Nearly one," he answered reflectively, and then turning to me, he added with a look I shall never forget.

"Now, Gurt, if you have any nerve, I shall expect you to show it. No flunking or crawling, mind! Do exactly as I say, and without question or hesitation."

I nodded assent, for I could not speak. I saw something bulky under his coat, and wondered what it could be; but it was no time for such an inquiry.

Torrence then opened the door into the hall softly, and put out the light.

"Follow me; but walk quietly and don't speak a word," he said, leading the way.

We walked along the passage until reaching the grand stairway, when, instead of descending, as we had been in the habit of doing, Torrence led the way above. We climbed several stories until we stood at the foot of a narrow flight of steps, which ended in a scuttle above. From time to time he looked around to see if we were observed, and then stalked ahead, apparently satisfied. Reaching the scuttle, which was bolted upon the inside, he slipped the iron tongue noiselessly back, pushed open the hatch, and told me to follow. I found myself upon the roof of the hotel with my brother, who quietly closed the heavy door behind us. At that moment an awful thought flashed upon me. Had the fellow become in anyway connected with a gang of burglars? Had all this vast wealth come by theft? I stood still, petrified. It was not too late to retreat. I would not be led thus blindly as an accomplice to a crime never even suspected by me! It was too horrible. I was paralyzed with terror at the thought. Seeing that I had stopped, Torrence turned suddenly and exclaimed in a low excited tone:

"For God's sake! what's the matter?"

"I will not go another step," I answered; "I believe you are bent on some damnable crime!"

Torrence positively laughed. Nothing he could have done or said would have been more reassuring.

"Why, you old fool, Gurt! Have you taken leave of your senses?"

"Swear to me that there is nothing of the kind," I replied, still without moving.

"Swear! Why, of course, I'll swear. Do you suppose with the money I've already accumulated it would be necessary to risk my neck in housebreaking, for the sake of a few paltry dollars more? Really you have less common sense than I imagined."

Something in the tone of his voice convinced me that I was mistaken.

"Torry," I answered, "I will believe you. We have lived together all our lives, and I have never yet found you doing a dishonorable act."

"And you never will!" he exclaimed with feeling. "You will soon know everything. Now don't make a fool of yourself, but follow me and look where you step, too, for we are at least a hundred and fifty feet above the pavement, and I don't want to be responsible for your scattered remains!"

We approached the edge of the roof, and looked out over the city of London. It was a grand picture with great masses of shadow, and small flickering lights through a sea of mist below. Torrence stooped and walked along the cornice as if looking for something. Presently he stood still and looked down. What was he about? Did he intend committing suicide? I entreated him not to go so near the edge of the roof.

"We've got to go over it in a minute," he answered, without even looking back at me. Then he struck a match and examined his surroudings more carefully. I was completely unnerved and called:

"I'll be damned if I'll follow you another step. I believe you've lost your mind!" at the same minute I turned to go back. Torrence ran after me.

"You'll regret it all your life if you don't come with me now!" he exclaimed excitedly. "I swear to you that neither of us shall be hurt, if you will only do as I say."

I hesitated and allowed myself to be persuaded. Again he approached the edge of the roof, and when I reached him I saw that we were standing above another building at the back of our own, but which seemed about two stories lower. Torrence did not now stop long, but reaching under his coat, drew out a coil of stout rope, with an iron hook fastened at one end of it. It was the bulky thing I had observed when he entered my room.

VIII.

WITHOUT further hesitation Torrence hitched the hook onto the cornice, and threw down the other end of the rope. He then, having obtained my promise to follow, commenced letting himself over to the building below. I slipped after him as quickly as possible, until we found ourselves standing side by side upon the lower level. It was here that I again demanded an explanation, though foolishly enough, when I had come so far; retreat being now out of the question, as the hook had been disengaged from above, by a dexterous twirl of the rope and caught without striking. He only answered by saying:

"If you value your life and liberty, you will follow me as quickly as possible!"

I saw it was no time to hold back. We slid from roof to roof, Torrence always unloosing the hook above, and catching it before it struck. At last we found ourselves on the top of a low building, overlooking an alley, at the head of which a solitary gas lamp was burning. Here we paused.

"I'd give a thousand pounds if that light was out!" said Torrence, not seeming to know how to proceed. Then he added:

"Now, listen! An officer will be due in about five minutes. We must stop where we are until he has gone; then we must get down into the alley and cut for our lives!"

We crouched in the shadow of a chimney and waited.

The alley and the street beyond seemed equally deserted. There was no sound, save for that of an occasional cab, or the shout of a passing reveler in the distance. Fortunately there was a light fog and if the wall below was not too closely windowed, I thought we had a fair chance of escape; though why he had not come by the front door of the Mustapha was a riddle I saw no prospect of guessing.

"Quiet!" said Torrence, suddenly pressing his hand against my shoulder, "he is coming!"

There was the slow even step of a policeman. I could hear him pause as he reached the end of the alley, and imagined him looking up it to see if all were well. Presumably he was satisfied, for the step gradually receded into the distance, and the street became quiet again. I was intensely excited and resolved to elude the vigilance of the officer if it were possible to do so.

"This way!" said Torrence, stepping softly along the edge of the gutter in search of a suitable anchorage for the hook. But the place looked dangerous. There was an attic window hard by, which we must avoid, and the gutter flared too broadly for a holding. Fortunately there was plenty of rope, as the drop to the ground could not have been more than twenty feet.

"Now don't make a sound for your life. I am going to take a loop around the chimney. There is a blank wall where we must drop, but whole families are asleep beneath us. Follow me and hold your breath. If we can once gain the air ship we are safe!"

It was the first intimation he had given of where we were going, and I was relieved to be assured that we were headed for our own property, though why we should be afraid to go there openly was the mystery.

We passed the line around the chimney and made a

loop with the hook, and then Torrence, grasping the rope firmly, disappeared over the edge into the alley below. I followed him as quickly as possible, but must have made more noise than I intended, for scarcely had I touched the ground than a window opened above me, and a man's head was thrust out.

"Hello, there!" he cried; and then seeing the rope, which was hanging in full view of the gaslight, shouted at the top of his voice:

"Police! Stop thief! Police!"

"Run for your life!" cried Torrence, "but don't lose sight of me!"

He led the way down the alley at a lively pace; I followed, though farther off than I liked. It was only a short distance to where a street crossed at right angles. Turning to the left we dashed down the thoroughfare at full speed, and before I had gone fifty yards, ran square into the arms of a policeman.

"No so fast, young man!" said the officer, holding me firmly, "what's all this about?"

"What's it about," I answered indignantly; "I'm trying to catch the thief, and there he is." I pointed to Torrence, who at that minute turned another corner, "and if you'd do your duty and *help*, instead of standing here holding me like an idiot, we'd have him!" I added.

"And what's he done? asked the man stupidly, evidently mortified at his mistake. "Has he robbed you?"

"I should say so. He's grabbed my watch and chain and made away with it; and we'll never get it back again either, if you keep me here much longer."

The man released his hold. Fortunately my coat was buttoned up so that the chain was covered. The policeman had only got a glimpse of Torrence, who passed while he was on the opposite side of the street, but he was now convinced that he was in error and had caught the wrong man, and so joined me in the pursuit. Scarcely had we turned the corner after Torrence than we met that gentleman walking very leisurely toward us.

"Did you see a fellow running this way?" asked the officer excitedly.

"Yes," said my brother; "he's just ahead of you! If you run I think you may catch him!"

Having delivered himself of this information, the gentleman walked on leisurely; not, however, without having given me the tip to meet him on the lower corner. And then to divest myself of all suspicion, should any still be lurking in the officer's mind, I feigned considerable feeling at the loss of my watch, and even went so far as to offer a reward for it, paying the man ten shillings down on account. Of course I gave him a fictitious name and address. It was a capital ruse, if I do say it myself, and worked like a pair of charms.

As soon as I was free I hurried down the street to join Torrence, who was waiting quietly for me on the corner.

"And now the sooner we get out of this neighborhood the better!" he said, leading the way quickly down the thoroughfare; "but mind, we must not run. Not a step."

We then hastened along all manner of back streets, till I thought we were lost, but suddenly emerged on the bank of the river, at a small wharf, where, to my surprise, I found the launch already waiting, with steam up. In an instant we were aboard, and in a couple of minutes more had shoved off, and were out in the channel of the river.

"Give her her head!" called Torrence to one of his men. "We have lost time, and must make it up!"

We were soon shoving down the stream at a tremendous pace; the ghostly houses on either side rushing by, and giving me a happy sense of relief after our scary adventure.

"I'm glad we're free at last!" I said, cuddling up to Torrence in the stern of the boat.

"Don't crow before you're out of the woods!" he answered. "We shan't be safe until we're in the air ship, above the heads of all of them!"

"Not knowing who the *them* are, I'm not in a position to disagree with you!" I answered.

"Nor to agree with me, either," said he; "but wait 'till we're up in the clouds; then I'll tell you all about it."

The launch trembled under the pressure of steam put upon her. The grim docks, just showing their heads through the darkness, and the black swirling water beneath, made it seem as if we were rushing down some giant millrace. It was the stillest hour of night, and Torrence said we must make Gravesend before dawn, which at that season of the year, would not be long in coming.

As usual, a tremendous fog came piling in from the sea, as we swept down the river; and before reaching our landing, we were enveloped in a dense cloud-like vapor which wet us to the skin. Luckily our pilot knew his business, and I believe that with points of the compass given, and revolutions of the screw, he could have landed us with his eyes shut. However that may have been, we got there without an accident; and when ready to go ashore, I saw Torrence put a pile of money into the hands of each of the men; at the same time, he said:

"Boys, she's yours! I shall never want her again!"

Then leading the way with his lantern, we hastened forward toward Wetherbee's barn.

The air was thick, and the road difficult to find, but

we stumbled along without a word, until reaching an old fence, where Torrence suddenly stopped.

"We are nearly there," he said, putting his hand on my shoulder, and speaking impressively. "The air ship is ready to carry us aloft at a touch from my hand; but for certain reasons which I cannot now explain, there is an obstacle in the way of our leaving which we must overcome before the approach of dawn. It is this. The barn is surrounded by a force of armed men, whose object is to prevent our escape. I will tell you all about this as soon as we are out of their reach; meanwhile, if you, Gurt, will stand by me, and do exactly as I say, we shall outwit them. No human being in this wide world understands the mechanism of this thing but me. At this hour we may reasonably expect those lubberheads to be asleep. We must crawl in among them stealthily, climb up into the machine and be off before one of them suspects that anything is wrong. If by any accident they should be aroused and attempt to detain us, why I intend to plow through them like a reaper in a wheat field. There are, however, two points in this programme which must be carefully observed, and adopted if necessary. The first is, if we are suspected, drop immediately on the ground, and assume to be one of the watchers by feigning sleep, and a due suspicion of the others. Second, if we find them awake and recognizing us, fight if necessary; but reach the air ship under any circumstances, for once in it we can plow them down like chaff. Whatever you do, be sure and take your cue from me, and follow close upon my heels."

Torrence blew out the light, and threw the lantern away as a useless encumbrance, and we plodded along through the dark. I confess that my anticipation of trouble did not put me in the most cheerful frame of mind, but I resolved to do my best and stand by my leader at all hazards. Presently we climbed a fence and I knew that I was in Wetherbee's field; the one in which the barn stood. We moved stealthily on, over a grassy sod, and once, as I looked aloft, thought I saw the faint flickering of a star, and called Torrence's attention to it as a good omen.

"We don't want any stars to-night," he whispered; "the denser the fog the better."

Suddenly he stopped.

"We are there!" he said; "now remember!"

We felt our way with utmost caution among the sleeping bodies around us, examining the ground carefully with each foot before setting it down. Our progress was naturally slow, but after awhile I saw the dark outline of the barn looming up through the fog, in the first faint intimation of approaching dawn. We were getting along famously, and beginning to congratulate ourselves upon our success, when Torrence reached for my hand and then with his mouth against my ear, said:

"Now, be doubly careful; we are about to enter the building. They are thick as hail upon the floor!"

We crept slowly forward among legs and arms. A dozen men were snoring around us, and one fellow turned over, muttering something in his sleep, as my boot brushed against his shoulder. The ladder was gained. We climbed up the side of the great machine without a sound, and took our places within, as best we could in the darkness. Again Torry's mouth was at my ear.

"I must wait a minute," he said, "until my eyes become accustomed to the light. As soon as I can see the outlines a little better we are off!"

The silence was only broken by the breathing of the sleeping men around us. I was in an agony of suspense fearing there would be some hitch at the last—something wrong about the machine which might prevent its rising. The time seemed eternal. But the great open end of the barn was growing in clearness of outline. The fog was friendly; but the dawn was approaching. Again my brother's hand was upon my shoulder.

"Now brace yourself!" he said; "we are going!"

The air ship trembled. It was a sensation never experienced before. The vibrations seemed to pass through the innermost fibers of my being. I felt that we were being lifted in the air, and then that we were slowly floating out at the open end of the barn.

There was a shout and a curse and a call to arms. Noiseless as our movements had been, the men were aroused, and in an instant a score of voices were calling and yelling in every direction:

"Stop thief! Surround the barn! Where are they?"

A hideous medley of curses, groans, and sounds of fighting rose through the darkness from every quarter of the field; but the air ship was far above, and hidden from sight in the dense gloom of the morning fog.

"Let them fight it out among themselves," said Torrence, drawing a long sigh of relief; "we shall never see them again!"

We rose steadily and slowly for several minutes, Torrence saying it would be necessary to be well above the houses, as we were going to pass directly over London and must take no risk of a collision in the darkness. Presently I could feel that we were sweeping ahead. The movement was perfect, and as we sped rapidly forward through the dense atmosphere, catching an occasional glint of a street lamp below, all sense of fear departed. The trembling had ceased; and I felt as though we were floating rapidly away on the breast of a cloud, or upon the back of some monstrous bird; only here there was no effort. It was the only element comprehended. I could imagine nothing more sublime, more exhilarating. It was the absolutely finished poetry of flight. Beyond this, there was a feeling of safety far surpassing that of earthly locomotion, possibly due to the knowledge that we were lifted clear above all obstacles; that no uncertain switch, or ill-timed train could affect us. On we swept, in an ecstasy of rapture, realizing neither our speed nor place, engrossed only with the novelty of our situation, and watching the coming dawn.

Suddenly a great, dazzling object not twenty yards away flashed past us.

"*Great God!*" exclaimed Torrence, rising, "I thought I was too high for that."

"What was it?" I asked in amazement.

"The cross on top of St. Paul's!"

We had narrowly missed it, and caught sight of it, just as it reflected the first rays of the rising sun, in a rift of the fog, and just as I was congratulating myself upon being above every earthly object. But it was a clear miss and no harm done.

Presently the fog cleared and we looked down upon the great city of London speeding away below.

"And where are we going, old man?" I inquired at last, hardly able to contain myself with the strange delight of this new sensation of flying.

"To the North Pole!" said Torrence, holding fast to his levers, screws, and steering apparatus.

IX.

With the rising of the sun the fog cleared, and the great city of London was spread out away beneath us. It was a sight I can never forget, and a sensation unequalled by any previous experience. Patches of smoke blocked out large areas of the metropolis, but there was promise of a day of rare, Spring-like beauty. As we floated aloft, above the smoke and grime, through an atmosphere of translucent purity, we watched with interest the shifting masses beneath, and drank in with delight the marvelous scene. On and on we flew, at one moment unscreened from the streets and houses of the city, at the next catching only occasional glimpses of a tower or steeple piercing an earthward cloud, like the finger of a submarine monster pointing heavenward. But far to the north the smoke had vanished, and the green fields of Spring would soon be under us. It was a dream of bliss, transcending the power of words to picture, or the imagination of man to conceive.

"It makes me shudder," said Torrence, "to think of what a narrow escape we had just now. A few feet more to the left and we would have banged into St. Paul's cross."

I admitted that it would have been an ugly collision.

"The truth is," he continued, "I miscalculated our height; and in the fog and darkness, we may have had some other close shaves, for all I know."

"Hardly," I answered; "the houses in London are not high, as a rule."

"There are the Queen Anne flats at Victoria station," observed Torrence.

"True; but surely we did not go as far to the west as that?"

"Indeed we did. I ran considerably out of our course intentionally. You see I wanted to take in London by daylight; and wouldn't have missed the sight for a barrel of money. I ran slow, as well as indirectly, or we would have been well out of Middlesex by now. But I really thought we were higher, and should have consulted the barometer; but in getting away from those hounds I never thought of it. But thank God we're all right now. How do you like the air ship?"

"It's the grandest thing on the earth or off of it!" I answered; "but you haven't told me why those fellows wanted us; and why we had to sneak out of the hotel like thieves."

"There's lots of time for that," he answered; "but let us not miss this sight while we have it."

And I did not want to miss it myself, but before we had quite passed the suburbs Torrence explained as follows:

"You remember Hart?" he began.

"Perfectly; you mean Wetherbee's partner; the fellow we had our first interview with."

"Yes. Well, do you know that when the scoundrel discovered that we were building the machine without his aid, and that we were becoming the talk of London for our wealth, and manner of living, he was consumed with envy, and fearing that he had lost a good thing, got out an injunction against our moving the vessel, on the ground of being Wetherbee's partner? Of course he totally misrepresented the facts, and——"

"Then you did violate the law after all!" I exclaimed, feeling that I had been deceived.

THE SECRET OF THE EARTH. 87

"Not in the least!" he answered; "the paper was never served; I took care that it shouldn't be. But there were men in waiting at the entrance to the Mustapha, who confidently expected to catch me as I passed in or out, and if I had not come by a private entrance and left as we did, we should be down there now, and perhaps for a year to come, waiting the settlement of a legal investigation. Now, I knew if I stopped to explain matters to you, we might not get off. You would naturally argue the point, and the precious time be lost. I was warned of this pending injunction by one of the gentlemen I introduced you to in the billiard room, who certainly did me a very decent turn in return for my favors in the money line. The fellow found it out quite accidentally, but he didn't forget me."

I was amazed, and greatly relieved to find so simple an explanation of what, but a few hours before had a painfully criminal aspect. If Torrence could explain the mystery of his sudden wealth as satisfactorily I should be more than gratified; and this I suggested to him.

"My dear boy," he answered, "every penny I have spent will be as satisfactorily accounted for as being my own legitimate money as what I have just told you. I have never committed an illegal or dishonorable act in its acquirement, and when the time comes to explain, I will do it; but not yet."

He touched a button on his left, and I was conscious of slightly increased speed.

The green fields were now beneath us, and the few clouds that hovered above only kept the sun from being too warm. The motion of the most perfect boat, gliding before an imperceptible breeze, would be barbarous compared with ours.

Our vessel was loaded with every luxury, including

such clothing as we should need in the latitudes we proposed to visit. And not only were there suits for cold weather but for warm as well, we having left our trunks at the Mustapha. Furs and eider-downs were here galore, beside every contrivance for Arctic comfort. Beyond these, we had abundance of fire-arms, and ammunition. Our sleeping apartments were luxurious. They were situated forward, with a comfortable bed in each, and separated by a curtain with rings which slid upon a brass rod, running parallel with the length. Our cooking arrangements were astern, and immediately before them our dining room or saloon—a cosy little apartment with sliding windows, which could be opened to admit the purest air in the world. Indeed the ventilation had been admirably planned, and nowhere, or in any kind of weather need we suffer from a fetid atmosphere. In the center, but below the main deck, was the motive power, controlled from a small table above, where Torrence manipulated screws, levers, and springs, utterly beyond my comprehension. The machinery was entirely out of the way, and the space utilized to admirable advantage. Cushioned seats surrounded the wall of the saloon, and above was an open deck which ran the entire length of the boat. This was surrounded by an aluminum rail, filled in with a fine net of the same material. It required more nerve than I possessed at first to mount the ladder and look out over the taffrail, although the sense of security below was perfect, so that I could inspect the country from the saloon windows with as much indifference as though I were on the deck of an ocean steamer. It was not long, however, before I could go above and lean over the bulwarks with equal intrepidity. Through the hatch the sky was always visible, even in the saloon, which was never closed except in cold or stormy weather.

In order to make the construction of our air ship perfectly clear, let the reader imagine a gigantic cartridge or cigar, tapering at each end. Now flatten the top of your cigar, and put a railing around it and it would represent our upper deck. Now, divide your cigar longitudinally halfway between the upper deck and the bottom, and from end to end; and you have our main deck; in the center of which is the saloon or dining room, or general living room, to the rear of which is the kitchen, and forward, our beds. Beneath this deck is the machinery, entirely out of sight, and operated from either the saloon or the upper deck.

Our larder was more than ample; comprising an endless variety of tinned goods, as well as quantities of such vegetables as would keep in the open. We had large supplies of both fresh and salt meats, and all arranged to handle conveniently. In short, it was a camping outfit upon an extended scale, including wines, fruits, medicines and implements which might become necessary during the voyage. Having to do our own work, the equipment had been planned upon the most judicious and labor saving lines, so that it was astonishing how little effort was required to prepare a meal; and having no back yard to keep tidy, it was only necessary to throw the scraps and refuse overboard.

At times when we hovered nearer the surface of the earth it was amusing to see what excitement we caused the populace. In passing over a village the entire population would turn out into the streets, and shout themselves hoarse before leaving them out of sight, and being unlike the ordinary balloon, we were naturally looked upon with greater astonishment. Torrence having set his controlling apparatus, it no longer required attention, until some change in speed, elevation, or direction was desired; so that he was as free to move about the vessel as I was. The landscape was passing beneath us, with a steady flowing motion, giving the impression that a considerable distance would be covered during the day, although the rate of speed was deceptive. It was interesting to trace our course over the charts, with which we were amply provided. Maps of each of the counties were spread out upon the table, and we were singularly well situated to test their accuracy.

I was wondering how fast we were going and inquired.

"About twenty-five miles an hour," said Torrence; "she is capable of much greater speed; but there's no hurry, and I don't want to strain her on her maiden trip."

"And how high are we?"

"About five hundred feet."

I was reflecting that it was no very great height, or extraordinary speed, when I heard the sharp swinging sound of a bullet, and looked down. I saw a man passing through a field with a gun in his hand and looking up. Evidently he had fired at us, not knowing what we were; possibly with the intention of finding out.

"He's going to shoot again!" I called to Torrence; but at that minute my brother pressed a button and we were swung aloft with great velocity, as if seized by some gigantic hand.

"I shan't give him a chance," he answered, as we plunged into a cloud, and then darted forward with increased speed. Again we were enveloped in a dense wet blanket, but as there was no fear of a collision, did not slacken our rate, but swept on like a hurricane unable to see a thing in any direction beyond the vessel.

"Now," said Torrence, looking at a small instrument on the governing board, "we are whirling along at the rate of fifty miles an hour. Risky business on land in a cloud like this, but here—thank Heaven—there is nothing on the track! When we lower ourselves out of the fog, and come in view of the earth again, our sporting friend will be lost to sight."

In about ten minutes we dropped to our former level, and reduced our speed. Of course there was no reason why we should not remain above, except that it was more interesting to have the earth for a companion.

"Suppose he had hit us?" I observed.

"There's not one chance in a hundred that he would hurt us if he had. I prepared for such enterprising fools by protecting her critical parts with asbestos and rubber; but it isn't pleasant to be fired at, and when one can move out of range so easily it seems the right thing to do."

Later in the day I went above and found it the pleasantest part of the boat, and was surprised to find how all fear had left me. I asked Torrence if he intended to land anywhere in England; to which he gave a negative answer, saying that it might not be safe, from the danger cf having papers served upon him.

"There is no necessity to halt," he added; "our course is probably watched, and the news of our landing will be telegraphed to London, and they might make it difficult for us to get away again. We are safe out of their reach now, and it would be better to let well enough alone. When I land it will be upon some uninhabited coast where they can't find us."

"How long can you keep afloat?" I inquired.

Torrence laughed.

"Forever, if I want to. There's no limit to our capacity in that line. When the chemicals are exhausted, or have formed new combinations, I have only to supply the proper proportions of air and water, and the original conditions are restored. So if for any reason it should prove inconvenient to land, all we have to do is to drop a line with a bucket over any river or sea, and pull up a pail of water, run the compressor into the generator with the chemicals—and presto—all the power is restored. It is perpetual motion, with the very minimum of attention. Rather it is gravitation neutralized; and so simple, it is a marvel men never thought of it before."

I had made no inquiry about the North Pole, supposing it was only a jest; not doubting, however, that he really meant to make an extended trip northward; but now, on alluding to the subject, Torrence declared that it was his serious intention to penetrate into the mysteries of the Polar regions, farther than any navigator had ever gone

"We may find it worth our while," he said, "and there is no reason why we should not.

I told him that while I felt some doubt about the ice barriers, I was ready to follow him anywhere; to which he answered with a good deal of force that so long as the vessel depended only on the atmosphere for her support, he could see no reason why we could not ride over icebergs, frozen mountains and continents, to the ends of the earth. All we had to do was to keep above all obstructions, and to prevent ourselves from freezing, against which possibility we were amply provided. He showed me how our saloon could be made perfectly snug, and heated to any temperature desired; and that the motive apparatus was entirely protected, and could likewise be kept warm.

"Should our upper deck become loaded with snow," he added, "we shall be obliged to put on our extra feathers and go above to clean it off; not such a very difficult

matter when you consider that we are well provided with
the appliances."

Indeed, it seemed to me that nothing had been overlooked, and as Torrence had all his life had a hankering for Arctic exploration, I was not greatly astonished at his decision. I reflected that the pole could never be reached except by balloon, and that the difficulty of ordinary ballooning was the impossibility of advancing against air currents, and that since our ship had overcome that point, it did really appear as if we might be in a fair way to accomplish something more than other explorers. I became greatly interested, and began to look for marvelous results.

At noon I went into the galley and prepared dinner, while Torrence kept watch above on the upper deck, where there was also a duplicate controlling board. We had eaten nothing since the previous night; the excitement of getting off having kept the thought of food from entering our heads, but now we were hungry. It was undoubtedly the first time since the creation that a meal had been cooked and eaten at that elevation over Northhampton, but it was none the worse for that, and two hungrier men could not have honored the occasion. From our seats in the saloon we had a good outlook upon every side. Forward we looked directly ahead through the cuddy ports—aft—through our stern lights in the galley, and upon either side were great sliding windows. The watch was, of course, only to guard against any unexpected elevation in the land, such as a hill, otherwise—or even had we been a little higher—we might have drawn the blinds and run on with impunity. After dinner we threw the scraps overboard, and went on deck for a smoke, and watched the country steadily slipping away beneath us. We were fanned by a gentle breeze, which might have been stiffer, but such wind as there was, was blowing dead aft.

"This," said Torrence, looking about him with pride, "is what I call the climax of living. Above your enemies; above your friends; and out of reach of all the petty annoyances of earth!"

I was as jubilant as he, and found it quite as difficult to conceal my emotions, which were altogether natural; for has not flight been always regarded as a prerogative of angels? and has not man aspired to it as the most perfect form of migration? The exhilaration was beyond description; and as we swept on through that long summer day, there was a sense of power and freedom which no other form of locomotion could impart.

"I could never be content to live down there again!" I said, flipping the ashes from my cigar overboard.

"Nor I," said Torrence; "not after this experience. The sky is good enough for me!"

Toward evening we could hear the tinkling of bells and lowing of herds, and catch an occasional shout of surprise from a frightened farmer, as we dipped a little nearer earthward, and then skurried aloft and away, before he had time to recover his equanimity. At a small village in the southern part of Lincolnshire we pounced suddenly upon a traveling circus, and stampeded the entire crowd, not one of which will ever forget us. It was the grandest game imaginable; to come swooping down to within fifty or seventy-five feet of the ground, over an unsuspecting congregation of countrymen, and then dart onward and upward amid their shouts of consternation. However, we did not indulge in this sort of thing often, not wishing to incur the risk of being fired at. It showed, nevertheless, the absolute control we had over the machine, and was interesting from a scientific, as well as a humorous point of view.

Toward sundown I smelled salt air, and knew we were approaching the sea. Then we ran into a bank of mist, and the earth was lost to view. I asked Torrence where we were heading for, and he said:

"I am going to run around the city of Hull; leaving it a few miles upon our right, so as not to attract attention, and then cross over to Norway."

"You surely don't intend to try the North Sea tonight!" I exclaimed in surprise.

"Why not? There is no danger," he answered.

I did not argue the matter, feeling safe in his hands. The fog bank continued for some minutes, and when we suddenly ran out of it, imagine my astonishment to find ourselves hovering directly over a large city, with the sea beyond.

X.

TORRENCE jumped up in consternation, and looking overboard, exclaimed with an oath that he thought we were at least five miles to the southwest of that town.

"And what difference does it make?" I inquired.

"Look for yourself!" he cried; "they are expecting us. I feared our course would be telegraphed to all sea ports; but they shan't track me out of the country," he added, looking aloft significantly, "that is, not if I can help it."

"I should say we had decidedly the whip handle of them!" I replied.

"So we have. Of course they can't stop us, but I think it will be just as well to give them a false scent for their trouble. It may be interesting to use a little strategy with these people, Gurt, although we are undoubtedly masters of the situation."

Looking down I saw that the streets were crowded with people gazing up at us; and around the Wilberforce monument, on both sides of the bridge, it looked as if a mob had gathered to intercept our progress. In the open square, probably not less than a hundred soldiers had been assembled under arms, and had a very threatening aspect.

"Surely they won't fire on us!" I exclaimed.

"Not a bit of danger, they wouldn't dare; and if they did, they couldn't hurt us. No, the red coats are only for show; but if they got ugly, we could clean out the crowd by simply dropping a lot of cartridges overboard, without taking our guns out of the racks."

He pressed a button, turned a lever, and we slowed down.

"They want to speak to us, and perhaps it will be just as well to give them a chance."

A man was waving a white flag, evidently intended to attract our attention. He appeared to be some high functionary of the town, judging from his dress and general deportment. He held a paper in his other hand, which he indicated was for us. Torrence waved his handkerchief in reply, and pulled the air ship down to a dead halt, about two hundred and fifty feet above the level of the street.

"It may be the injunction!" I suggested.

"Too late for that now," said Torrence; "they can't enjoin me after I've left. But I don't want them to know my course, and shall therefore humbug them a little."

He looked earnestly above at a great white cloud that had crept up from the southwest, and which had now nearly covered the sky. He then took a pencil, and with a writing pad resting on the rail, wrote:

"If you have any communication to make I will let down a line."

This he threw overboard. It was picked up immediately, and handed to the official who was standing quite separate from the others. Shouts of "lower your line!" were now heard distinctly, and in another minute we had dropped a cord overboard, with a screw tied to the end for a weight. It did not take long to draw up the line again, at the end of which was an official looking document. Torrence tore open the envelope hastily, and began reading. In a minute he thrust it into his pocket and said;

"Rot!"

"What's the matter?" I asked him.

"That blackguard, Hart, wants to get me back to London. Pretends I've committed a crime by moving the air ship without his consent. Promises forgiveness—the lunatic—if I'll return; and—of all the gall in creation—says he will pay down a handsome sum, as he calls it, for a half interest in the air ship, if I'll come back and make it over to him; and then to cap the climax, has the effrontery to threaten me if I don't do it. The fellow must either be a dolt himself or take me for one. But I'll make it interesting for him, nevertheless!"

"They must take us for a brace of nincompoops," I replied; "but is it in the form of a summons?"

"Seems to be a kind of *capias* for my arrest, but how on earth can they execute their orders while I'm up here?" said Torrence.

"You surely don't intend to return," I said, looking over his shoulder.

"Of course not; but I'm determined not to be tracked out of the country. The man has done all he could to thwart me by foul means. He has tried to entrap me in a pretended form of law. He endeavored to prevent my sailing by procuring an injunction issued upon false representations, and if he's fool enough to suppose that I'd return to London—why let him suppose it, and wait, and sweat!"

He now headed the air ship toward London, and rising, sailed away from the town.

"Let them think what they please!" he said. Torrence got up on the top deck and waved his hat, and then every one shouted. I think there was some doubt, however, as to whether we really intended to return, until they saw us gradually head about, and point our prow toward London; then there was an unmistakable yell of delight from every throat.

We were soon running against the wind, due south. The cloud bank which had been steadily pushing up out of the southwest now nearly covered the sky at an elevation of many thousand feet. The city of Hull was fading in the distance. It would soon be lost to sight. I looked at the earth below, and saw that we were steadily ascending upon an inclined plane.

"When we are wrapt in the bosom of the clouds," said Torrence, "I intend to put about, and run directly over their heads out of sight, and be far to seaward before the sun sets."

The clouds were still at a great altitude above us; and to prevent our real intentions being discovered we made the ascent very gradually, still steering south, but on an ascending plane, so that upon entering the cloud bank it would be apparent to all that we were still headed for London. The elevation might be easily accounted for on the hypothesis of air currents, so that no suspicion of insincerity would be aroused on the part of those watching us.

"Now," said Torrence, "as we are going up to a great height, we might find it more comfortable to slip on warmer clothing; or at all events to get out some top coats."

This we did, and then seating ourselves on deck, watched the great feathery mass into whose bosom we were gradually ascending. All at once the earth, the sky, and the greater part of the air ship vanished. We had plunged into the cloud, and I could not even see Torry, who was sitting only a few feet away. Luckily we had on tarpaulins, or we should have been wet to the skin. It was like unaided flight, not even our support being visible. Torrence's voice came out of the invisible, producing a weird sensation, and I could feel that we were still being borne rapidly upward.

"Still ascending?" I inquired, feeling as if I were addressing chaos.

"Still ascending!" came the answer.

"How much higher do we go?"

"Clear above this bank. It will be pleasanter."

The words had a strange unnatural sound, as if coming from under the water. My body was the only objective reality in all creation, and even the more distant parts of that showed a tendency to evade me. Still onward and upward, with nothing to prove our motion save the feeling which the vessel imparted. Suddenly a flood of sunlight enveloped us, and we rose like a duck out of the water into another element. A milk-white sea was spread beneath; a dazzling sky above. Again Torrence was at his screws and levers. We halted, and trembled for a moment in midair, preparatory to changing our course; and then, with the rush of a sudden gale, went swirling ahead in the opposite direction. A minute later he looked at the register and said:

"Altitude, eight thousand two hundred. Speed, a mile a minute. Course, northeast by north!"

And now the Hullites could amuse themselves speculating how long it would take us to reach London, while we swept on to the North Sea.

Our present altitude was unpleasantly cold, and the atmosphere perceptibly rarefied, but it was not the intention to remain at such an elevation longer than necessary, and when well beyond the English coast we would descend to our former level. It was here that a strange sight attracted our attention.

As the sun went down, our milky ocean became transfused with color. At first the change was slight, merely a rosy flush caught against the higher points; but quickly the entire surface was emblazoned; flooded with a million dyes of liquid fire, of a depth and splendor that was dazzling. Such purples, greens, and violets—vivid, intense, pale, and shadowy. It was as if we had suddenly discovered the polychromatic sea of an unknown planet, but a sea whose waters were strangely lacking in specific gravity and from whose surface a myriad eddies of violet and other colored smokes arose like incense, curling, twisting, and falling, and constantly changing tone, shape, and density over the entire mass.

We were bewildered—dazed. While looking down upon this marvelous panorama we were suddenly startled by a sight I shall never forget. Far down to the east another air ship was following at tremendous speed. Black and forbidding it plunged along through the fiery waves, as if bent on running us down. It was the counterpart of our own vessel. We seized each other's hands in amazement, overcome with horror. So brilliant was the scene below that it was an instant before we realized that the awful object was our own phantom, or shadow, cast upon the clouds beneath; but during that instant it was a terrifying sight.

When the sun disappeared we were left in the dull gray of twilight, and as the cold was increasing began at once descending to a lower level. Again the cloud drift was about us, darker and denser than ever; but we quickly passed through it, and I was surprised on emerging, to find the North Sea beneath, and the bluffs of Scarborough fading in the distance.

"There is no danger of our being sighted from land now!" said Torrence, checking our descent, and fixing the altitude at about five hundred feet above the sea.

He also reduced our speed to its former rate, twenty-five miles an hour, which he said was fast enough. The temperature here was warm and pleasant, with light breeze from the southwest, which, by the by, we did not catch, as we were moving faster, in the opposite direction, making our own wind. The sea was deserted, and the land barely visible. It would still be some time before dark, and we took places on deck to watch out for vessels. We had purposely taken a course away from the track of the Wilson steamers, which ply between Drontheim and Hull; not that it was a matter of any vital importance, but Torrence wanted to keep our movements from the public if possible. This was easily done, both by reason of an extended horizon and the enormous speed we could develop if necessary.

As darkness came on we went below, closing the shutters to all lookouts, so as not to reveal our position, and then lighted a swinging lamp, deriving all necessary ventilation from above, whence no light was visible. Having thus shut ourselves in from the observation of the world, we set about getting supper. Nothing could be more cosy; suspended in midair, and surrounded with every luxury, while partaking of our evening meal. The consciousness of absolute independence of the world; the sense of power, which our command of the situation imparted, was, to say the least, extremely gratifying. The feudal lord in his castle might be harried and captured by an enemy; but our enemies could be laughed at with impunity. After supper we amused ourselves with an experiment at dish washing, which proved very satisfactory. The plates were simply piled into a net and lowered to the sea by a cord. After swishing about for a while, they were drawn up clean. Of course we dropped our level to within forty or fifty feet of the water, and greatly slackened speed during the performance, but it saved a lot of trouble. On completing these housekeeping arrangements we climbed up on deck, for a chat and smoke before retiring.

The night was dark, there being no moon, and the sky overcast, beside which the air was misty. We kept our position well above all mast-heads, should there be any, and took extra precaution to prevent a certain nimbus-like reflection against the mist by putting out the lights as soon as supper was over.

Torrence touched his controller, and we rose to our former altitude, remarking that our course only insured us against collision with steamers; and that sailing ships were liable to be found wherever there was water enough to float them.

"And there is no danger of dropping to a lower level unawares?" I asked.

"Such a thing is impossible!" he replied. "The air ship has just such an antipathy for earth as her vibrations impart. It is like the negative pole of a magnet, and unless my controllers move of their own accord, which is an impossibility, the vessel must remain upon just such a plane as I put her."

"How about our being discovered in the morning? Will you run up into the clouds again?"

"No," he said, "let them discover us. I was only anxious to delude those Hullites into the belief that we had really gone back to London. If we are seen tomorrow, they won't find it out until the next day, and they are welcome to all the satisfaction it will give them. One thing is certain; they will never follow where we are going!"

"No," I replied, "not if we succeed in reaching the Pole!"

"There is no *if* in this matter," said Torrence, "for straight through the Arctic regions we go, and without many stations either. I know the road. We 've got the machine. We're stocked with provisions and clothing. The great mystery will be solved at last. By the by, old man, hadn't you better keep a record of our trip?"

"Decidedly!" I replied.

From that time, whenever possible, I wrote up the account of this voyage, beginning with our landing in London; and the present voluminous paper is the result.

At 11 o'clock Torrence insisted on my going below to bed, while he continued the watch above. It was a strange sensation, this crawling into a bunk to sleep on an air ship, but I was exhausted with the excitement of the day, and soon fell into a sound slumber, rocked by the gentle swaying of the car. Nothing could have been more soothing than the situation; though why I should have felt no fear of falling was a mystery, possibly induced by the negation of gravity which pervaded all my surroundings, and perhaps, to a certain extent, even penetrated my own body; though this is only a surmise.

If I dreamed, I do not know it, but was awakened while it was still dark by the sound of music. Sitting up, I listened in amazement. Several instruments were distinctly audible, and these were accompanied by half a dozen voices. Probably every one is familiar with the ravishing charm of music while sleeping, and I awoke enraptured with this unearthly fascination, believing at first that the sound had only been in my dreams; but to my amazement it continued. I recalled immediately where I was, and my astonishment was only increased on remembering our singular isolation. There could be no doubt about it—there were musical instruments, and there were human voices—but where out of heaven or earth did they come from. Slowly I crawled down from my bunk and groped my way through the dividing curtains to Torrence's; but he was not there. I thought it must be nearly morning but evidently he had not come to bed. Had he crossed the North Sea and landed without my knowledge? I could not believe it; nor could I think that we had returned to England. I pinched myself and bit my finger to make sure that I was awake, and then slowly felt the way into the saloon, and having reached the ladder, commenced climbing above, with a horrid dread of some awful catastrophe having befallen us. I stepped out upon the deck and looked around. The dull red glow of Torry's cigar caught my eye; for there he was in the gloom, still sitting where I had left him, his chair against the rail, and his arm hanging over. Evidently he was looking at something below, and leaning outward, did not see me. Here the music was even clearer than it had been below, and I paused for a moment in dumb amazement to listen. The instruments were well played, and the voices strong and thrilling, with a wild pathos. I glanced out over the taffrail. The misty waters were still spread around us, and the swish of the waves was distinctly heard. Feeling as though suddenly bewitched, I groped my way toward Torrence, who at that moment caught sight of me. He raised his hand, and said softly:

"Hush! Do not speak a word!"

I moved cautiously along to his elbow.

"What is it?" I whispered; "where are we, and what does this music mean?"

Taking me by the arm, he said in a low voice:

"We are floating just above the masthead of a Norwegian bark. The men are having a little frolic on board, and are playing and singing!"

He then went on to explain how he had overhauled the bark shortly after I had gone below, and hearing the music had dropped a little and slackened speed to enjoy it.

I looked over the rail and a weird sight it was. Just below, through the turgid atmosphere, was the huge silhouette of the ship, magnified in the fog. A few lights were visible along her deck, and near the center was a reddish glow through which shadowy figures moved and danced. No detail was visible. Nothing but the shifting shadows and the light, and the great mass of the vessel. It was like a huge kinetoscope, with the addition of music.

"The fellows are having a good time!" said Torrence; "sometimes in rifts of the fog we can see them more distinctly. Far from home, and with a good-natured skipper, there is nothing to prevent their enjoying themselves!"

At one moment the shadows would form a circle, when one would step into the glowing center and perform some fantastic evolutions to the music. The whole scene was wild and weird in the extreme. A pink nebulosity from out which dark mysterious figures were forever coming and going, dancing, falling, and jumping.

We lingered quite awhile, looking and listening without their having a suspicion of our proximity, and then Torrence, with a sudden burst of enthusiasm over one of the performers, shouted "Hooray," at the top of his voice. Instantly the music stopped, and every man, seized with panic, looked aloft; but we were dark and silent, and gave no token. Slowly we rose again in the air, and in another minute had left the Norwegian bark far behind. It was a queer experience, and I have often wondered how those people explained the mystery of the heavenward voice.

XI.

The morning was radiant; not a cloud in the sky, nor a hatful of wind. It was Torry's turn to rest, while I kept watch, and that he needed it was shown by the fact that he slept until noon. Meanwhile I got my own breakfast, and set his aside; and then resumed the lookout above. From my lofty perch I caught the occasional glint of a sail, or the dark trail of smoke from a southerly steamer, but these were quickly dropped astern, no matter what their course. Our rate of progress was uninterrupted, and the fascination of flight grew with familiarity. When Torrence came on deck he decided to increase our speed, wishing to make the coast of Norway before night, on account of the intricacy of the mountain channels to be encountered there.

"Once in sight of land," he said, "we can shape our course and elevation accordingly."

I agreed with him, and the water was soon rushing beneath us at a fearful rate. Both sailing ships and steamers were now passed like stationary objects, but the wonder with which we inspired the passengers unfortunately escaped our observation. The day was warm, and the speed agreeable, allowing us to remain on deck in comfort.

While racing, we passed a fleet of schooners loaded with lumber. The consternation caused on board was made apparent by the blast of half a dozen trumpets, which reached our ears in a chorus, although we left the boats so rapidly that the sound was only heard for a minute, and in a quarter of an hour the fleet was out of sight.

At 4 o'clock we caught the first glimpse of the island peaks, off the coast of Norway, and knowing that it would not be dark until after ten, we slackened speed.

Nearing the land the sight was singularly beautiful. The dark blues and greens against the black rocks of those mountain islands, made an intensely vivid picture. Between these lofty heights were revealed far-stretching vistas of bluest sea, bounded again by other islands and other mountains.

Torrence said he should not venture in any of these channels, but proposed running entirely outside the cordon of islands, keeping the coast well in hand upon the right. Fortunately there would be but two or three hours of darkness, or it might have been expedient to seek a higher level to avoid the possibility of accident by collision; as it was, a sharp lookout would be all that was necessary.

After sailing up the coast for a couple of hours, I went below to prepare supper, which we decided to eat on deck, so as not to miss the magnificent scenery. This we did, and later I was instructed in the art of aerial navigation, and after changing our course a few points to seaward for safety, Torrence went below to sleep, leaving me in charge. During this watch our speed was materially lowered, as we did not deem it wise to run rapidly along this dangerous coast, while I was alone on deck.

The feeling of power as I sat there with absolute control of the vessel was exhilarating. I had never had such a sensation before. Like a visitor from another planet I floated on above the sea, inspecting the most exquisitely weird and beautiful scenery, made doubly entrancing by the lingering twilight, which seemed as if it would never fade away. The intensity of the coloring, the purity of the atmosphere, and the marvelous shapes of these mountain islands, made impressions not easily obliterated. There was an endless variety of fiords and water vistas opening between them, and each vista and each island showed something new.

Torrence slept soundly until 10:30 o'clock when, as the twilight had deepened into gloom, I thought it best to call him, and went below to sleep myself. The night was quickly passed, as there was little of it, and in the watches we rounded the headlands of the Sogne, the Geiranger, and the Romsdal fiords, and then steering a little more to the east with the trend of the coast, made for the great bay of Trondhjem, which we reached about the middle of the afternoon. Skirting the opening of the fiord, Torrence asked if I thought it worth while to pay a visit to this historic city of the Norwegians— Trondhjem being one of their most important and beautiful towns. If we concluded to go, he said it would be best, in order not to attract attention, to land upon one of the lonely island hilltops near the town, and thence make our way by foot and boat. We talked the matter over, but finally decided to let all towns alone, it being possible that the authorities held orders for our detention, as they had in Hull.

"We are quite safe where we are," said Torrence, "and when we stop, let it be away from people."

Having decided to stick to the air ship, we went directly on past the mouth of the bay without entering it. The town itself is a number of miles further up the fiord.

We now headed straight for the North Cape, which we reached in about five days from London. We passed the

Lofoten isles, the Vest fiord, Tromsöe, Hammerfest, and other points of beauty and interest along this marvelous coast, without stopping at any of them, and landed upon the northernmost point of Europe without accident. On this desolate headland we decided to make our first landing, to overhaul the machinery, stretch our legs, and have a general pow-wow on Mother Earth before proceeding further.

An elevated plain, lopped off at one end by a wall of granite, hundreds of feet high, and overlooking the sea, stood ready to receive us. No human habitation is visible, but thousands of pigeons living in the crannies of the cliff were frightened at our approach, and flew about wildly in all directions. Above this plain we halted, and then slowly began our descent.

At the water level on the east is a steamboat landing, where the Olaff Kyrre stops once or twice during the summer for the benefit of tourists who find their way to the top by a winding path cut in the face of the wall. Thence to the northern cliff is a level walk of over a mile across this plain, along which a wire is stretched to guide those who happen to be caught in a fog, which at times is very dense and sudden.

This plain afforded the isolation we sought, and with a slow and steady movement we descended upon it. We touched the ground so lightly that I was not aware of our landing until Torrence threw out the ladder and stepped over. I followed immediately, and then we sent up a shout of triumph for the success that had so far attended our journey. We walked around the air ship, admiring her from every point of view, and then went away to see how she looked at a distance. She was perfect! The grandest thing ever constructed; the most powerful engine for the advance of man's material welfare ever executed. Torrence made a careful examination of her working parts. Not a screw or bearing was out of place; and not withstanding the way we had speeded her on occasions, she was none the worse for it. She was carefully oiled, and where necessary lubricated with graphite, and we had the satisfaction of knowing that she was in quite as good condition as on leaving London.

"I am willing to trust my life in her across the frozen sea!" said Torrence, observing her with intense admiration.

"Now is the time to decide if you're not," I answered; "though for my part I believe she is safer than dry land!"

"That is exactly my idea," said he, "although if you should feel inclined to change your mind, there is another chance at Spitzbergen, where we shall stop again before the final leap."

"I have not the slightest intention of doing so, old boy, in fact I am quite as anxious to get to the pole as you are; and strange as it may seem I feel safer in the air ship than standing here."

We were unanimous in our determination to go to the pole, and I will guarantee that no expedition ever started for there with so good a prospect of reaching it, or with greater comforts than we had.

We cooked our supper near the edge of the cliff overlooking the Arctic Ocean, and we both felt that it was a solemn occasion, for we should soon be placing an impassable gulf between ourselves and the land of human habitations, and entering the great solitudes of the unexplored North.

As there was no wood for fuel, we used an armful of our own kindling, which we had brought for just such occasions, and while drinking hot coffee we discussed the past, and the prospect of the future.

"I am absolutely certain of success,' said Torrence; "nothing but an air ship can reach the pole, and an air ship has never yet tried to get there. What's the use of an old water-tank endeavoring to screw her way through a continent of ice. She might as well run her nose against Gibralter, in the hope of coming out on the other side. The mystery to me is why no one has ever tried this before."

"You're not there yet, old man," I answered; "don't crow before you're out of the woods."

"Ah!" said Torrence, smiling, "I believe the worst wood we had to get out of was London; and having shot the rapids at Gravesend, I think we can go the rest of the way."

I was quite as enthusiastic as he, but being without his knowledge, had not the same convictions.

"And so Spitzbergen will be our next stopping place?" I observed, between mouthfuls of coffee.

"Yes, when we shoot off this cliff to the northward we'll set neither eye nor foot on land for five hundred miles. So make the most of this boggy sward while we have it. Five hundred miles to the north of this is pretty far north—and then——"

"And then our real journey begins," I interrupted.

"You may say so," he answered, broiling a piece of bacon with a fork over the coals. "Certainly the most interesting part begins after leaving Spitzbergen. I flatter myself that the entire voyage from that point will be one of unusual interest."

I had every confidence in our ability to reach the pole, for without the difficulty of ice to encounter, I could see no good reason why we should not. Moreover, the season of the year would insure pleasant weather in high latitudes; there would probably be no detention, as in

THE SECRET OF THE EARTH. 113

other expeditions, and it seemed a reasonable presumption that we should reach 90° north, while the summer was yet at its height. Presently a dense fog came rolling in from the sea, and in a few minutes the air ship was lost to view, although not more than forty or fifty yards from where we were sitting. We continued eating our lunch like a couple of specters on each side of the fire, until, finding that we were getting wet, I got up to go after some oilskins. I thought I knew exactly where the machine was, believing that I had sat down with my back toward it, and at best did not suppose it possible to lose so large an object so close at hand. I walked until quite sure that I had covered the distance separating me from it, and then continued to walk on farther. Suddenly I stopped, convinced that I had mistaken the direction. I started upon another course, and after another unsuccessful tramp stopped again. Then I called for Torrence, and told him that I was lost. His voice sounded much farther than I thought it should, and I tried to get back to him by following it. Presently he called out imperatively:

"Stop! don't try to find me. Stand perfectly still until it clears!"

"Why not? if you'll keep on talking I'm sure to find you."

Then he shouted vehemently.

"Stop! for God's sake, stop! You're risking your life with every step. Have you forgotten that we're on the edge of a precipice?"

I had not forgotten it, but his words startled me into realizing the danger of my position, and I stood perfectly still. Strangely enough I had not thought of the possibility of tumbling over the cliff, believing all the while that I was walking in the opposite direction; but now the murmur of the sea on the rocks below convinced me that I was nearer than I had supposed.

"If you move at all," shouted Torrence, "go only one step at a time. I mean, look carefully at each step before you take it."

I could not imagine how I had come so far, for his voice sounded strangely distant.

"Have you moved from where I left you?" I called.

"No," was the answer, "and don't intend to."

"That's right. I think I can find you if you keep talking."

"All right; go ahead; but watch the ground carefully at every step!"

The truth is I could not see much above a yard at a time, and a misstep would have been fatal. Torrence continued to talk, and I slowly advanced in the direction from which his voice seemed to come. Suddenly my way was blocked by a solid wall and in another instant I saw that it was the air ship. I now perceived why the voice had been so faint, for I had wandered clear around the machine, which had intercepted it.

Feeling my way carefully to the ladder I called out that all was well.

"No matter about the skins," came the answer, "let us get off as soon as possible. Go into the saloon and fetch a ball of twine from the locker; tie one end to the step, then make your way slowly!"

I found the twine; groped forward with the ball in my hand, and reached camp without accident. Then we commenced carrying our cook tools back to the boat.

"There is no place like home!" yelled Torrence, returning with the last load. In another minute he had climbed over the side, and drawing a breath of relief, added:

"It is fortunate we travel by air instead of land or water, because we shan't have to wait for the fog!"

A few minutes more and the ladder was hauled in, the gangway closed, the hatch to the upper deck shut down, and we were comfortably established in our cosy cabin. Then Torrence going to his controlling board, pressed a button, moved a lever, turned a screw, and we were swung gently up, and resumed our journey north, 11° west, headed for Spitzbergen, which Torrence said we should reach within twenty-four hours.

I don't know why it was always such an indescribable pleasure to feel clear of earth; and yet this was the fact. The first sensation of being above the ground was a thrill of inexplicable delight. It seemed as if we were lifted into a higher plane of being, morally as well as bodily, involving a certain arrogant sympathy for those left behind. The poor creatures knew so little about life, and it even amazed me to think that I had been one of them for so many years without realizing the depravity of my state. Life without an air ship was not worth the living; but with it, I could answer Mr. Mallock's question without thought or hesitation.

When the fog cleared we were many miles to seaward, and the rock-bound coast of Europe showed only as a dark line against the horizon. Torrence said there was nothing to prevent our going into the cuddy for a sleep, which we needed, that in our present position there was no danger; that collision was impossible, and falling equally so. That the air ship was headed for Spitzbergen, and could take care of herself—in short, that we should be just as safe as if sleeping in the Mustapha. I suggested the possibility of icebergs but he explained that we were above the altitude of the highest ever known in this quarter, and that, moreover, it was improbable that any would be passed at this season and this locality. And so, taking his word for it, we both turned in and slept ten hours without waking. At the end of that time we felt like new men, and climbed up on deck to look out.

A dull gray sea, bounded only by the sky-line, was rushing away beneath, and so far as I could tell, our speed and elevation had remained unchanged. Despite my brother's assurance, I could not help feeling that we had taken an awful risk about the icebergs; but when he told me that the ice masses formed off Spitzbergen were greatly inferior in size to those coming down from Greenland, I was better satisfied. Indeed, it was very rare, he said, that an iceberg in this part of the ocean was more than one hundred and fifty to two hundred feet in height; they were differently shaped, being flat on top, and covering considerable area, but never high; while our own altitude was more than a thousand feet. Torrence had made quite a study of the polar regions, and I had great confidence in his judgment.

On we sped—I cannot say during the day, for there was no night, although we kept a record of the time, and at regular intervals darkened our sleeping apartments to delude ourselves into the belief that it was night above. While on watch we sunk to a lower level, as being warmer, although it was getting to be the time of year when the mercury seldom falls below freezing even in this latitude. Occasional masses of ice were now passed, though none of any considerable size, and I can truthfully say that, except when above the clouds, we had not, so far, suffered from cold.

About thirty hours after leaving the North Cape of Norway the irregular, saw-shaped outline of Spitzbergen peeped above the horizon. Our passage had been uneventful, and as we neared the barren shores of the west island, there was nothing to invite us to linger. We decided, however, to land for a short time before pursuing our journey northward.

Proceeding with care we entered the channel to the east of Prince Charles Foreland, known as Foreland Bay. Moving up this passage to its upper terminal, and then crossing King's Bay, we effected a landing opposite Cape Mitra, on the eastern shore of Cross Bay. The whole country was desolate beyond description, and we only halted for another examination of our vessel before plunging into the great unknown beyond.

We touched earth on a shelly beach, and congratulated ourselves on having reached this high latitude in safety.

Drift wood abounded, and we soon had a roaring fire, with the prospect of a good meal ahead. We took care this time to guard against fog by carrying a line from the air ship to our encampment.

Torrence wanted to shoot a reindeer, an ice fox, or a polar bear before leaving, although neither of us cared to make a sporting tour for fear of getting lost; moreover, the time was valuable. There were no indications of life from our point of landing, although we knew the islands abounded in Arctic game, and that the animals mentioned were plentiful. Torrence seemed particularly anxious to run across a herd of deer, and when I suggested that a white bear would be a finer sight, he shrugged his shoulders and said:

"Perhaps; but I have special reasons for wanting a deer, which I will explain later; meanwhile let us get dinner."

And so we set to work upon the best our larder afforded, feeling that it would probably be our last meal on land for a very indefinite time. Indeed when I thought of the future and the unexplored regions ahead, and the mysteries of the unknown awaiting us, I confess to some nervous apprehension.

The realm we were about to penetrate had been from all time screened from the eyes of man; was it not sacrilege to force the hand of Providence and expose it now?

· · · · · · · · ·

XII.

We were in the midst of dinner when down the beach came a great, white, swaggering bear, sniffing the air from side to side, for the fumes of bacon, sausage, and fried potatoes which happened just then to be in the pan. The suddenness of the apparition froze every drop of sporting blood in my veins; but this perhaps, is not so much to be marveled at, when it is remembered that we had left our arms and ammunition in the air ship, full fifty yards away, though fortunately in the other direction. Dropping the remains of dinner on the ground, we ran with one accord and mortifying speed to the big machine, tumbled in over the side, and hauled up the ladder with a dexterity never before equalled. Here we armed ourselves with a couple of Winchester rifles, and then crawled up on deck to watch the enemy. It was a painful sight to see our excellent repast scattered right and left, nosed, pawed, and devoured before our very eyes; but it was satisfactory to observe that the beast burned his mouth and paws in his greediness. When he got through licking his chops and sucking his fingers he had time to look around, and catching sight of the air ship, was surprised. Evidently he was familiar with that part of the coast and had never seen such a thing before. We decided to wait until curiosity had brought him nearer, which it was not long in doing. Still sniffing, now probably for danger, the monster slowly approached, and when two-thirds of the distance had been covered, he stopped suddenly, overcome with astonishment. It was our time to fire, and crack went the rifles, almost at the same instant. It had been previously agreed that I was to aim for the head, while Torrence was to shoot immediately behind the shoulder. The animal started up with a snort, surprised and wounded. He showed his teeth and snapped as he caught sight of us, and then turned and began licking his wound. I was surprised that he had not keeled over stone dead, for as the blood trickled down over his long, dirty, white hair it looked to me as if it issued from a vital point, but it was difficult to tell. Presently the sound of our voices renewed his anger, and he came at us, on a gallop. We waited until he touched the vessel, when, just as we were about to fire again, the bear raised himself upon his hind legs as if trying to get a foothold to board us, and rolled over dead without a struggle. We discharged our rifles into the animal's skull as he lay there, and then after a few minutes went to work upon him. It was a great find, as he was large and fat. We soon had him bled, and cut up into convenient sizes. We left the skin for other explorers, not caring to bother with it, but the principal part of the meat was carefully stowed on board. After this adventure we went back and finished our dinner, or rather we cooked another; this time being careful to carry the rifles with us.

As we sat smoking our pipes around the camp fire, after finishing our repast, I asked Torrence why he had been so anxious to kill a reindeer.

"For marks!" he said, blowing a volume of smoke into the air.

"Marks!" I exclaimed in astonishment; "what marks? What are you talking about?"

"Ear marks," he answered, still puffing away at his pipe.

"And why are the ear marks of a Spitzbergen reindeer especially interesting?" I inquired.

Torrence looked at me thoughtfully as he answered:

"Because they have been made by the hand of man!"

"And why shouldn't they be?"

"For a very simple reason. Because man does not inhabit these islands!"

"Then how is your theory supported?"

"By an enormous array of accumulated evidence that there are vast continents to the north of us, which are inhabited both by man, reindeer, and other animals!"

"You mean *continent,* not *continents,*" I suggested.

"On the contrary; I believe there are continents fully equaling in size Europe, Asia, Africa and the two Americas!"

Had the fellow lost his mind? I looked carefully to see if he were serious, and observing no indications of a joke, answered:

"Your theory might be all right if there was room enough around the pole for all the land you speak of; but as there isn't, I am afraid you'll have to be contented with one very moderate-sized continent, which I will admit it is barely possible may exist. As for its being inhabited, I don't believe it."

"It's a pity, Gurthrie, for you'll have to believe a great deal more than that before you get through with this journey. But speaking of the reindeer, do you know that immense herds of them roam over these islands; and that the enormous numbers which have been killed in former years—amounting to several thousand sometimes, in a single season—tends to support the theory that they have migrated from another land? But that is not all; for these creatures carry with them stronger evidences of a habitable region to the north—for they cannot have migrated from the south."

"And what is that evidence?" I asked.

"The ear marks we were speaking of," continued Torrence, "thousands of these reindeer are marked; that is, they have their ears cut in a way to indicate that it was done by the hand of man. It is the opinion of many hunters in this region that these animals have emigrated from an unknown country to the north; and that is my belief also!"

"But you spoke of *continents!*" I urged.

"And I still speak of continents. But wait; I do not wish to startle you, or shake your faith in my sanity. What I know, I know; and what I know, you shall soon see for yourself. But mind, we are going into a warmer climate, and we shall find all that I have intimated. But a little at a time; do not strain your mind with thoughts you have never yet learned to assimilate."

I admitted that if it were a fact about the ear marks it was certainly a curious one; whereupon Torrence declared that it was only one out of many reasons for the theory, which he would explain later. Altogether there was a conviction in his manner which was very impressive. I listened to him talk for more than an hour, and must confess that he produced an array of alleged facts that were startling. He ended by declaring that our discoveries would vastly exceed those of Columbus in their magnitude, and that we should go down to history as the greatest of all explorers!

When Torrence stopped talking, our pipes had gone out, and the fire was reduced to a few glowing coals. We got up to make preparations for a final departure into the great unknown, and I confess, with a good deal more awe than I had previously thought possible. If Torrence was oppressed by the contemplation of what we were about to undertake, he only showed it by a more earnest and serious demeanor than he had yet exhibited. For my part, I dreaded to leave the island, overcome with the thought of what might be awaiting us. Beyond this, I was seriously puzzled by my brother's remark about *continents*, and their size, but could not bring myself to insist on an explanation, which he seemed, for the present, disinclined to give. We had started together, and we must pull together for the rest of the journey, come what might.

We now made a thorough and exhaustive examination of the machine, and were gratified to find that everything was still in perfect order, as we did not wish to land upon an unknown continent without the means of returning. The vessel had been so thoroughly built, regardless of cost, that she seemed as staunch as when she first came out of the hands of the contractors at London. We took aboard several casks of fresh water for drinking, besides our bear meat; put everything to rights, and then shutting ourselves inside, concluded to take a long sleep before resuming our journey northward. Nothing disturbed us; not even a polar bear discovered our position, and when we arose at the end of twenty hours' rest, we partook of another hearty meal, and were ready to move.

Taking our places on deck, Torrence touched the controllers, and in a minute we were suspended a couple of hundred feet above the beach. Then slowly we commenced navigating the tortuous coast, first bearing eastwardly across the bay, and then following up the shore line as far as the Norwegian isles, a reef of rocky keys off the northwest coast. Here we took careful bearings; made allowances for the rather singular behavior of the compass, and then heading the ship due north, bore away upon our course.

I felt as if I were about to sail over the face of an unknown planet, and in a great measure, it was just this that we were destined to accomplish. I was fully alive to the terrors of that mysterious, strangely isolated quarter of our globe, where it seemed as if the Almighty had set his ban against man's advance, by encircling it with an impenetrable barrier, to cross which, every effort, of which history holds any record, was fruitless.

When the granite cliffs of Spitzbergen were fading from our view, Torrence turned to me, and said with emphasis:

"Mark my word! We are going to find a better climate ahead than we have left behind. We are going to find land, and a race of men who are unknown to the world. We are going to find many other things; but put that much down as a record if you will;" and so I have entered it.

We were alone, and with a loneliness never felt before. The last-saw like edge of Spitzbergen had sunk below the water line to the south. Yes, even that terribly Northern foothold must now be looked upon as a southern home, when compared with our present resting place. Should we ever look forward to reaching it, as a tropical paradise—the bourne of all our hopes and expectations? For Spitzbergen had known men; it was a part of our own world, and as I watched it fade and sink away it seemed close to all I had ever known and loved in my dear old earth, where nothing could ever be so solemnly, so *awfully* foreign as where we were, and where we were going.

Suddenly it became cold, and looking down we saw that the ocean had grown strangely quiet, the sparkle and motion of the waves having left it. Descending to a lower level we saw that we were passing over a field of pack ice, solid and impenetrable; and we slackened speed, and sunk still lower to examine it. As we slipped along close above its hummocky surface, at the rate of ten or twelve miles an hour, we could appreciate some of the difficulties with which Arctic explorers have had to contend. What a herculean task to forge ahead through such an obstacle, whether with ship or sled! And yet with what absolute ease we seemed about to solve the puzzle of the ages. However, we were still a long way from the pole, and there was no telling what might happen before reaching it. At times I would be seized with a superstitious dread of some awful impending calamity, or of some horrible condition of the earth's surface or atmosphere, which would make it impossible for man to live where we were going. But Torrence was firm and resolute, and if such thoughts ever troubled him, he did not speak of them. I could scarcely believe that we should continue to the end as easily as we had begun, and advance without hindrance into the forbidden mysteries beyond.

It grew colder, although I can truly say, so well were we provided against the weather, that neither of us had suffered, and we continued to sit on deck in our top coats without inconvenience. Torrence made half a turn in the screw controlling our elevation, and we rose slightly higher, as there were dangerous looking inequalities in the ice ahead. We also moderately increased our speed, keeping, however, low enough, and running with just such headway as would enable us to see to the best advantage the formations below and around us.

Presently it began to snow, and the ice field became covered with a tattered sheet, the uneven protuberances sticking through in dirty patches. But it was only a summer shower, which we ran out of in a dozen or twenty miles, leaving the sea of frozen waves and hummocks bare again. Then we came to floes, or extended areas of ice that had not packed, wind-driven into the solid masses behind, but were still shifting about with the current, undecided as to their future course. The crunching and roaring of these masses was horrible. Detached areas, miles in extent, would rush at each other with Titanic power, and meeting, rend the air with deafening crashes like the wrecking of a thousand trains.

Next came the piling up into strange, fantastic shapes. Pyramids, towers, and grim fortifications would threaten each other for a minute, and then slowly advancing, meet with a report like thunder, splitting the air from earth to heaven, and melt into each other, to be again squeezed and piled into new designs. It was an awful, yet fascinating sight. But the worst had not come. Onward we swept over this crunching and grinding world, roaring in agony to free itself from the embrace of the demon Cold, which was slowly but surely stiffening it into immovable forms. And as we advanced, the thundering of the under world grew less, for there was no more movement. The forts, the towers, and the pyramids had become fixed and silent, and a city of weird architecture followed. A city of frozen monuments, deserted streets, of isolated villas, cathedrals, parks, and gardens, lakes of dazzling whiteness, turreted battlements with mounted guns commanding open spaces, and distant rivers threading the land beyond. But a deathlike silence reigned. It was a marvelous change, but a greater still was coming. Looking far to the north we observed that these singular ice forms were growing in size and splendor, so that it seemed advisable to rise a little higher to avoid a collision. But they grew. The forts became lofty houses; the houses cathedrals, and the cathedrals great ragged mountains of ice, with pinnacles reaching skyward.

. . . .

"This," said Torrence, turning toward me with great solemnity, "is the Palæocrystic Sea—the sea of ancient ice—the sea which man has never crossed. We have passed the limits of the known; beyond lies the mystery of the undiscovered world. A world which you will soon admit is greater, and of far more importance than our own!"

Although I could not gather his meaning, there was an import in his words that appalled me.

. . . .

And now the scene grew more terrible with each mile of advance. Ages of freezing and thawing, accumulations of snow and ice, had produced a spectacle more awful than words can picture. A sea of mountains and valleys; of cañons black in eternal night. A sea of silence. A sea of death.

. . . .

But I will not dwell upon the horrors that separate the known from the unknown. The Palæocrystic is simply an unexplored belt of ice surrounding the poles. Indeed it is not known to be unbroken, or to be of equal severity throughout. It might be termed a ribbon of ice mountains, which has been ages in forming, and which probably will not average more than fifty miles in breadth, and at some points, doubtless much narrower. Beyond it we came upon free ice again, and further reached the open polar sea.

Here was a marked change in the temperature, and as the air currents were from the north, the frozen area had little effect. Our thermometer showed a few degrees above freezing, and a tendency to rise still higher.

We now felt that we were fairly launched into an unknown world. A placid ocean stretched beneath to an unexplored horizon.

"Now!" exclaimed Torrence with enthusiasm; "if there are any discoveries to be made, we ought soon to make them.

Taking out a pair of field glasses we searched the skyline from the upper deck.

"No land in sight!" said Torrence; "but if I am not mistaken, yonder is a flock of wild geese, leading our course, and not more than half a mile ahead.

"They might be petrels! I suggested.

"Whatever they are, I propose to give them a chase. A bird or two for dinner wouldn't be a bad idea!"

Although I had never hunted wild geese in an air ship, I agreed that it ought to be good sport.

XIII.

STEERING directly after the geese on an ascending plane, we put on a tremendous spurt and soon had the whole gang squawking and floundering before us. There were hundreds, and when pressed, set the pace at a rate that made the air whizz by like a hurricane. It was intensely exciting. But the air ship was too swift to afford the slightest chance of their escape. In a few minutes we had overtaken them, broken their columns, and flown directly into the flock. Our shotguns were ready, but, strange as it may seem, we did not use them, because more than a dozen of the birds fell dead upon our deck from sheer fright, and we let the others escape. It was a strange experience; a method of hunting probably never indulged in before; and it was not at all surprising that the birds should have been frightened to death. The geese proved to be fat and a great delicacy.

We then dropped to our former level and speed, and resumed the lookout for land. Ice floes were still occasionally met, though steadily diminishing in size and apparent solidity. A few hours later we passed the last of them, and then met only an occasional chunk, or hummock, which seemed to be floating northward. We determined the direction by descending close to the surface of the water, and making a careful examination. There could be no doubt about it; the currents which carried these ice masses were trending northward. It seemed to imply some mystery, as yet unconsidered, although Torrence thought it possible that they might be vortex in character, returning again to their starting point.

At the usual hour we went below to partake of our midday meal, having first reduced our speed to a rate not exceeding ten miles an hour, not wishing to run upon anything startling during the stay below. It was fortunate we had done so, for upon coming on deck again, we saw a small blue line to starboard, apparently not more than a dozen or fifteen miles away.

"Land!" We both shouted in a breath.

Immediately we changed our course in the direction of this island, as it appeared; and while drifting toward it, considered whether we should call it Attlebridge Land or Torrence Island. Suddenly Torrence, clapping his hand to his head, exclaimed:

"If it's what I now believe it to be, we have not the right to name it!"

"And what do you believe it to be?" I asked.

"An island," said he.

"And why have we not the right to name it?"

"Because I believe it has been already discovered. Because I believe it is inhabited!"

"Inhabited!" I shouted; "and by whom?"

"By a man."

"By a man, or by men? Which did you say?"

"I said by a man—by one man—I believe that island has a *single inhabitant*, but we shall see!"

Again I looked at my brother with curiosity, half-wondering if he were demented.

"I understood you to say that the Palæocrystic Sea was the dividing line between the known and the unknown world.

And you understood me correctly, he replied,

"There is but one man in the world who knows anything about this island; in fact he is the only man living who has a right to name it."

"I should imagine that the inhabitant you speak of would have an equal right," I observed.

"That is just where you make your mistake," said Torrence with a knowing look. "Were he an ordinary man he might have; but under the circumstances—hardly!"

"And what are the circumstances? Why should he not name it?" I insisted.

"Because he is an idiot!" said Torrence.

I started.

"And how do you know that?"

"If I am wrong we shall soon find out. If I am right we shall equally soon know it!"

He was searching the point of land with his glass, and seemed disinclined to continue the subject, so with rather unpleasant emotions, I concluded to wait for developments. It could not now be long before I should know if there was any foundation for Torrence's talk. Certainly what he had said savored of lunacy.

We now bore down upon the island rapidly, and saw a rocky ledge surmounting a narrow beach, where we concluded to land. The promontory had a flat top, about thirty feet above the sea and we lowered ourselves gently down upon it. Scarcely had we done so than Torrence said:

"We shall probably have to explore in order to find traces of our inhabitant; and I wonder, therefore, if it would not be wiser to sail around the island before disembarking. It would certainly save trouble."

We concluded therefore to take a leisurely tour of discovery, and ascertain the size and general contour before landing; and so without further ado, we rose again, almost as soon as we had touched the ground.

The island was rocky, but not without vegetation, its arable parts being carpeted with vivid green. There was also a quantity of small trees, bearing a peculiar fruit, which neither of us had ever seen before. Inland, it rose into billowy hillocks, to probably an elevation of a couple of hundred feet, near the center. Its shores were indented with a number of bays or inlets, some of which made considerable inroad upon it. To the best of our judgment it was about four miles long, and of very irregular width, as in places these inlets nearly cut it in two. Thousands of pigeons flew out wherever we approached their rocky nestings, but there appeared to be no other animal life.

"And where is your inhabitant?" I asked, when we had gone around the greater part of the coast.

"We may not be able to find him at all," he answered; "I said we should probably discover traces of him if we searched. For my part, I have not given that up."

But the words were scarcely spoken when he sprang to the governing board and halted the vessel. I saw that we were hovering over a green sward which sloped gently to the water's edge near the head of one of the inlets described. Lowering ourselves gradually we landed on a grassy knoll, and Torrence immediately threw out the ladder and went over. I followed him, and in a minute saw what had attracted his attention from above, but which had entirely escaped mine. It was a rough looking stone, set on end, in the sward, and there being no other stones in the vicinity, it presented rather a peculiar appearance, inasmuch as it seemed almost certain that it had been placed there by human hands. We examined it with growing interest. There was something uncanny in finding such an object in such a place. It looked like a monument intended to mark a tomb, or the headstone of a grave in some country churchyard. It was about three feet high, nearly covered with a green mould, and had the appearance of great age.

"This," said Torrence, "is the first indication I have found!"

He was passing his hand over the face of the stone.

"Your single inhabitant must be a giant to plant such a rock as that!" I observed.

"Not at all," said Torrence; "I have no idea that he even touched it."

"Then you think nature placed it there?"

"Neither; but what is this?"

He was still examining the face of the thing studiously, with both hands and eyes. I stooped down to examine it. There was a roughness or indentation, which did not seem to be natural. Scraping the moss away from the crevices, we discovered to my amazement the following inscription, which I herewith give from a careful copy in my note book

ZEIZEA

There could be no possible doubt about this being an intentional design, but in what tongue, or what it meant was a mystery. We puzzled over it for an hour, when Torrence suggested that they might be English letters, rudely and ignorantly carved. "For instance," he said, "the first might very well be an N. The second is evidently an E; while the third is unmistakably intended for an I. Now the fourth is the same as the first. The fifth cannot well be other than an L. The sixth is the same as the second, and the last is a T." When we looked at it in this way, it seemed clear enough. Indeed what else could it be? But what the word meant, remained a mystery. Suddenly it occurred to us that it might be more than one word. "Suppose," said Torrence, "that the last five letters are intended to form the word 'Inlet'—a pronounced feature of the coast of this island—and that the first two stand for North East. There we seem to have it—North East Inlet—the stone probably refers to something of interest in, or about the North East Inlet of the island!"

Surely we had solved the problem. But when I reminded Torrence that we had been searching for traces of his alleged inhabitant, and that he should not be surprised at this discovery, he said:

"True enough; but exactly where they would be, or what they would look like, or even if this was the right island, I could not tell; but now I feel sure that I am right."

"The stone was evidently put here by some one," I remarked.

"Undoubtedly. There is not the slightest appearance of its having been deposited by nature; and the letters were cut with rough tools, by ignorant hands."

"And you believe a human being could have reached this spot without an air ship?"

"There is not one chance in a million that it could have been done," he replied; "certainly *never* by the course we have taken. But there are stretches of land reaching far to the north; and in certain seasons, under the most exceptional circumstances, possibly some lost scout of the Arctic seas might have drifted here, had he once pushed his way across the frozen belt. I say it is possible; but that is all. Before we leave we shall know whether it is a fact."

We lingered a few minutes while I made the copy of the inscription, and then climbed back into the air ship, bound for the North East Inlet.

Skimming slowly around the shore we soon discovered the indentation we were looking for, and following up its course for a few hundred yards above the mouth, reached another of those turfy knolls, with which the island abounded. Around this the water ran directly into the land, forming a diminutive lake a little higher up, with grassy slopes upon every side. It was a beautiful spot, entirely protected from the surf, and screened from the winds as well. Indeed, so sheltered and peaceful a nook was it, and withal so inviting, that we decided to descend and look around, having observed nothing extraordinary from above.

"If I do not discover something interesting here," said Torrence, "I shall be disappointed."

Having landed on the hillock above the lake we separated, walking in opposite directions. The ground was covered with a brilliant, mossy turf, where the black bed rock did not protrude; but where it did so, only served to enhance the intensity of color by contrast. I had not walked far when I heard Torrence call:

"Hello! Look at this!"

I hurried over to where he was. There was no doubt about it. He had made a discovery. On a grassy knoll, not far from the water's edge, was a small structure like a tomb, built of rough stones to the height of a man's breast, and about five feet in diameter. It looked old, was moss grown, and covered with a heavy cap stone. We felt convinced that in this cairn was concealed some important secret, and that it was undoubtedly the place referred to. We went immediately to work to remove the upper stone, which we found quite difficult, but by working an iron wedge which we secured from the air ship, it slowly yielded to our endeavors. The stones were closely knitted together, having been set in a rough mortar, made out of some tenacious kind of mud, but we gradually worked them loose, and one by one rolled them on the ground. In half an hour we had an opening large enough to look into. It was dark, but Torrence leaned over the edge and groped about with his hands. Presently he was tugging at something and exclaimed:

"I believe I've got it."

A minute later he pulled out an iron box by a ring in the lid. It was covered with rust, and had a keyhole but no key. We shook it gently. There was something inside, and we tried to raise the lid; but it was immovable. I proposed to pound it open if possible with some of the stones at our feet, but before doing so, we decided to examine the crevices of the cairn for a key. It was well we did, for our search was rewarded by the discovery of an old brass key, covered with green oxide. We polished it up with some sand, but before it would open the box we had to go to the air ship after a little oil to lubricate the chambers. At last we were successful, and turning back the lid looked in; but I drew back with horror at the first glance, for directly under my eyes was the rough, though strongly executed picture of a madman. It was one of those crude, intense drawings that gives the immediate impression of lifelikeness. Old and stained as the picture was, it was evident that the artist had seized upon the most salient features of his subject, and reproduced them with terrible effect. It was the simplest sketch imaginable, but the wild and painful glare of the eyes was intensified by a reddish brown scar, which ran down the middle of the forehead. Directly under this picture, which, by the by, was done upon a piece of old cloth, was this extraordinary inscription

Examining the box again we found directly under the picture another paper which upon examination proved to be an outlandish, water-stained document. At the first glance it looked like a foreign language, which we had no doubt it was, but our attention being attracted by certain words that looked like English, we examined it more carefully, and to our amazement discovered that the paper was really in our own language, though evidently executed by such an ignorant hand as scarcely to be recognized as such. We took possession of it, and I here give a careful copy of it, without attempting to reproduce the handwriting, which is almost unintelligible.

"Tu thim az finds these roks and kontents plese rede with kare an in charty's nam help ef he bee livin the pore kretur we shipreke saylers is kompeled to leve on this lonsum plase. Us 3 abil Bodid seamen was reked in the ice from the Brig John W. Saunders, whaler, of the city of Hull. There was 13 others of us wen the ship squeeched and busted, levin us wid nothin but sum vittels and a few valybles, wich we tride to save. We bilt some sleds outen her timbers, and loded thim with sich vittels an truk as we wanted tu sav and started over the ice. God amity nos how fur or wher we traveled tu, hevin no berins no nothin tu go bi, and God amity nos the orful sufferins we suffered. All on us dide but us 3. We traveled over montans ov ice, and it seemed like we kep a travelin fur yers, tho in koors we nos it went so long as thet. Bimby we finds oursels a flotin on a chunk o ice ni az big az a farm. Our vittels was ni gone afore we struk the flotin' ice, and all was ded but us 3 Ned Merrick, Jo Niles and Jan von Broekhuysen who is uf dutch parents but English birth. We kep a flotin on the ice

138 THE SECRET OF THE EARTH.

tel the long nite past and the day kum agin; but we sede as how Jan was doin quer and one day he went plum mad and tried to kil us. We tide him down, and then we sited this iland, tho in wut part uf the erth we kan't tel. We sede we wus flotin strate fur here and the sea was ruf but not so kold as before. We dun wut we kud fur our chums as dide but we kudent help oursels, lesen them, and so lef, thim bak on the ice tu rot. Wen we got close tu this iland the sea wus up, and our ice chunk struk a rok and busted afore we landed. Jan von Broekhuysen struk his hed agin a rok and we brung him ashore levin a bludy streke behind. His fored got split in tu and he wuz the orfulest site we ever sede—he warnt moren abut 20 yers o age and that lik he got in the hed or his goin mad wun, plum noked the reckolecshun outen him. He node uz not—nor wher he hed bin, nor wher he wuz, nor his own nam, nor nothin—nor yit kud he speke a single word. We hev heered as how a nok in the hed wud sometimes strik the memry outen man, but niver is we seed one in sich a fix afore. Jan van Broekhuysen node nuthin'. He wuz like tu one jes born—the rok wut split his hed made the terriblest lookin skar we ever seed, and we washed it out and dun the best we kud for him but waz not fix to sow it up agin. He seen us drink the water outen the spring, and he dun so 2. he seen us ketch the birds in the roks and ete um and he dun so 2, he seen us ketch the fish and he dun wut we dun. The frute here is bitter but it helps tu kepe us aliv. Now how long we has lived here we kan't tel, but we iz goin awa in a bote we bilt outen skraps o drift wood and stuff we found preferin tu resk the orful sea and ice agin than tu liv and rot on this place wher man kums not. Jan von Broekhuysen has grode afeerd o us and runs awa wenever we gos ni him and we seldum ketches a site o' him. We has lost all kont o time and don't no how long we has ben here nor wen we kum nor nothin—but ther has ben 1 dark spel and 2 lite spels, and we think it must a ben a yer sence we kum. Siknes and hardship has ni ruined us mind and body, and we don't keer wut bekomes o us. We bilds this ere rok hut around this box wich we fetched with us havin' sum o' our valybles.

We makes a pikter of Jan von Broekhuysen and paints that skar on his hed wid our own blud but we douts ef eny man will ever see him agin az he is wilder and skeerier nor a gote. We haz also razed a rok in anuder place for a sine. It is with sorro that we leves our ole kcmrade—but we kan nether ketch nor tame him. Ef we node wut part uv the erth we wus in we wud no wher to strik fur, but we don't, and rekon we will both be drownd afore gettin any whers. Ef eny person finds Jan be kind to him. We leves here amejetly. Jan is livin' on birds eggs, birds, and fish, and sum o them qur apples there ain't mutch else tu ete. Kind frends we saz farewel

"Yours Truly,

(Signed) { "NED MERRICK, "JOE NILES."

The original is very difficult to read, both on account of its peculiar orthography and from its being smirched and weather-stained. We went to the air ship where I recorded this discovery, and then sealed it up in the cairn, carrying the original paper with us.

"Sailor like," observed Torrence, "there is not a date in the paper from beginning to end."

I had not thought of this before.

"He may have been here for years," I added.

"He may," Torrence replied, and then producing a paper from a large packet, asked me what I thought of the signature.

I started, for I recognized it at once. It was one of those I had seen through the keyhole in the hotel Mustapha, and the signature was the same as the one before me—Ned Merrick. I then recalled the fact that I had heard my brother address the mysterious stranger—I mean the sailor we had first met upon the Thames boat, and whom afterward I had seen at the Mustapha—as Merrick. Could it be possible that he was the same who had escaped through the ice belt to this island? I was amazed, but before I could make an inquiry Torrence continued:

"I now am certain that this island is inhabited, as I told you, unless, perchance, the man has died. I am also sure of the continents; for the man Merrick having told me the truth in this most amazing case, it is probable that he has not lied in other matters, especially as he gave me proof, and as his story coincides with my own views. Let us look for Jan von Broekhuysen, then we will proceed upon our voyage."

We made a careful search for this extraordinary individual, but not finding any traces of him, we returned to the vessel and prepared to go.

As we were clearing the coast a creature of scarcely human aspect, clad in a robe of feathers and covered to the waist with a mass of tawny gray hair, appeared to rise out of the sand. He probably emerged from the shelter of some neighboring rock, and stood for a moment looking at us in amazement. On a motion to alter our course, as if to pursue him, the creature disappeared as suddenly and strangely as he had come. He was simply invisible, and it would have been useless to waste our time in an effort to capture him. There was no doubt to our minds that this was Jan von Broekhuysen.

· · · · · · · · ·

XIV.

Northward again we proceeded on our journey, and from the upper deck surveyed the solitude of an ocean unknown to human eyes. All traces of ice had vanished; the sea was tranquil and the air pleasant. Naturally enough our conversation fell upon the mysterious cairn and its contents.

"In my opinion," said Torrence, "this Jan von Broekhuysen is the most unique creation of our planet. He is the only human being of his kind since creation. I will guarantee that not in a million years has the earth produced such another!"

I asked him what he meant, and suggested the possibility of others having been lost under like circumstances, while admitting the improbability of their having reached such a latitude.

"That is not it at all!" he exclaimed; "Jan von Broekhuysen stands alone, and for this reason. Because he is the only living creature of our race who has been put alone in an uninhabited world, and who has never seen nor communicated with a fellow-creature!"

"You mean since he was twenty years old, for I believe the paper says that was his age," said I.

"No," replied Torrence, "I mean nothing of the kind. I mean that never, for a single instant, has he seen or communicated with a fellow-being until he saw us!"

"I don't understand you. Doesn't the paper say he was twenty years old when wrecked?"

"Certainly. But doesn't the paper say that when he struck he lost his memory?"

"But what of that? he's sure to have seen plenty of people in the first part of his life."

"Gurt, that fellow never had any other part to his life. His life began afresh after landing on that island. His past having been wiped out, he was born again. His memory being gone, the past had no existence for him. He knew no more about a previous existence than you or I know about a life before this. Practically he was reincarnated, inasmuch as his brain had lost every picture and every record of the past. He came as a new man to a new world, knowing nothing. The first twenty years of his life was no more his than if it had belonged to another body. I claim that Von Broekhuysen is the most unique creature that ever visited our planet!"

I was impressed, and thought some time before answering. Finally I said:

"It is doubtless a remarkable case, but you must be accurate in your statements, and when you declare that the fellow has never either seen or communicated with a fellow-being since losing his memory, you must not forget his comrades, Niles and Merrick, who were with him for a year afterward; surely he must remember them."

"Not at all," said Torrence; "when those men left him he was only a year old, so to speak. He had entered his new existence but a twelvemonth before; and although he had the size and strength of a man, he was but an infant, so far as his mind was concerned, and I defy any one to recall anything which happened at that time of their lives. No one can remember what happened when he was but a year old. I have thought it all out, old boy, and Von Broekhuysen ought to belong to a museum!"

There was no gainsaying what my brother said. I wanted to ask him how Merrick had made his escape, and what had become of the other fellow, but a look warned me that an appropriate time had not come for these questions. I was impressed with the marvelous way in which Torrence had been prepared for our discovery by this extraordinary man, Merrick, who must have seen more of the mysteries of the Arctic regions than any human being alive.

We were sailing over a sea of vast extent, whose shores were mythical. Whither would it lead us? Although it was the time of year when we might reasonably expect to find moderate weather, even in high latitude, we were amazed to find the air so temperate and pleasant as it was. We sat on deck nearly all the time, when not engaged in eating or sleeping, and often without our top coats. We kept constant watch on the horizon, the water below us, and the sky above; expecting at any moment to discover the outline of some unknown continent, but as the monotony of sky and water continued we began to sympathize with Columbus.

Twenty-four hours after leaving the island, which we agreed to call Von Broekhuysen, we estimated that we could not have come less than four hundred miles, and yet there had not been the slightest indication of land, although we had not changed our course half a degree. It was the same placid, unmarked, and unknown ocean. Whither were we drifting?

It was about here that the meteorological conditions of the atmosphere began to strike me as peculiar. The northern horizon had been subjected to a singular phenomenon for a good many hours, which I ascribed to one of those effects of light so common in these latitudes. It was simply a crescent-shaped cloud, growing in height as we advanced. At first it subtended the segment of an arc of about sixty degrees across the horizon, steadily ascending toward the zenith with our progress. But gradually this form lost its definiteness, and melted into the sky in a mellow haze, which softened the light and obscured the sun. We were glad enough to have the glare off the water, as it had been quite trying, but I was at a loss to account for the phenomenon which had abolished it. If Torrence understood this he failed to explain it to me—advising me to wait and see what would happen. I mention it here as an important fact bearing upon our future discoveries. I had never before seen so peculiar a cloud, retaining a definite form for so long a time, fixed in density and character save that the arc grew as we proceeded; and I naturally puzzled myself a good deal meditating on it. But it was not until later that I ascertained the cause of this astounding phenomenon.

. . . .

Forty-eight hours after leaving the island we were still floating over the same placid sea, and without indication of land upon any point of the horizon. We were working our way along at the rate of five and twenty knots, under perfect conditions, when a thought struck me.

"How far have we come since leaving the island?" I asked.

Torrence looked at the indicator.

"About six hundred miles," he said.

"Exactly; and as Von Broekhuysen's island is not more than two hundred and fifty from the pole, we must have passed it, and be running down on the other side of the earth. It surely can't be long before we strike the frozen belt again; indeed we ought to be there already. But there hasn't been a block of ice, or a bit of cold weather to speak of yet. How do you account for it?"

"Don't bother about the ice," said Torrence; "you ought to be glad we haven't got any?"

"But we ought to have it," I insisted, "according to my calculations——"

"Damn your calculations," he answered laughing; "didn't I tell you I was going to show you a new world, and new continents!"

"Continents! I should enjoy even a shovel full of mud at present."

"Have patience; if Merrick could cross this sea in a dugout, with a cotton sheet, we surely have an equal chance of doing so; although I confess I think he must have struck a strip of land to the east or west which we have missed. But we are on a straight course and bound to come out all right if we keep on."

"You expect to run down then over Alaska?" I inquired.

"I expect nothing of the kind. Wait and you will see."

And I had to wait, for he would say nothing more just then, although I asked him numerous questions.

It was shortly after this that I observed another most singular phenomenon in the sky, which struck me with such amazement that I was filled with awe. About twenty degrees south of the zenith there appeared in the heavens an enormous disk of pale light, only distinguishable from the rest of the sky by being brighter and more of a bluish tinge. I should say it was a hundred times as large as the sun, distinctly defined, and though not brilliant by contrast with that luminary, was probably twice as luminous as the surrouding parts of the sky. There was something so utterly amazing in this sight that I could not take my eyes from it, and even Torrence was impressed, although I could see that he had a plausible explanation in his own mind. When I had stared long and earnestly without observing the slightest change in the appearance, he said:

"When you have got a little more used to things here I will talk plainer. There are mysteries about our planet not even realized; and we are on the high road to solve one of the most astounding."

The disk of light continued. It did not seem to grow larger or smaller, or to change its position in the heavens, and after I had grown weary of looking at it, directed my attention again to the horizon, and was startled by the unexpected appearance of two very singular objects. They were small and very distant, but the glass revealed a couple of dark spots four degrees to the port of our course, and hard upon the sky-line. Later a more careful observation showed a pair of black columns rising directly out of the sea. These objects, whatever they were, now absorbed our entire attention, and we steered directly for them.

. . . .

Our compass had behaved so strangely of late that we depended in a measure upon the triangulation of the rudder, which we knew was inviolable in a still atmosphere, such as had favored us since leaving Spitzbergen. This feature of our steering apparatus was really very clever, and entirely original with my brother, who had devised it for the special purpose of obviating the difficulties mariners often encounter in Arctic waters from the extreme sensitiveness and uncertain freaks of the magnetic needle. It consisted in a semi-circular dial, accurately inscribed with degrees, minutes, and seconds, upon which an indicator, connected with the rudder bar, acted. Thus any deviation from a given course was accurately recorded by this index finger, and while unaffected by air currents, was thoroughly reliable. Another great advantage in determining our position, lay in the fact that we were enabled by the aid of our speed register to know exactly how fast we were traveling. Of course in a high wind it would be more difficult to utilize these contrivances with accuracy, as another computation that of estimating the velocity and direction of the air current would have to be entered upon, a condition which fortunately had not troubled us.

We continued, head on, for the points mentioned, the nature of which, we were unable to decipher, even with the excellent glasses at our command. Although running at a good rate, it was impossible to tell at the end of half an hour whether these dark projections were any nearer than when we had first seen them. The air was clear, and the field of vision extended. The light appeared to differ from that of our own day, being less intense and exceedingly restful and pleasant to the eyes. I can compare it to nothing I know of, although in an inaccurate way it might be said to resemble, on an exaggerated scale, that charming blending of moonlight with the gloaming. It was here that I first noticed what seemed to be an electrical condition of the atmosphere that filled me with the most agreeable sensations. I felt lighter, stronger, in every way healthier, and in better spirits. Torrence also spoke of this, and I am sure that I am right in ascribing it to our environment. The sun itself continued invisible, while the luminous disk referred to remained unchanged. We were indeed entering an unknown world. Where would it end?

After an hour's run we could just perceive that the dark columns ahead were a trifle nearer, though still thoroughly indefinite as to character. Torrence looked at the register. Twenty-five miles an hour.

"They are still at a great distance," he said, "and I propose to hasten my acquaintance with them."

He moved up the speed controller five miles faster, and then we took seats and lighted cigars.

"Why should we not push her up to a mile a minute," I suggested, "and satisfy our curiosity so much the sooner?"

"I don't know," he answered, "there is no reason except a strange apprehension that comes over me sometimes lest we have an accident. We seem so far from all we know."

"I thought you had every confidence."

"So I have. The truth is I am excited. We are on the verge of an astounding discovery. I am dead sure that Merrick is right, and that I am right—but hush—do not ask me yet. I do not want to unnerve you. A little later!"

"You unnerve me a great deal more by not telling me than by telling me. What is it?"

But he was quiet; with his glasses trained carefully on the objects ahead.

At the end of two hours more we appeared only a trifle nearer the columns, although we were undoubtedly seventy miles closer than when first sighted. Torrence was growing nervous. He walked the deck, chewing his cigar. Presently he stopped, and said:

"I can't stand it. I'm going to give her five miles an hour more," and moved up the controller accordingly.

We were now moving at the rate of five and thirty miles an hour, but even at this rapid pace, it was three good hours before we could decide with any certainty the nature of the columns; and then we saw that they were twin mountains of extraordinary height, rising directly out of the sea. In another hour they were much more distinct, though still very far, and I was at a loss to account for our having seen them at so great a distance at first, except upon the ground of the many singular effects of light and atmosphere which we encountered. Among these was a strange indefiniteness about the horizon, totally differing from the prevailing conditions in other parts of the world. The sky-line blended with the heavens in a kind of atmospheric veil, self-luminous, and illusive. The effect was altogether pleasing, though entirely novel. Occasionally the clouds would be rosy as after sunset, which I again attributed to some electrical condition of the air, possibly the aurora, which, had it been the Arctic night instead of day, I imagined would have made a wonderful display. But this was purely hypothetical on my part, and when I suggested it to Torrence, he looked at me with surprise and said:

"Night! There is no night here!"

"Not now," I replied; "but six months hence there will be."

"Never!" said he; "there is never any night here. It is always as light as this!"

I saw from his mood that it would be useless to argue, and so continued my investigation of the twin mountains, which had grown near enough to be easily inspected with the naked eye. Torrence calculated that they must have been more than two hundred miles away when first seen.

When we had approached near enough to observe them in detail, we slackened speed. Rising directly out of the ocean, they presented a marvelous picture; for their stupendous height and rugged grandeur is surely not equalled in the world we inhabit. We moved slowly toward them, wishing to take in the scene from our deck to the best advantage. We photographed them at different ranges, and were always surprised to find that our last picture had been so remote. We moved more slowly as we approached, finally reducing the rate to five miles an hour, believing we were within half an hour's run of the shore, but were undoubtedly ten or a dozen miles away at that time.

A stupendous wall of black granite rose before us, to a height which we estimated to exceed twelve thousand feet. This was the mountain upon the left; the one on the right was nearly as high, though not so absolutely precipitous. Between these mountains was a channel about a mile wide. Coming to a halt before these appalling objects, two hundred and fifty feet above the sea, we stood on deck, overwhelmed at the awful sight. Below stretched a crimson beach, running back to a chaotic sand hill, strewn with huge masses of broken stone, from the top of which towered in one unbroken wall the palisade or face of the mountain itself.

Lowering ourselves gently to this beach we landed in a new world and language cannot picture the appalling sublimity of the scene, or describe our emotions.

"Surely these cliffs must mark the end of the earth!" I exclaimed.

"Hush!" said Torrence solemnly; "it is only the beginning!"

He was pale, and I could not help wondering if my face were as white as his.

Craning my neck backward I looked up. A cloud had hidden the top, and I felt dizzy.

• • • • • • • •

XV.

IMMEDIATELY on landing we made another careful examination of the air ship, and to our intense satisfaction found that she was still in perfect condition. We had come a long journey, and thoroughly tested her powers in varied temperatures and atmospheric conditions, but the distance was as nothing to what was to come. As we stood on this brilliant beach and looked back at the southern sky I observed that the disk of blue light was a little smaller, and a very little higher in the heavens. Still there was no sun, but this great circular shield was a focus for the dissemination of light upon every side. I stood marveling at it until Torrence called me. He was examining the crimson shells a little higher up the shore.

"Come," he said, "and look at these!"

I walked over to where he was.

The shore was literally covered with pink mollusks, a large percentage of which contained true pearls of extraordinary size and beauty. Torrence was pounding them open with a couple of stones.

"Within a hundred yards of this spot," he said, "lies a fortune greater than the combined wealth of the Rothschilds. In the pearl fisheries of the old world not one shell in a thousand contains a pearl of any value. But here, in these strangely colored mollusks, ninety per cent. enclose gems of extraordinary merit."

He held one up for my inspection.

"Here," he said, "is one which I have opened at random. It is of the first water; of perfect skin and orient; the most delicate texture, and without speck or flaw, and is worth at the lowest estimate one hundred pounds. Without going a dozen steps we can find ten times that value. Some of these pearls are pink, and from what I have seen and heard of them, I do not think they will ever fade——"

"From what you have heard?" I interrupted; "what do you mean?"

"My dear fellow, the shores of this continent are strewn with these shells for hundreds of miles at a stretch, as its mountains are filled with gold and diamonds. Do you not know that Merrick had the value of millions in them. It was from him that I heard of them, and from him that I bought millions of pounds worth."

"Bought!" I exclaimed in astonishment.

"Yes, bought!"

"And with what pray?"

"With a promise," said Torrence "Money was of no use to him, but fame he valued. As you know, he and Niles escaped from Von Broekhuysen Island. Niles was lost, while Merrick alone reached the world we are now in. How he got there, or what his adventures are, it is not necessary to relate; but he did it, and I now know that he found land much nearer the island than we have —but that is unimportant. How he reached his home again is even still more wonderful, and a volume might be written about the man's terrible sufferings and adventures; but his life was embittered by the incredulity, the cold skepticism, and indifference with which he was greeted on every hand, by those who were too bigoted and ignorant to heed his story, or even investigate the proofs of the new world, which he brought with him.

The geographical societies of a dozen cities either listened to him as they would to the ravings of a madman, or turned a deaf ear with scorn. And this treatment he received wherever he went, and at the hands of organizations termed scientific, whose plain duty was to listen to the words and test the affidavits of the applicant. But the nature of Merrick's claims was so astounding that no one, high or low, would heed him, and yet he only discovered that which I have always believed in. I, alone, of all the world, gave the fellow proper audience. I saw at once his claim to credence. I promised what he demanded in exchange for his wealth—notoriety. He saw that with the air ship I should be able to prove all that he had ever said, and that I could make his name great among coming generations. He saw that I could upset the position of the wiseacres who had refused to hear him, and make them the butt of their fellows. All this I promised to do, if able, and in exchange for that promise he gave me the few millions in pearls, diamonds, and other precious stones he had brought with him as proofs of his discovery. Gurthrie, have you not yet guessed the nature of that discovery?"

"I should hope so," I answered

"And what is it?"

"That the North Pole has a continent around it which is blessed with a temperate climate."

"And is that all?"

"That the sky has a luminous disk as big as a cart wheel, that takes the place of the sun!"

"Nothing more?"

"That the electrical condition of the atmosphere is highly beneficial to the nerves."

"Go on!" said Torrence impatiently.

"That pearls and precious stones are as common as dirt!"

"Tell me what else he discovered," exclaimed Torrence, "and be quick about it!"

"Not being Mr. Merrick, I'm sure I don't know," I answered.

"Don't know!" roared Torrence, "do you mean to tell me that you don't know where you are?"

"Somewhere about the pole I suppose. I might say ninety degrees north."

My brother looked at me with a singular expression of pity, and then stooping down resumed his work of opening shells with an indifference that exasperated me.

"Where in Heaven's name are we then?" I shouted.

"No matter just now," he answered. "I thought perhaps you would have guessed. I don't want to shock you. Perhaps the truth will dawn on you later; if not I will tell you. Meanwhile, let us gather a few bushels of these pearls. They are of no value here, but they will be if we ever go home again."

And so we set to work under the shadow of those awful cliffs, and in a couple of hours had secured unestimated value in the most perfect specimens conceivable. We packed these away in the air ship in a small sack, and then Torrence proposed that we name the stupendous headland before us "Mount Horror."

I agreed that it would be an excellent name, well adapted to our feelings on approaching it, and descriptive of the gloom and phenomenal aspect of the mountain itself. The one on the opposite side of the channel he suggested we call "Mount Gurthrie," to which I also assented, and entered the names in our chart of discoveries.

It was upon this desolate shore that we cooked our first ration of bear meat, brought all the way from Spitzbergen.

Climbing into the hill beyond the beach among the sand and rocks, we found a quantity of dried seaweed, which we carried down to the shore for a fire. It burned with a crackling noise and pungent smell, so pleasant that we decided to carry some of it away with us, filling some bags, and throwing them on board before leaving. We had quite a picnic over our bear steak and coffee, although it was impossible to divest ourselves of a certain gloom, resulting from the lowering heights above. The air was still, and only the tiniest ripple of a surf came rolling in upon our rosy beach, and the stillness, the cessation of motion, and our extraordinary situation, made me for the first time long for home.

A bird of an unknown species came flying toward us from over the water. Its plumage was brilliant with trailing feathers of red, green, and yellow; while upon its head was a topknot of the same colors. Torrence thought he should like to have it and so fetched his gun. The bird circled above, full of curiosity. Perhaps we were the first human beings it had ever seen. Descending spirally it came at last within easy range, but we had not the heart to kill it. Then, apparently satisfied with its investigation, commenced an upward course, circling away again, just as it had come; only this time aiming its spirals toward the top of the cliff, until lost to view. Torrence then discharged the gun in the air to hear the reverberation from the rocks. The sound was impressive, coming back to us like thunder from the heights. It was probably the first time a gun had ever been discharged in this desolate quarter of the globe, and I was glad it was not in the destruction of life.

When the smoke had cleared away and the echoes ceased, we were attracted by a whirring sound above, and looking up saw thousands of pigeons which our shot had frightened from their nests. We watched them while they skurried about in dismay, until, finding that no harm had been done, they settled back among the rocks again.

. . . .

We had made a hearty meal and were beginning to think of going when Torrence suggested that we ascend the face of Mount Horror in the air ship instead of taking our way up the channel, or following the precipitous and rugged shore line for another exit. I reminded him that it would probably be cold at such an elevation, but agreed that it would afford a magnificent view of the country. Beside, we wanted to inspect the crater, feeling sure the mountain was an extinct volcano, and so determined to ascend to the highest elevation first, and then continue our journey northward over the country beyond, or through the channel which offered a clear passage in the direction of our course. This chasm through which the river ran was sublime and terrible. A rent in that stupendous rock formation which seemed to dwarf and threaten the very foundations of the earth on which it rested. We could but regard it with feelings of awe. An overpowering desire to escape its depressing influence possessed us.

Safely aboard the air ship we began ascending the wall as if passengers in a huge elevator, which in fact we were. Again the birds flew out, terrified at our approach, some falling dead from sheer fright, a few of which we secured on deck. Hugging this terrible escarpment we were enabled to examine its formation with accuracy. Large blocks of syenitic granite hung loose, ready to drop at any minute and we saw how for ages the cliff had been slowly disintegrating, and receding from the sea by action of storm and catyclism. Lightning had also played its part, and its handwriting was visible on every side. Ledges large enough to hold a house were loaded with nests and eggs of every color and size. We consulted about the feasibility of capturing some of these, by halting and climbing out after them, but concluded to let them go, as the danger was too great. It involved not only the risk in scrambling from the vessel to the ledge, but the additional chance of being smashed by a falling rock from above. Of course in our ascent we were careful to keep far enough away to obviate that possibility.

When we had risen clear above Mount Horror we looked down into the fearful chasm that separated us from Mount Gurthrie. It was a sight never to be forgotten. To the south lay the unspotted ocean; but to the north the land sloped away rapidly, and beyond the highest elevations which, in themselves, were mountains of no mean height, but so far below as to seem trivial; beyond these, I say as far as the eye could reach, extended a beautiful country, with rivers, valleys, lakes and hills, with forest, plain, and mountain. The panorama was entrancing, and the effect on us profound.

Hovering over the crater, which we found just as we expected, we looked down into a black abyss, so vast and awful, that we had no inclination to investigate it, although it was large enough for us to have descended bodily with the air ship. There was no smoke, nor were any sulphurous fumes emitted. Evidently the volcano had been extinct for ages; and we passed rapidly on upon our north bound course, glad enough to have dry land under us once again, and to descend to a lower and warmer level. We were soon down among the foothills, and traversing a well timbered country, rising from time to time to clear the elevations encountered. The panorama that now stretched away before us was one of ravishing beauty, and we took our places on deck with lighted cigars to enjoy it. I suggested that we name the new land "Torrenzia," but Torrence only declared that while people might call it what they pleased, the credit of the new world must go to the man who had first seen it.

"You seem to think there is only one scrap of a continent here," he said, "and Torrenzia may do well enough for one; but remember it is a new world we have entered; and if I am not greatly mistaken we shall find it studded with civilizations equal to any we know. Certainly you are dense, Gurthrie, and stupid to a degree, not to have guessed by this time where we are!"

I did not answer; in fact I was provoked that he should be so secretive with the information he possessed. I confessed to my bewilderment at what we saw but was still in the dark as to the truth.

We now ran rapidly forward over a picturesque country, and through an atmosphere not only temperate but exhilarating. About a hundred miles inland the timber and water courses were less prolific, and fifty miles farther we merged upon a great, treeless plain, covered with short tussocky grass, sand, and rocks. At intervals were to be seen the bones of animals bleaching where they had fallen, the entire skeletons being generally intact. More than once we descended to the ground to examine them, but could not decide whether they were buffalo or some other creature. What surprised us most was the fact that there appeared to be no living ones. But we did not waste our time upon this arid plain, fearing to run short of water, and being particularly anxious to discover if our new world was inhabited. As we sat on deck smoking our cigars, rushing into the gentle breeze ahead, we felt like monarchs, or rather god-like creatures, who owned and ruled a world from above.

THE SECRET OF THE EARTH. 159

We had little time for sleep, our excitement being intense, and the short intervals we spared for an occasional nap, were taken alternately, the one remaining on deck promising the other to wake him as soon as anything of special interest occurred. I had just come above after one of these short siestas and joining my brother observed him looking with unusual interest through the glass at something below.

"What is it now?" I called, leaning over the rail.

At a glance I saw that the nature of the country had changed. No more skeletons; no more sand and rocks, or arid desert, but a great sheet of water lay to our right, while below and beyond were trees and fields, which looked as if they were cultivated; and here and there, at intervals of a mile or two, were undoubtedly the walls of human habitations. I do not say they were houses, for houses have roofs, whereas these edifices were roofless.

"I am sure I have discovered houses," said Torrence; "and I am trying to see if there are any people!"

I took the glass from his hand.

"There is no doubt about it," I exclaimed; "and what is more, they do not appear to be ruins, but houses in perfect repair, judging from their similarity and the condition of the grounds around them. But what kind of climate must these people enjoy to require no roofs? Certainly it can never rain!"

"Nor snow!" he added with a smile.

"What made you think of snow?"

"I thought, perhaps, you were thinking of it," he replied.

"Why?"

"Because you said it was high time we were in the ice belt again!"

I started.

"And how far have we come?" I asked.

"From where?"

He looked carefully at his register and made a calculation. He then said:

"We are now one thousand three hundred and eighty miles from Von Broekhuysen's Island, and about one thousand one hundred and thirty miles north of the North Pole—if you can imagine such a thing—I mean that we have advanced upon a straight line for this distance; and as you see, we have met neither ice, snow, nor cold weather yet!"

I looked above. The great disk of light was still bright in the heavens; I thought a little nearer the zenith than before. Unless there had been some gross miscalculation in our speed we had got to face a physical problem of the most stupendous nature. A problem so appalling that I began to dread the explanation as much as I had recently sought it.

"Yes," I answered in a weak voice, "there is certainly neither ice nor snow here!"

"Nor cold!" added Torrence.

"Nor cold!" I admitted.

"Nor undue heat!" he continued.

"Certainly not. The temperature has been perfect."

"And the air has a vitality unknown to us in the old world," he pursued.

"I grant every word you say. This may be a dream, but it is a paradise!"

"It is not a dream!" cried Torrence; "it is another world; a world within our own. Yonder disk of light in the sky is the opening at the pole through which we have sailed. The earth is a hollow globe, with an opening at each pole, through which the sunlight always

THE SECRET OF THE EARTH. 161

enters. For six months it comes through the northern opening, and for six months through the southern. But the change is gradual. With the advent of the southern day, the disk is in the south, fading imperceptibly as the northern light supplants it, and *vice versa*. The great aurora borealis which illumines the Arctic regions of our world is simply the sunlight pouring through from the southern hemisphere, or the light which enters the earth at the South Pole, discharging itself at the north. For ages our world was believed to be flat; but time and study proved the fallacy. In the days of Hipparchus and Ptolemy, and for centuries after it was believed that the sun revolved around the earth; what a stupendous change in man's knowledge when the opposite was found to be the case. From the days of Columbus to our own—with a few notable exceptions—the world was supposed to be filled with a mass of molten material; but within recent years facts observed in the boiling of water have compelled men to abandon that theory and substitute that of a world solid to the core. One by one the theories which have stood on the bed rock of science and been held as irrefutable by the wisdom of the age, have crumbled to pieces, and been supplanted by others; and now the faith in a solid earth is to be shattered, for you and I know that it is hollow—light and inhabited. But let us see what small beginnings led to the change in men's views in the past, and observe how similar they are to those operating now——"

"What!" I interrupted, "do you mean to say that we have sailed through an opening at the pole, and are now in the interior of the earth?"

"That is exactly it," answered Torrence.

"I can't comprehend such a thing. What is the diameter of this opening; and where is the North Pole?"

162   THE SECRET OF THE EARTH.

"The North Pole has no existence except as an imaginary point in space, at least five hundred miles from the surface of the earth. The openings at the so-called poles are more than a thousand miles in diameter, admitting the light of the sun and holding it with a denser and more highly electrified atmosphere than our own, making perpetual daylight, for, as I have told you, when the sun crosses the line, its light is derived through the opening at the opposite pole. The frozen belt surrounding each of these openings mark the regions of the verge, and the distance across this ring is about fifteen hundred miles.

"But the polar regions are declared to be slightly flattened."

"That is because men have penetrated far enough into the verge to mark the change in the earth's convexity, but not far enough to perceive that they had actually begun to enter the sphere itself. But I am coming to that presently. I wish to show you why certain men, in advance of their time, have believed that the earth was a hollow globe, luminous and desirable for man's abode, as we now know it to be; and how, as in some of the greatest discoveries of the past these views have been based on the study of facts as we find them, and not upon theories, which distort facts to maintain themselves. About the year 1470, a Portuguese sailor by the name of Vicente found a piece of curiously carved wood more than a thousand miles to the west of Algarve, a province of southern Portugal. This relic was discovered after a westerly gale of long duration. It set the fellow thinking. It also set Christopher Columbus thinking. Another mariner, by the name of Correa had observed certain flotsam and jetsam under similar circumstances, and was impressed by the fact. Then there was the belief in the mysterious islands of St. Brandam; and nearly a thousand miles west of the Canaries was supposed to be the lost island of the Seven Cities, upon which theme you remember Irving's charming story, 'The Adalantado of the Seven Cities.' These and a few other facts led Columbus to stake his life and fortune in sailing into the unknown West for the new world. I now want to show you some of the reasons for believing in a hollow, habitable globe, and to ask if they are not equally as strong as those which guided Columbus."

I was astounded, dazed, and stood trembling by the taffrail, while Torrence proceeded.

XVI.

· · · · · · · ·

"Do not be appalled by our discovery," he continued; "it is as simple and natural as that which proved the earth a sphere, when the wisdom of the ages had declared it flat. The old arguments against its rotundity were quite as potent as any ever brought to refute the theory of a hollow globe, first advanced by Captain Symmes. How could the earth be round? Would not all the water run off on the underside? The thing was absurd. 'How could the world be hollow and habitable? Would not the inside be dark? and would not the water drop from the upper to the lower half?' Why does not the moon drop? The land and water above us are so distant, and so screened by the atmosphere as to be invisible even if we were thousands of miles above our present position. The center of gravity lies somewhere within the crust, which is probably nowhere more than a hundred miles thick.

"The inner world is better in every way than the outer. The climate is more uniform and temperate. The electrical conditions of the atmosphere more conducive to longevity and health, and the struggle for existence far less than with us. Here are some of the arguments in favor of a hollow globe, which the so-called wise men have ignored. The uniform migration of herrings to the south. Whence come they, if not from the interior of the earth, for they are never known to return? The assumption is that in search of their food supplies they constantly advance against an opposing current, which takes them through the earth, from pole to pole.

"Arctic explorers have observed in the long night of the polar regions that the north star rises to the zenith at a certain latitude, and then declines over the stern of their vessels as they advance further northward, which is directly in contradiction to what it should do, had they not already reached the verge and begun to pass inward toward the interior. This in itself should be a convincing fact. The Aurora Borealis has never been explained satisfactorily, but you and I know its meaning. Strange plants and birds unknown to our world have from time to time been found upon our most northern shores. As I have already told you, the reindeer of Spitzbergen are marked by the hand of man, but what man no one knows, as the island is uninhabited, and as they could not have come from the south, they must have crossed the ice from some undiscovered country to the north.

"Almost all of the civilized nations have from time to time expended large sums of money in determining the figure of the earth. Arcs of the meridian have been measured again and again; and observations of the pendulum, as well as weight experiments, have been made to determine the force of terrestrial gravity in different localities. The result of these experiments has been to prove that the bulk of the earth, as determined by gravity, differs greatly from the result reached by measurement. This discrepancy has never been satisfactorily accounted for, nor can it ever be, with the present view of the earth's interior, but with Symmes' theory of a hollow globe, as we know it, could be easily explained. But I am coming to still more extraordinary data.

"In the early part of this century two human corpses were found incased in an iceberg, which had presumably floated down from the eastern coast of Greenland. The bodies were perfectly preserved, and clothed in garments entirely different, both in design and material, from those worn by the Esquimaux, or any known race of people. Beyond this, neither the form, shape of skull, or color of skin resembled that of any nationality with which we are familiar. Their discovery created quite a sensation at the time, but as no clew was ever established to their identity, the circumstance was gradually forgotten. Might not these men have been daring explorers, dwellers of the inner earth, and wandering beyond the possibility of return, been lost in the ice and so preserved, perhaps, for centuries?

"About twenty years ago, one Niack Dolê, a Norwegian whaler, discovered in a block of field ice, after a northerly gale of many days' duration, an extraordinary animal, differing from any which he or any of his companions had ever seen before. The little creature was carried home at the end of the voyage, and although thousands of men of experience, and travelers from many parts of the world, saw and examined it, it was impossible to class it with any known species.

"In the year 1855 four wild men were found by some sailors on the ice to the north of Cape Tchelyieskin, in the Tamyr Peninsula, Siberia. They could give no account of themselves, as no one could understand their language. They were cared for, and visited by many people and afterward sent to St. Petersburg where strangers from all parts of the world saw them; but not a single individual was ever able to communicate with them except through the language of signs. They all died within two years of their discovery, and the only

THE SECRET OF THE EARTH. 167

established fact concerning them seemed to be that they came from somewhere across the frozen sea to the north, where they had always lived. In appearance these men were unlike any we know. They understood each other perfectly, had a racial resemblance, were fairly intelligent, and would doubtless have mastered the language spoken around them had they lived long enough.

"You may say that this is all very well to show that there is an unknown continent somewhere about the pole, but that it has no bearing on the hollow globe. But the arguments in favor of that I have already shown you from an astronomical, geographical, meteorological and scientific point of view, and yet there is one more I wish to present, which in my opinion is profound and unanswerable.

"In the transit of Venus observations are taken at various points upon the earth's surface. The path which Venus describes across the disk of the sun varies with the position of the observer, so also does the angle of her axis vary with that position. The projection of Venus against the sun occurs when she is at her inferior conjunction, and approaching either node. The node is one of the points where the orbit of a planet intercepts the ecliptic, or the orbit of its primary. In this condition the body of Venus will appear as a dark spot crossing the disk of the sun. Now, in the last transit of Venus, two gentlemen of great ability—Herr Von Pultzner, and an American by the name of Breslyne observed it from a point quite remote from all others. I will give you the exact locality of their observation later, and the reason of their choosing it. I am not going to bother you with scientific terms, but will merely say that when the dark body of Venus was interposed between the earth and the sun, an extraordinary phenomenon presented itself to these men—a phenomenon entirely different from that seen by any other observer. In the center of the planet was a brilliant point of light, around which the opaque substance of the star was visible. Von Pultzner and Breslyne examined this light carefully, and identified it with sunlight. To be concise, they perceived that they were looking directly through Venus at the sun. There was no disputing the fact—the light was analyzed and proved identical with sunlight, the same as that beyond the dark circumference of the planet. These men—both of whom I know to be intelligent and truthful—looked at each other in amazement.

"'We have made a most astounding discovery,' said one.

"'It is nothing less than that Venus has a hole through her center, from pole to pole,' answered the other.

"'Yes, and a thousand times more,' continued the first, 'for if Venus is a hollow sphere, *all the planets are hollow.*'

"This I know to be a fact, and yet, because unsupported by better evidence—I mean the evidence of professional astronomers—the testimony of these men was turned aside."

"And why should all the planets be hollow because Venus is hollow?" I inquired.

"Because it is inconceivable that they were not brought into existence and formed by the same law. An hypothesis which accounts for the formation of Mars or Venus upon one theory, and that of the earth upon another, would never be countenanced by science. The solar system was the result of law, of unalterable and immutable law, working for manifestation. It could not produce a solid globe in the one instance and a hollow sphere in the other. No—all the planets are hollow—the earth is a mere bubble floating in space. And now I want to ask if the evidence I had accumulated was not equal to that which fired Columbus?"

"Why did you not tell me all this before we started?" I inquired.

"Because, being an average man, you would have discarded it, as other very wise and average men have done before. You would have taken me for a fool, and left me in the lurch. But we are here at last, and my dream is true. We now know that the earth is hollow, bright, and habitable."

I was dumfounded at the awful significance of our discovery. If I had suddenly found myself a visitor upon the planet Mars, through some newly devised means of transportation, my bewilderment could have been no greater. Not only was the evidence overwhelming that the earth was hollow and open at the poles, but the fact had been established by the testimony of our own senses.

We were in that world, and there could be no further speculation regarding its existence.

. . . .

"Beyond all that I have told you," continued Torrence, "Arctic explorers have observed the crescent-shaped cloud which we saw above the northern horizon, and which is simply the opposite side of the verge across the polar opening. Few navigators venturing beyond the eighty-second parallel have failed to observe this phenomenon.

. . . .

"Now I have told you some of the most potent causes which influenced Symmes and others in the adoption of this belief; but there are other reasons, quite as forceful, not necessary to enumerate at present, as we should be on the lookout for wonders ahead."

. . . .

Passing beyond the shores of the lake we entered a rolling country, watered by a broad river with numerous minor tributaries. The course of this stream proved the same as our own for quite a distance.

. . . .

The small roofless houses were again observed, and we thought they were possibly the huts of herders, as occasional glimpses of animals were to be had in the distance.

. . . .

Tracing the course of this river for more than a hundred miles we encountered a sight that thrilled us to the core of our beings.

. . . .

Sailing on the quiet water below was a ship of unknown build. In the most romantic imagining of fairy tale this vessel could never have been surpassed. Slightly resembling the Pinta and Santa Maria, she suggested them, but the likeness was not sustained on closer examination. She was of greater beam and depth, and of loftier bow and stern. Her prow rose to unusual height, receding gracefully, and again projecting outward in a superb figurehead in the form of a swan, whose beak was gilded, and whose head and neck were set with jewels in laminated gold.

. . . .

The masts were short, two in number, and placed upon

THE SECRET OF THE EARTH. 171

each side of the deck, instead of down the center as with us. Stretched horizontally across from mast to mast was a sail of many colors. It possessed a sheen transcending that of the finest silk and was striped perpendicularly. The masts were gilded and set with jewels. Wherever we looked the ornamentation was extreme and extended to every detail. Colored sparks flashed from remote and unexpected corners, where gem-like stones were set, and the vessel glowed and burned and blazed with creeping fires as of scintillating phosphorescence of green, yellow, red and gold.

But this was not all. There were living creatures upon the deck clothed in the soft undulations of watered silk. No Eastern potentate, or denizen of Aladdin's palace, was ever half so gorgeously attired, as the passengers aboard this extraordinary craft. The flash of powdered mica on cloaks of transparent fineness produced the impression of liquid glass. The headgear was high, and terminated in a point like a cornucopia, and ornamented with odd designs, fore and aft, in precious stones. Some in green, like emeralds, others blue, like sapphires; while what appeared to be rubies, diamonds, and gold flashed among them in dazzling profusion. On no theatrical stage had I ever seen such a sight, and we hovered low to take in the singular scene.

Naturally, we caused great excitement among those on board, who pointed up at us, shouting in a tongue unlike any we had ever heard. One old man who had a long, gray beard plaited in three strands, each strand held together by half a dozen jeweled rings, seemed particularly anxious to communicate with us, and made signals for us to descend. But Torrence thought it safest to remain above, and so we simply looked down upon them from an elevation of about sixty feet, adjusting our speed to that of their vessel. We realized more than ever that we had entered another world, for a more strangely fantastic scene was impossible to imagine. The wildest consternation reigned on board while we remained in sight, and Torrence waved a white cloth, and made signals to show that we were friendly. We embraced one another, and extended our arms toward them as an indication of brotherly love, and we had to convince them with some difficulty that the air ship was not alive. It was evident that they did not understand flying machines in the new world.

We hovered above this strange vessel for more than an hour, exchanging signals, and endeavoring to communicate; but, finding it quite as impossible to impart information, as to acquire it, we waved them a farewell, took a snapshot with the kodak, and lifting ourselves high above, swept onward upon our journey.

The mysterious craft was soon out of sight, and we hurried forward, following the sinuosities of the river, about a hundred and fifty feet above its surface. As we sat looking out upon its beautiful shores, and the exquisite country beyond, meditating upon the marvels that had befallen us, I almost doubted my bodily existence. The revelation had been too profound and stupendous to be credited in so short a time.

"Is this thing real, or is it a vision of death?" I inquired, turning on my brother suddenly.

"I am not surprised at your asking," he replied; "I have been afraid to tell you the truth of our discovery before, although I have known it and believed in it for years. Merrick's story only confirmed me in my own views."

"And have you never felt a doubt as to the result of the enterprise?"

THE SECRET OF THE EARTH. 173

"Scarcely; the arguments were too strong in favor of the hollow globe for me to have any serious misgiving. But long before I spoke to you I was absolutely convinced. By the distance we had traveled. By the genial climate. By the strange light. By the crescent cloud. By the absence of recurring cold, and by the accumulated knowledge already mentioned. My dear boy, I fully appreciate what a shock this must be to you—even greater than it is to me, and for the reason that I have studied the question and believed in it half my life. For fifteen years I have been convinced that if I could ever find a way across the Palæocrystic Sea I should be able to sail without difficulty into the interior of the earth. There is really nothing more stupendous in this acquisition to our knowledge than was that of the spherical globe to the ancients. When a race of people has been bred for thousands of years to believe that the world they inhabit is flat, it must seem wildly absurd to be suddenly confronted with a theory which advances the possibility of their being able to walk upon the under side of it. Think of such a statement being made to sensible men!"

"And how do you account for the fact that these people have never found their way into the outer world?" I asked.

"For the same reason that we have never found our way into theirs," replied Torrence. "The difficulties of crossing the ice belt are very nearly insurmountable; and yet that they are not quite so we have seen in the case of Jan von Broekhuysen and his two companions. Neither is it by any means certain that dwellers of this inner region have never reached us. Remember the wild men discovered off Cape Tchelyieskin. Where did they come from? Beyond this there are isolated cases of communities that point to unknown regions in the far north, as well as the far south, as their hailing place. These have traditions of having once inhabited a land of more genial climate, and affording better conditions for the human race than ours, and moreover, a land where day was eternal! True, it may not be once in thousands of years that the ice barrier has been threaded, but what is more to the point, it is probable that those who have crossed it did not know it. The change is so gradual, the mind so fixed in its normal conception of the earth's character, that only a few eccentric, or peculiarly educated persons, among the very few who may have accomplished the feat, ever suspected it. There was a time in the world's history when one might have circumnavigated the earth without a suspicion that he had done so."

We now took our meals invariably on deck, not wishing to miss any of the strange and beautiful scenery constantly passing. On one occasion, while preparing some food in the galley, I was struck by what appeared to be a secret panel in the wall. Asking Torrence about it, he said:

"Push it up one inch, and then down two. Then if you press it gently inward it will slide open of itself."

I did so, and found that the aperture contained ten small canvas bags, in each of which, as Torrence told me, were a thousand English sovereigns.

"And what on earth have you brought this amount of coin here for?" I inquired in amazement.

Torrence simply said:

"Because I thought we might need it before we got home again. Gold talks, you know, and we may be able to communicate with these people through its medium. Gold is current throughout our world, and I wanted to see if it were good here. If it is valuable we may not expect to find any very abnormal deposits; if not, look out for a bonanza, provided the air ship holds together, so that we can carry it out with us. I have my theory about it."

"And what is that?" I asked.

"Why simply that our little stock of sovereigns won't buy bread enough for a square meal!" he answered.

XVII.

This circumstance reminded me of Torrence's financiering and the discovery of pearls upon the beach. It seemed trivial to concern ourselves about gold when precious stones were to be had with so slight an effort, and I asked why he should care to carry any of the yellow metal away with him.

"Merely to convince the outer world of its existence, and to confirm a theory I have always held," he replied. "To my mind there can be no reasonable doubt that we shall find deposits here exceeding anything our people have ever dreamed of!"

"And why?"

"Because gold is heavy," he answered.

"Nonsense. Do you mean to say that the center of gravity is not quite as far below our feet here, as on the outer crust?"

"Probably not. When our globe was in process of forming, two great forces moulded it—the centrifugal and centripetal. These produce various vibratory conditions in different masses, resulting in gravity or affinity upon one hand, and repulsion upon the other. Bodies having the greatest specific gravity grouped themselves about the inner surface, forming an arch, being thrown off in a gaseous state from the center. But from the very reason of their gravity were unable to descend any great distance into the crust; and therefore the heaviest substances should be found upon the inner or under side of the earth's canopy."

"I fail to see it," I answered. "Why should not a heavy weight sink deeper than a light one?"

"It doubtless would on our side of the world," he replied, "but here the conditions are different, and for this reason. The great mass of earth above our heads is drawing us upward, as the mass below is drawing us downward. Not, to be sure, to the same degree, or we should not be able to walk on the ground. I believe that all things here are lighter than with us. You and I probably weigh several pounds less than we would in the United States or England. Gold, too, is doubtless lighter, for it is lifted up, as well as pulled down; whereas upon the outer surface of the earth it is drawn only one way. I may be mistaken, but I expect to find it in large quantities."

"Why, then, did you bring so much with you?" I inquired.

"Simply because I didn't know what might happen. If we find it, well and good; if not, the interest on fifty thousand dollars won't be any too much for a couple of men to live on, in the event of our being stranded here and unable to return."

All this time we were passing over a country where water, timber, and pasturage abounded, and where the grass was variegated with large patches of brilliant flowers of unknown varieties. But if the flora differed from that of our own land the fauna was no less remarkable. We saw herds of diminutive deer, feeding in the open country. Birds abounded, and some with a strange plumage, in which the pink of roses predominated. The topknots on certain of these looked as if a rose had blossomed there; add to this a body and tail of red and green trailing feathers, it appeared as if a flower spray was floating through the air. We caused the greatest consternation among these creatures wherever we went, and the four-legged beasts would at first run on catching sight of us, and then, overcome with curiosity, huddle together and look up, with cries of amazement and terror.

But we were approaching a remarkable sight. In the distance was a fleet of boats, similar to the one we had passed, and beyond them, looming in the denser background we saw a magnificent city of white and gold. We brought our glasses to bear upon this strange vision of the new earth. As we approached, the fleet presented a vision of splendor impossible to describe. Whereas before a single vessel had so impressed us, we were now confronted with a vista of hundreds, which stretched away down the wide avenue of this unknown river as far as the eye could reach. Flashing sails in a thousand strange designs of form and color. Decks loaded with men, women, and children, in such fantastic and magnificent apparel that we were startled and bewildered at the sight. On nearing this extraordinary scene, we hovered above, and caused the wildest excitement. Trumpets were blown at us. Bells were lifted on poles and jangled. Chimes were sounded that came floating down the water from ship to ship as if each vessel had its own special note, and then were answered back again, receding in the distance, until they faded on the air. In all the sounds there was a singular harmony, a softness of tone strangely gratifying. We moved slowly down the line—above the mastheads, above the music—for I cannot call it noise—to exclamations of joy and wonder. Here was a revelation awful to contemplate. Had we been living just above these people, in such close proximity for the unnumbered ages of man's creation, and never even guessed of their existence? But why was it any more remarkable than that they had not discovered, or even thought of us? A double world indeed; a shell, a bubble, a hollow ball; and yet neither had given a thought to the other's existence.

We hovered above this scene for hours, trying to communicate with the people, and examining their surroundings; and then, having learned but little, hastened on to the distant city.

. . . .

Another singular feature of our new world was the fact that there were no shadows. I do not mean that there were no shady places, but a shadow, in our sense, with clear cut edges did not exist. And indeed it was impossible that it should, the sun itself being nowhere visible from the inner side of the globe, the light entering from the poles, and being disseminated throughout the interior, as after sunset with us. The facilities for this distribution are vastly superior to anything we know, both from the electrified air, and a certain humidity, which seizes the rays of the great luminary, and equalizes and softens them most agreeably.

As we neared the great white city it grew upon us in splendor. Minarets and towers, arcades and domes, hanging gardens, tiers of arches rising one above another, majestic colonnades leading to palaces of regal magnificence, delighted and bewildered us. Although white was the predominating color, every conceivable hue and tint was used in ornamentation. Green domes with golden devices. Lapis lazuli columns. Malachite archways communicating with gardens where flowers of a thousand tints mingled in the spray of colored waters, whose trembling waves of iridescent mist would alternately hide and reveal them; where birds sang, and throngs of gayly attired people loitered. These were mere glimpses through the arches; but the parks, the great public spaces of the city where thousands of citizens met for pleasure and recreation, these were a vision of glory which word painting cannot approximate; for dreams of paradise were they, beyond the power of man to conceive. Here the very atmosphere was alive with song birds, whose plumage sparkled like jewels. We were entranced. The sights, the perfumes, and the sounds made the brain reel in its effort to absorb them. When the sense of vision would weary with the shifting pageant beneath, the nerves would be soothed with strange perfumes, whose origin was unseen, but whose effect was marvelous, creating an inexplicable sense of rest and quiet. When this power of enjoyment had reached an apparent climax, it would be relieved by such music as only the voices of the dream-world can equal. Was the place heaven? I do not know; but can only affirm that it was too utterly marvelous, too glorious for language.

As we moved slowly above the glittering streets, listening to the musical voices of those below, and watching the excited gestures of the populace, electrified at the sight of us, we marked the varied monuments of beauty, and saw that all were heavily decorated with gold and flashing with precious stones. Not only was this the case, but there existed a grace of outline and proportion nowhere to be found in our world of to-day. Beyond this was a majesty in height and size, eclipsing the creative genius of the most famous architects of history. The ancient Egyptian colonnades must slightly have resembled some of those we saw, judging from the drawings we have of them, but even these were crude, heavy, and cheerless by contrast. The city was indeed a vision of glory and magnificence, whose streets, if not paved with gold, were ornamented with it, and gems beside. I can never give the reader even the faintest conception of what we saw, nor can I recall to my own mind the fullness of the vision. Over all was thrown that rosy haze we had sometimes seen before, and which added distance and dreaminess to the picture.

We hovered over a park near the center of the city, and brought the air ship to a stand, while holding a consultation as to whether we should descend, and risk our lives among the inhabitants, who seemed so anxious to have us among them. Golden trumpets emitted notes of singular sweetness, and seemed to invite us to come down. Words, signals, and banners all spoke of the same hospitable thought, and we deliberated long and earnestly.

"I am willing to risk it!" said Torrence.

I acceded to the proposition, and slowly we began to lower ourselves into the midst of these unknown denizens of the inner world.

On perceiving our intention pandemonium reigned below. Trumpets sounded a harsher note than before. Bells jangled, and shrieks of applause rent the air. Crowds flocked into the space beneath, making it unsafe for a landing, as we were particularly desirous that no one should be hurt. We motioned the people away, but they surged to and fro, directly under the air ship, regardless of their lives, and with apparently no more intelligence than animals. This, of course, was the rabble, which the better portion of the populace tried to control, but without effect. Indeed it is not to be wondered that so marvelous a sight should have made them lose their heads.

Coming to a halt again about fifty feet above the ground we leaned over the rail, shouting to the crowd to disperse, not daring to touch the earth for fear of injuring some unseen person beneath, and with the further apprehension, lest in their frenzy of excitement they should climb upon our decks and overpower us. We were manifestly looked upon as visitors from another world. Some pointed above, others to the north and south as if to inquire whether we had come over the regions of eternal ice. We could neither make ourselves heard nor understood in the jargon of voices, and hesitated whether to descend further or not. While poised above their heads, Torrence threw a handful of gold sovereigns into the crowd. They were picked up with avidity, and passed from hand to hand as souvenirs.

"Just as I thought," said Torrence; "the coins are not valued on account of the metal, but merely as mementoes."

It was evident that St. George and the dragon, and the head of the ruling monarch of England were regarded with peculiar interest.

"Yes," I replied, "it is clear that gold is of no such value with them as with us."

They continued to solicit our descent by unmistakable signs, and we concluded to drop a little lower. Immediately a shower of gold coins, much larger than ours, was hurled up at us, and fell rattling over the deck, whence many fell to the ground again, although we secured quite a number. The pieces were stamped with strange devices, few being similar in design. There were dragons, sea serpents, leviathans, and other beasts of mythological fame. The people seemed to say:

"Have you any animals like these in your world?" at which we held up our own pieces and nodded. It was difficult to exchange the simplest idea with them.

Gathering up a few of these coins we offered to throw them back, and did indeed return a few, dropping them into the crowd; but when it was discovered that they were only their own no interest was shown in them, many falling to the ground unnoticed.

Presently a plaited rope, like the finest silk, was thrown across our stern, catching on one of the knobs of the rail. A man who looked like an athlete was quickly climbing up it, and half a dozen others followed his lead. The rope broke and they all fell to the ground in a heap. Seeing the danger which might ensue if we went any lower, we decided to leave this strange city behind without landing, and then amid the shouts and lamentations of the populace took our upward and onward course once more.

I was not without regret that we waved farewell to this first great imprint of the most wonderful civilization ever inspected by a man of our earth, and one perhaps never to be seen by him again. The city was a witness to a higher order of society than we had expected to find; at least I must speak for myself, for Torrence had committed himself to nothing. Not alone were the indications of wealth beyond compare with anything known in our own world, but withal, it was clear that the artistic and not the barbaric instinct had been appealed to. As we passed on through the environs, monuments of great size and beauty were constantly met. Gardens full of sculpture, strange flowers, and unfamiliar trees were seen. Temples, whose lofty summits were surmounted with amazing figures of nondescript beasts, eccentric dragons, and wonderful creatures with spreading wings, and all wrought in dazzling combinations of gold and varicolored marbles hove in sight. As yet we had seen no horses or domestic animals, unless the deer could be counted as such, and I remarked upon their absence to Torrence.

"The horse is a later development, he said, "and I am also inclined to think the dog is.

"And what do you mean by that?" I asked; "you speak as if these people had a prior existence to our own!"

"They had," he answered, with an air of conviction that amused me, considering his short acquaintance with them.

"One might almost imagine," I continued, "that you were familiar with their history."

"Not in the least; only I believe men first existed inside, and afterward outside of our planet."

He was sweeping the adjacent country with his glass, while my eyes were still fixed in a regretful gaze at the last magnificent portal of the city, now rapidly fading from our sight. I can conceive of nothing grander of its kind than this arch. Full of *bas-reliefs*, deep-cut intaglios, and surmounted with a gigantic god-like figure in gold, with a flowing robe ablaze with precious stones, it was a sight to hold one spellbound. The head was bent slightly back, the arms stretched heavenward, as if calling down a blessing upon our heads, or perhaps the wrath of the Powers above for having left so abruptly. When it had faded into the hazy atmosphere I turned to Torrence with a touch of superstition and asked what he meant. He did not answer immediately, but called my attention to the fertility of the soil. The great beauty of the country, the marvelous climate, and health-giving qualities of the air.

Indeed, these things had been impressed upon me from the beginning, and as we advanced into the interior their perfections seemed to increase. The hillsides were covered with verdure, and throughout the great parks fruit abounded in such variety and beauty that we were

THE SECRET OF THE EARTH. 185

tempted to descend and gather it more largely than, we could have used. Twice we dipped earthward and threw on board several bushels of pink, green, and yellow things, which, in addition to their extraordinary taste, had the quality of being cold as ice. There was no appearance that any of these were cultivated, nor was there any indication that the ground had ever been disturbed with a plow. All was spontaneous, beautiful, and perfect. The fields—great open plains—grew at intervals a grain which was always ripening and falling, judging by its look. It formed itself into a head which could be gathered and eaten at once without further labor or preparation. This we tested, after observing that both men and animals partook of it. Everything was produced so abundantly and brought to such a high state of perfection by nature, that no room was left for man's improvement of it.

. . . .

Distant outlines were softened by the mellowness of the air, and the clear-cut effects of the outer world were wanting. In no place did our range of vision exceed twenty miles.

. . . .

Billowy hills were grouped beneath us, where the vine and fruit tree flourished, and where streams of crystal water flowed.

. . . .

Herds of wild goats of a pinkish hue were passed, but they ran away so rapidly between the hillocks that it was difficult to get a good view of them.

. . . .

Human habitations were far between. There were no

roads; neither were there fences. All was pastoral, primitive, and restful. From the fact that the houses were but partially under roof, we concluded that rain did not fall, moisture being supplied directly through the atmosphere in the form of impalpable humidity, without condensation from above. In this way the disintegration by the washing of the soil, so common in our rain storms was entirely obviated. The conditions of life seemed wonderfully happy, and it looked as if man had only to breathe the life-giving air and eat the incomparable fruit and grain provided so abundantly to continue an existence of the utmost blessedness.

Turning to my brother I asked why he believed that the interior of our planet was peopled before the exterior. He looked at me queerly for a minute and then asked if I had ever heard an old fable about the Garden of Eden, from whence men, for certain reasons had been expelled. I told him that I was familiar with the story, but could not allow him to capture the whole inside of the earth for an Eden.

"And yet," he answered, "there is much to support such a theory. Mind I am not stipulating for garbled accounts of creation handed down from an ignorant age; but there are often some grains of truth in a mass of absurdities. Let us say that in here was the Garden of Eden. Now those who were compelled to leave it, or who did leave it, from whatever cause, naturally looked back to it as the hailing place of their race, and taught that fact to their children. The conditions of life upon the outer world are difficult, compared with those we find here. The story of their lost home would grow in beauty as it descended from generation to generation; and I verily believe that at one period in the earth's history there was a family driven forth which preserved its records, and that this fact has given rise to the Persian and Scriptural accounts of Adam and his family and the garden they left behind them."

"And how do you suppose they crossed the ice?" I inquired.

"I don't know," he answered; "how did Jan von Broekhuysen cross it? And do you know we have also discovered the gate of the garden, where the angel stood with a flaming sword?"

I started.

"What on earth are you talking about?" I exclaimed.

"Mount Horror and Mount Gurthrie! If ever there was a great natural gateway between two worlds it is there. I am sure one is an extinct volcano, and while it may not have been active in thousands or millions of years, it was once; and its awful eruptions of fire were doubtless the flaming sword of the angel!"

It was impossible to help being impressed with Torrence's ideas, because they were generally fresh, and often right.

"There is another point I wish to make," he added, as we hovered close above a field of purple berries, "it is this. Several of our most ancient civilizations have been sun worshipers. Look at the superb temple of the Syrians at Baalbec! Look at the Phœnicians, the ancient Greeks, the Peruvians! Now, why was the sun worshiped? Because it had not been always known. Because it was a new figure in the heavens, of marvelous powers, among which was that of locomotion, hitherto only applied to living organisms. Because it carried directly with it the power of light and heat, and because darkness followed when it went away; darkness being a condition previously unknown. Had the sun always been present in the heavens of the ancients, it would have been too commonplace, too familiar an object to have been deified. But it was new, strange, and apparently endowed with life and intelligence, and that is why it was worshiped. Gurthrie, there can be no doubt about it, we are in the Garden of Eden!"

"Possibly!" I answered; "but you must remember that we are in a new world, nearly as large as our own, and we must expect to find every variety of climate, and many different conditions, as with us."

"True," said Torrence; "I by no means believe that the Garden of Eden was an entire world. There are doubtless many strange things awaiting us."

We descended into the bosom of the purple field, and made a hearty meal of the berries.

. . . .

XVIII.

* * * * * * * * * *

An hour after leaving the city a range of ragged mountains loomed up ahead. We stood on deck watching its beautiful coloring and outline until the foothills were reached, when we reduced our speed. Nearing a purple cliff, streaked with crimson, we halted, and then rose slowly to a grassy ledge, where we landed. The mountains were not lofty, but presented a rugged aspect by reason of a series of rocky precipices, like steps, upon the top of each of which was a narrow belt of green, where the fertility of the ground was evidenced by a prolific growth of grass and fruits in wonderful profusion and variety. The grapes we found here deserve another name, by reason of their superiority; and the fruits which greeted us on every side beguiled us into lingering for hours to enjoy the piquancy and delicacy of their flavor. Indeed we felt the poverty of the human system in our inability to do more than taste the countless varieties which loaded these hills upon every hand. There were fruits to quench the thirst of every degree of lusciousness and acidity, and there were others which partook of the nature of solid food. Others again had a singular effect upon the spirits, lifting us into a state of exaltation, as though due to the presence of alcohol. But I am talking of things that must be experienced to be realized. Language fails to describe them.

Resting on this beautiful escarpment we looked out over a dreamy landscape, and then settled ourselves down for a nap. It was our intention when rested to look for gold in the peculiar tinted rocks below. Being tired we were soon fast asleep, and were surprised on waking to find that several hours had elapsed. We were greatly refreshed, and started out at once to prospect for the yellow metal with a couple of hammers.

Finding a natural pathway we began scrambling down the rocks, clinging to the bushes and long grasses that grew in the crannies, and chipping occasionally at the craggy protuberances around us. Torrence was ahead, while I was close behind him. I don't think it could have been ten minutes when I heard him call out:

"Color!"

Before I had time to let myself down to his level he held up a great chunk of reddish stone filled with yellow nuggets, as large as my fist. I had never beheld such a sight, and on reaching his standing, was electrified at the vision that greeted my eyes. This was not quartz mining; it was simply bending one's back and picking up wealth faster than a bank teller could deal it out over a counter. We chipped away as hard as possible for a few minutes, and then stopped to consider what we should do with the metal. It was evident that in an hour's time the accumulation would exceed our capacity for removal. It was clear enough how the inhabitants could afford to use gold in such wild profusion. Indeed the metal could not be so valuable here as the peat on an Irish bog or coal at a Pennsylvania pit. We were discouraged at our inability to turn the world wrong side out, or that we had not a railway at our command. But what must we do? Our early education made it impossible to leave the place without taking with us all we could carry, and so we resumed our efforts, determined to do our best. We pounded and hammered for an hour. Nuggets were in sight that were of greater value than all our stock of sovereigns. The mines of Solomon were trifling by contrast, and we stopped occasionally to survey the field and stare at each other in amazement. It was evident that whatever we succeeded in removing must be carried in the ore, as we had no machinery to separate it; and had this been of an ordinary kind, it would have been a serious consideration, but the gold was nearly as plentiful as the rock itself. All we could hope to do was simply to loosen the quartz with our hammers and knock out the kernels, which left us a really very insignificant residuum of rock to transport. It was not necessary to dip into the ledge or to go below the most superficial outcroppings, as more pure gold was to be had upon the surface than we could ever hope to remove.

"We can easily get out a million of money with our hammers," said Torrence, "and it would be folly to trouble ourselves with any but the richest and easiest handled."

We now saw the necessity of returning to the air ship for sacks to remove the treasure, and it became at once apparent that it would be impossible to haul it up the precipice. This led to a consultation. The ledge immediately below was rough and shelving, and unfit for a landing, but the vessel must be anchored there in order to receive her cargo. The place where we were standing was barely wide enough for a footing.

"I have it," said Torrence; "we must bring her to a standstill underneath without landing."

It was the only thing we could do, and although the face of the cliff was an awkward halting ground, we must manage it. And so we returned for ropes and gunny-bags, and a boathook, which we thought would be useful.

In less than half an hour all was ready, and while I lowered the precious cargo down to Torrence, who stood ready to receive it, and pull it out from the face of the cliff with his hook to a position where it could be lowered into the vessel, the air ship stood balanced in mid-air about forty feet beneath where I was working. Bag after bag was swung aboard and stowed away, until Torrence called out that it would be unwise to load with any more. I then let myself down and scrambled aboard, when we rose gently again to our former level, where we landed for another rest.

"Is she as buoyant as ever?" I asked him, meaning the ship.

"Quite!" he answered; "and we must surely have several millions in gold quartz aboard of her."

When we had rested for an hour we got up to go, but Torrence said he had an impression of having seen a nugget of such extraordinary size that he should not like to leave without making an effort to get it, being anxious to carry it home for exhibition. And so we decided to crawl down the cliff once more. We found the nugget, but it was difficult to loosen from the mass, so that we tugged and worked away for quite a while, and were about to give it up, when on straightening my back for a rest I looked out over the plain and saw a sight that startled me.

Far down among the foothills a great living mass was moving toward us. I called to my brother, and we both stood watching it in wonder. We had left our glasses above, but it was not many minutes before we decided that it was a crowd of natives coming our way; possibly they had followed the line of our flight from the city, hoping to overtake us in the mountains, believing that we would halt there. We could form no idea of their number, though evidently it was large.

"It's the rabble of that city!" exclaimed Torrence. "They've been overcome with curiosity, and no doubt think to capture us among these hills. It would be interesting to see what they want, but the vessel will be the safest place for us. There's no telling what superstition and curiosity may lead to. Even without hostile intention, such a crowd might easily overpower and destroy us in a good-humored effort to investigate!"

And so we began at once to climb the cliff again, discarding our nugget in the cause of self preservation. But the ascent was difficult. We missed the trail and wandered off in the wrong direction. Twice we stopped to examine the ground, but the natural pathway by which we had descended was undiscoverable, and there appeared no other route. We beat the bushes, lifting the dense growth right and left, but what had been so plain before, was quite hidden now. There was no time to be lost, for already a murmur arose on the air—a babel of voices from the valley—and it was evident the crowd was scrambling up the first rugged declivities beneath.

"We must get back to the air ship," said Torrence, "even if we have to go up the face of the precipice!"

"It is impossible!" I exclaimed; "we shall risk our lives, and may be dashed to pieces before reaching the top!"

It had all been simple enough before by the other route, and with the aid of the bushes to lower ourselves by, but now the only growth we could find grew on ledges that projected outward, and the roots had so shallow a hold that we dared not risk our weight upon them. Those we tried gave way immediately. The natural pathway was lost, and we could not stop to rediscover it.

"It's that or nothing!" cried Torrence, pulling off his boots and stuffing them into his belt. He then with a literal toe-and-finger scramble commenced a climb of what must have been nearly fifty feet up a perpendicular wall. My head swam, but there was no time to think, and so, following his example, I found myself immediately beneath him, in the same act.

The sound of trampling feet, falling stones, and the roar of voices now approached with sickening rapidity. What if they should reach the air ship first, by some safer and better route known to them only? What if they should destroy it, and leave us lost and alone in this strange world, with our only means of returning gone? The thought of such a possibility was more terrible than that of death; for even if these people were friendly, we could never become one of them. A Chinaman or a Thibetan, or even some undiscovered race in Central Africa would be allied to us by every tie of life beneath a kindred sky, the same sun and moon, the same stars and clouds throughout the ages; but here was another world, compared with which nothing in our own could ever be looked upon as foreign.

But Torrence climbed slowly and steadily, and I kept my grip beneath him, not daring to look below, or speak a word. I was overpowered with the agonizing fear that each step might be his last, or, that reaching a spot where, unable to proceed for want of a foothold, he would be compelled to retreat. And all this time the crowd was gaining on us at a sickening rate. I could now hear the individual voices of those clambering up behind. How near they were I could not think. We dared not touch the shrubs that grew in the crannies about us, for the soil was mellow and they broke away in our hands. There was nothing to do but cling to the rock with tooth and nail, and trust to luck. Suddenly the jangle of bells rang out on the air; why had we not heard them before? Surely it was an ominous sound—possibly the token of victory. But Torrence stuck to the wall and I was close behind him. The vanguard of the crowd had already commenced climbing the cliff below us, and I could almost feel their breath upon my neck.

"Be quick!" I called to Torrence, speaking for the first time. But he turned upon me a face pale with horror and said:

"I can go no further!"

It was what I was dreading. The cliff above was smooth and slaty, offering not the slightest projection for a foothold. And there we hung in mid-air, listening to the rabble pouring on behind. Death seemed inevitable. for we had nearly reached the top, and could not have survived a fall to the jagged rocks below, to say nothing of dropping into the teeth of the enemy.

How long we hung thus it is impossible to say, but it seemed like an eternity, and I remember looking at Torrence's boots tucked in each side of his belt and observing that the one upon the right was not as well secured as the other, and wondering if he would lose it. Then an angel's hand seemed suddenly let down from heaven, as I saw for the first time the limb of a tree, which hung over the cliff in line with my brother's head. He had not seen it, so intently were his eyes fixed upon the rock, but I now called out loudly for him to grasp it. Even this was no easy task, the bough being several feet above his head, and it required all the nerve he possessed to jump into the air from his precarious foothold and seize it.

I trembled, and every nerve in my body quivered as he leaped upward. I sickened, and felt the earth give way beneath me, but at the same instant I saw that he had caught the limb with one hand and was swinging clear of the rock. Would he be able to draw himself up? Yes, there he was struggling along the bough with both legs and arms, and in another instant the top was reached. It was now an easy matter to bend the limb down for me. But the men were close upon us.

"Run for your life!" cried Torrence; and although exhausted, we ran as we had never run before, with shouts of "Kyah! Kyah!' resounding in our ears. I stumbled; I fell; but picked myself up again, and rushed ahead with "Kyah! Te Kyah!" creeping closer and closer behind me. I did not dare to look, but felt as if an army were rushing upon us with every creature in it shouting "Kyah! Te Kyah!" The panting of the men grew louder; still I felt that we might cope with the vanguard, if we gained the air ship first, although conscious that the race would be a severe one. Moreover, in those few seconds of intervening time I calculated every chance, and weighed to a nicety how much of our advantage would be lost in boarding the vessel, hauling in the ladder, and getting under weigh. The ship had always responded promptly to the touch of the button, but now I was full of the gravest misgivings, knowing that the slightest hitch would undo us. A horrible sinking seized me when I saw a large body of men approaching from the opposite direction, and observed that the leaders were nearly as close to the vessel as we were. They had climbed the cliff from the other side, and were now rushing through the timber frantically. I redoubled my efforts. The air ship looked as if it were a mile away, judging from the difficulty of crossing the intervening space, but I knew it was not thirty yards. Another instant I had a vision of Torrence bounding over the side and disappearing within, and how it was done I scarcely know, but I was tumbling down beside him, and then came the swing of the great hull beneath me and I knew that we were safe.

As soon as we had the strength we pulled in the ladder and closed the taffrail, and then looked down upon the enemy. They had gathered in great force, and we estimated there were more than a hundred.

It was impossible to guess what they wanted, but there was that which bespoke a deeper emotion than mere curiosity. Had we violated any statute of their municipality in sailing unsolicited above their palace walls? We were sure we had committed no other offence. It was a strange picture they made, assembled upon that mountain ledge, in such brilliant clothing and magnificent jewels, and the pow-wowing and jabbering that ensued was delirious. They constantly pointed up at us, evidently anxious to communicate, though ignorant of how to do so. We were suspended about fifty feet above their heads, but concluded to come a little nearer the ground, at which they gave unmistakable signs of pleasure, and motioned us to descend all the way. This, of course, we would not do, but made every effort to understand what was desired. Gradually it began to dawn upon us that they were anxious for our return to the city; the signals were pleading and imperative for our immediate departure, and could not be misinterpreted, though it was impossible to guess why we were wanted there.

"It can do no harm to return," said Torrence. "It cannot be more than twenty-five or thirty miles. We can run back in an hour or less and find out what is the matter."

I agreed with him, and when we signalled our intention, they were wild with delight. One thing more they begged; it was that we allow one of their number to go with us. So far as we could judge this request was simply that we might have one capable of explaining their demands. After a consultation we decided that the man, if carefully watched, could not possibly harm us or the ship, and we consented, if a way could be found to take him on board without landing. With this end in view we came within about twenty feet of the ground and dropped a line overboard, signalling that if he wished to come he must climb the rope. This seemed satisfactory, and the most gorgeous specimen in the crowd approached for the honor. Above the waist he wore but little clothing, but about his neck was a triple necklace of dazzling stones of such unmistakable genuineness and splendor that, had it been in our world, its value would have been inestimable.

His hair was long and black, and jeweled rings were knotted into it at intervals. Upon his wrists were bracelets of a metal I had never seen, and around his girth was a belt of aluminum. We imagined the fellow's name was "Tuzu" from the sound by which the others addressed him, although this may have meant something else, but knowing no better, we spoke of him in that way. Tuzu climbed the rope with the agility of an athlete, and swung himself aboard in splendid style. Torrence motioned where he was to stand at the bow, and he did as he was bid. We then headed the air ship for the city.

As we floated out over the cliff a great shout of applause rent the air, and the crowd began scrambling down after us. Tuzu stood motionless, holding fast to the rail. He was too much impressed to heed the demonstrations of his less fortunate comrades, who were obliged to find their way back afoot, a journey of at least six hours.

We decided to impress the man with our power, and so the machine was made to rise and fall alternately in stupendous curves of flight, and with the wildest velocity. The motion was unnerving, and yet Tuzu never flinched, but stood quietly facing the city, holding fast to the forward rail. His position was a trying one, and as his black hair flew upward in some of the downward swoops he made a striking figurehead.

When the great golden monument over the city gate hove in sight, we slacked our speed, and going forward, offered the man our hands. Evidently he did not understand the meaning of the salutation, but after a moment's hesitation, examined them with curiosity.

"Tuzu, I am proud to know you!" we said; "whatever your lingo and religion, human nature is the same outside the world as in it. Shake!"

The man did not smile; he only looked with increasing wonder, and we regarded him with growing admiration.

As we drifted into clearer range of the city's portal we were more impressed than ever with the splendor of the figure surmounting it. With arms outstretched to heaven, it seemed appealing for the descent of some blessing upon its people. The statue alone must have been more than a hundred feet high, while the arch supporting it was doubtless four or five times as much. It was a creation far exceeding any similar design of our own world, and one which can never be forgotten. We stopped before this monster with feelings akin to awe.

"What is it, Tuzu? What do your people want?" we signalled, while suspended at an elevation less than halfway up this noble arch.

He pointed to the monument, and assumed an attitude

of reverence. Then throwing back his head and lifting his arms, imitated the figure. He then looked at us, and with unmistakable signs entreated our doing likewise. Was it some ritualistic ceremony with which all foreigners were expected to conform? Although puzzling, we did as we were asked, each in turn, and a look of pleasure came over the fellow's face. We repeated the performance, always careful to imitate the attitude of the model, feeling sure it was the right thing. Meanwhile another crowd had come pouring through the gate, a happy, interested crowd, which shouted with delight each time we repeated the ceremony. Suddenly Torrence, turning to me, said:

"I have it! I know what it means!"

He then went on to explain.

"Simple enough; these people take us for gods come from the sky, and in part they are right. Chock full of superstition, they want our blessing before we return to the unknown. This colossal figure is a statue of one of their deities, perhaps their only deity. Being gods, they give us credit for knowing what it is, and want us to bless the town and the people. Tuzu and his gang were sent to urge our return, and now that we have come they are satisfied. I am quite sure that this is the explanation."

It seemed as if he were right, for although the inhabitants repeated their request that we descend, they were now willing to let us go in peace, having bestowed our peace upon them. We declined their invitation, but signalled our hope of returning at a later day. We could no longer doubt the kindness of their feelings, but having an unexplored world ahead, were anxious to hurry on, and so waved them a second farewell.

．　．　．　．　．　．　．　．　．

XIX.

Before turning our backs for the last time upon this splendid monument of an unknown civilization, an incident occurred which is worthy of record.

As Tuzu was about to descend the gangplank—a stout, manila rope provided for that purpose—Torrence asked leave to examine the magnificent necklace he wore. The fellow appeared pleased, and when my brother, who is an excellent judge of precious stones, expressed his conviction that they were gems of rare merit, he insisted upon our accepting them, together with other decorations. This, of course, we would not do, but the man threw the jewels at our feet, and could not be persuaded to touch them again. The metallic ornaments upon his wrists and the girdle he would not part with. It was evident that the stones were not valued as with us, and that the blessing we had bestowed upon the city was considered sufficient remuneration for them. Tuzu then looked over the rail and said something to the citizens below, and in a minute a shower of jeweled ornaments began pouring in upon us, in the wildest profusion. The deck became covered with precious stones of such magnificence that their aggregate value could hardly be estimated. I would not like to say what amount of wealth was thus heaped upon us, as the most conservative estimate would sound wild and extravagant, but it was something fabulous. The air was thick with bracelets, neckbands, anklets, belts, earrings. They fell upon the vessel in heaps, in piles; they caught upon every projection, until the trembling of the air ship in rising shook some of them loose, and we began to ascend beyond their reach. This shower of wealth had probably not lasted more than ten minutes, but during that time we accumulated inestimable treasure, and stones of every color and size. It was a dazzling sight, but when I reflected that these were not a tithe of the wealth of the city, my brain fairly swam at the thought.

"After all," said Torrence, "it is simply the inversion of values; for what could be more beautiful than some of our Rhinestones, or even than some of our colored glass? No emerald is really as beautiful as a true Rhine crystal, but it is more rare, hence its value. The conditions here favor the formations that are most discouraged with us; why this should be is very evident, on the theory of inverted molecular action. The grinding and cooling of the earth's crust resulted in certain products upon the outer surface, and in others upon the inner. I have always believed we should find exactly this state of things here, and should really have been surprised if the results of creation had been similar in kind and quantity upon both surfaces. No doubt with little effort we could find diamond mines that would entirely destroy their value with us."

"Shall we get Tuzu to show us where they are?" I replied, feeling as if the gardens of Hesperides must be within our reach.

"I think not," he answered reflectively. "We have already more treasure than we can conveniently carry. I would rather spend the time in a superficial inspection of our new dominion than in digging wealth out of a hole which cannot be transported. If we should ever return it will be time enough to look up the mines, but where their product is so easily obtained as from these people, it seems hardly worth while to work for. However, if you wish it, we will go on a mining tour, and stake our claims, though I am sure no one will ever dispute them."

I agreed with him that we would better pursue our journey, as vast distances were to be traversed ere we could form the most indifferent conception of what awaited us in the continents, oceans, civilizations and cities. As yet we had only seen one little corner. We must make our way as rapidly as possible, and be content, for the present, with a bird's-eye view. And so, having retreated to a short distance from the gate, we lowered Tuzu to the ground.

When fairly upon our way again we sacked up about fifteen bushels of jewels, which in addition to the gold, made us very short of room. Indeed, our saloon was so crowded that we went stumbling about over bags of treasure, like the miser of Benadin.

Torrence now put on high speed and we swept over the country at the rate of forty miles an hour. We soon passed the noisy crowd returning to the city, with jangling bells and flowing mane, and they sent up a shout as we flew over their heads that spoke of good humor and general satisfaction. We had lost some valuable time, but were in a fair way to make it up, and looked forward to the great unknown with a keener interest than ever.

"How far do you propose to penetrate into the new world?" I inquired, as we sat on deck smoking our cigars through the rushing air.

"All the way," he answered.

"You must remember it will take us as long to return as it does to go," I replied.

"Return!" he exclaimed with surprise; "surely you don't expect to return."

"Rather! Do you intend to live here always?"

"Not at all," said Torrence; "I expect to go out through the opening at the South Pole!"

This was a new idea to me; but suddenly a thought struck me with horror.

"Do you not know it will be the depth of winter, and dark as Erebus when we get there?" I exclaimed.

"I admit that it will be both dark and cold," he replied, "although not quite the depth of winter, if we maintain anything approaching our present rate of speed. You must remember we shall have left the shortest day—June 21st—behind us."

"At best it will be but a matter of a few weeks, and I still claim that it will be the depth of winter."

"Practically," said Torrence, "it will."

He spoke with as much indifference as if he were merely going to walk down the street.

"We shall be frozen corpses if you attempt such a thing, and I must beg you to give up an idea so thoroughly impracticable."

"It is not impracticable, Gurt," he answered seriously; "do you not know that we are prepared for all kinds of weather? We can shut up the cabin and heat it to any temperature desired. Do not be alarmed; everything shall go well. While here we ought to see as much as possible. We shall sail through the darkness in a warm and brightly lighted cabin, and if I mistake not, there are sights in the antarctic regions which will amply repay our visit. Remember that no human being has ever penetrated their awful solitudes, and that none is ever likely to do so unless equipped as we are!"

There was something horrible in the thought of plunging into those regions of ice and darkness, but I could see the force of his argument. However, the great bulk of the interior was yet to be traversed, and there would be plenty of time to think of those terrors before we reached them.

The purple hills proved to be a country of minerals, grass, and timber, was broken and picturesque, and abounding in lakes, parks, and diminutive rivers. The habitations were few and scattered, the houses but half under roof. Occasionally we sighted a village, brilliant in coloring, and strangely rich in architecture, and the inhabitants would invariably stare up at us and shout. There were greens and crimsons and flashes of gold among the rocks, and lumps of iridescence that looked like clusters of gems of marvelous size and beauty; but we had not time to examine them. We were sure, however, from all we saw that gold was among their least valued metals, and that those natural products most highly prized with us were here regarded as drugs.

We hastened through this mountain country, not because we did not appreciate its beauty, but from a desire to get a rapid bird's-eye view of the new earth, and reach again our old home.

A rolling country was now beneath, which we speeded over at the rate of a mile a minute, not wishing to waste time upon extended areas that could be comprehended at a glance. Here we saw, herds of cattle carrying four horns and tailless. Probably there were no flies to annoy them, and tails would have been useless. There were also more of those diminutive sheep of a pinkish hue, and wool like silk that trailed upon the ground. One and all they scampered away upon catching sight of us, but we quickly passed beyond their range of vision.

. . . .

Here were great parks of magnificent timber and

brilliant flowers, and limpid sheets of water. Occasional palaces of reddish stone under partial roofs of a dark yellow metal were also encountered. Dropping earthward to examine these we were saluted by the occupants, who coming out of the buildings would wave banners, and blow upon a powerful, sweet-toned trumpet, whose music would linger in the air for quite awhile after the performer had removed it from his lips.

. . . .

Howbeit, our speed was so great, that these heavenly strains of music were lost by reason of their distance, while other sounds would greet our ears ahead.

. . . .

Our anxiety to learn something of these people and their history was ungratified, from the impossibility of communication.

. . . .

It was easy to see that our air ship was an object of intense curiosity both to man and beast. We were as great a wonder to them as they to us, which, to be sure, was true of our vessel upon the outer world, and it showed that aerial navigation was as little understood here as above. We received various unmistakable invitations to halt, but these we declined on the ground of haste. We determined, however, to accept one before our final exit.

. . . .

A striking feature in the lives of those we saw was the fact that there was no evidence of work. So far we had seen no plowing, or tilling of the soil, neither was there any sowing of seed or reaping of grain, nor building of houses; and yet we had the evidence of our eyes that superb structures and cities had been erected. On speaking of this fact to Torrence, he said:

"The climate and soil seem to render agriculture unnecessary; and possibly the buildings belong to a previous age. I doubt if material rots and disintegrates, as it does with us."

I asked how he had reached such an extraordinary conclusion.

"The atmosphere," he answered; "it never rains, I am sure, and I am equally convinced that there are comparatively no changes in the climate. The atmospheric conditions, which with us cause rust, disintegration, and decay, are here neutralized, or altered, by an absorption of electricity, pertaining only to the interior."

"But does the population not increase, requiring more houses to keep them?" I inquired.

"Probably not as it does with us; but even in our own world there are large regions where the death rate keeps pace with the births; and the tendency is undoubtedly in that direction. When population ceases to increase, which I believe is the case here, building will stop. Where the term of man's natural life has been greatly prolonged, there is less concentration of effort. The inner surface of the earth was undoubtedly peopled millions of years before the outer, and we are barely beginning to approximate conditions that have existed here for untold ages. After all, it is the swing of the pendulum, and the next move will be a vast exodus for the interior. The marvelous fertility of the soil, the singular qualities of the atmosphere, make it possible for these people to live without labor. I should, however, like to see their household arrangements to gain a better knowledge of their lives. One thing I am convinced of: it is that man's highest physical development, the acme of his material civilization, is only reached under adverse terrestrial conditions. Where nature coddles him he doesn't work, because he doesn't have to, and while he thus fails in some of the results that a harsher world would encourage, he gains in the poetical and spiritual side of his nature because of the time afforded for reflection."

"And yet have we not witnessed the grandest monuments to a material civilization ever dreamed of, in the strange city behind us?" I asked.

"True," said Torrence; "but I am firmly convinced that that city is millions of years old, and that we have not yet seen a house which has not existed in its present form and position for untold ages of time. With us a city flashes up in a moment of energy. Here the energy is applied directly to the result—pleasure—as life is assured, while the city is the growth of ages. Houses are not built here, neither do they rot!"

We were flying over a pastoral country without roads or fences, but where temples peeped from flowering trees, and houses, red and golden, stood by sheets of limpid water. Many of these were small, and looked as if they had been shoved above the earth by magic.

· · · · · · · · ·

We crossed lakes, seas, continents, and mountain ranges. We caught the occasional note of a distant trumpet, indicating that the inhabitant of some isolated dwelling had seen us. At intervals the glimpse of a village would enliven the solitude, and herds of the same diminutive sheep would scamper across the plain.

* * * * * * * * *

But we could not expect that beauty and fertility would reign supreme throughout an entire world, and there was a time when, looking down from our lofty perch, we became aware that the trees had disappeared from our range of vision, and that the grass was tussocky and stunted. The change, to be sure, had been gradual, but with it had come the departure of the human residence, and of all animals, neither was there any water. It was clear enough that we were hovering upon the borders of a barren land, perhaps, even a desert. We looked to our water supply, and concluded there was enough to carry us over any ordinarily arid region, especially at the rapid rate at which we were traveling, and so settled ourselves down on deck to our cigars and fieldglasses.

* * * * * * * * *

We had been chatting along quite pleasantly, constantly scanning the horizon, when we became aware that the air was perceptibly warmer, and at the same time saw that even our scrubby patches of grass had been entirely supplanted by the sand, which lay thick and red beneath, with a peculiar luster. At long intervals there were rocks of the same color, indistinguishable, except from their elevation, and in their crevices grew a coarse, thorny plant, nearly as red as the rock itself. Dropping earthward, we found these plants greasy and bad smelling.

At the same time we discovered that the ground was

unpleasantly warm, and that the sand *crawled*, covering our footsteps as soon as made. We wanted to take some samples of this cactus-like leaf, but feared it might be poisonous and so let it alone. Gradually even this loathsome weed disappeared, and only the sand remained. It was clear that we had entered upon a desert, where nothing grew, and where nothing lived. True, there was no sun, but nowithstanding this, the air was hot and sultry. We were unable to account for this change in the temperature, and the heavy incinerated atmosphere, but the rapidity of our flight created a draught, which kept us fairly comfortable.

The smoke from our cigars trailed rapidly astern, and then sank to the ground in a condensed form as if weight laden. We watched it with interest, puzzling over the cause, which Torrence thought might be some peculiar quality in the air, coupled to the strong draught of the vessel. Dropping to a lower level, and going astern, we were amazed to see a pale-blue, thread-like line marking our course in a path over the ground. It seemed incredible, but it was nothing more or less than a smoke path, formed and fed by our cigars. Not a breath of air disturbed its rectilinearity. It was a phenomenon neither of us could understand. We stood watching this for a long time, observing how the smoke, as we blew it from our mouths, would sweep earthward with the draught of the vessel, and then immediately be drawn out into the thin, blue, concentrated line described.

Even the last vestige of rock had now vanished, and we were speeding over a plain of red sand, above which the heat-laden air quivered. The temperature was steadily rising, and our Fahrenheit thermometer recorded eighty-six degrees. Torrence and I took off our coats, and renewed our search of the horizon in the hope of discovering hills, or any indication that we were approaching the end of the desert, but there was nothing but the red sand as far as the eye could reach with the aid of our strongest glasses. We were moving at a high rate of speed, and felt sure that a few hours would bring a change, but in this we were disappointed.

We had penetrated more than a hundred miles into the solitudes of this desert when an extraordinary sight presented itself. A bird of such magnitude and terrible aspect swept across the sky that Torrence and I trembled with horror. There is nothing in size that I can compare it with, save the roc of the "Arabian Nights," and even that mythical bird, although possibly larger, had neither the plumage nor frightful countenance of this. The bird was flying diagonally across our path, although much above it, and to the best of my belief must have measured fifty feet from tip to tip of wing. Its feathers were of a dirty red, and its beak was hooked and powerful. Its eyes were fiery red, set in a circle of white, and as it looked down upon us there was a sinister expression, almost human in its intelligence. It was flying at terrific speed, and apparently without effort, and as it passed away we observed an unpleasant odor, which hung upon the air for some minutes after. It uttered no cry, but had evidently seen us, and left an impression bordering upon the supernatural, which was not easily effaced. It was the only living thing we had seen since entering the desert. The bird seemed to spring into the air from nowhere, and crossed our bow with such velocity—at an altitude of probably a couple of hundred feet —and vanished with such marvelous speed into the distance that ;had we not both seen it, I should have been inclined to ascribe it to some optical illusion. But there was no doubt that here was a creature unknown, or undreamed of in our own world. Could it be possible that the stories of the roc were founded upon any obscure tradition of this strange animal? Torrence believed that it was. He declared, moreover, that not a fairy tale existed but was built upon the conscious, or unconscious, knowledge of some past existing fact.

Five hours after entering the desert our thermometer registered one hundred and four degrees, and the heat was becoming intolerable. The deck was the coolest place, as we got all the draught of motion, and there was no sun to shine upon us. We looked anxiously ahead for relief, but there was nothing save the red sand and the quivering atmosphere in view. Even the sky had a pinkish tinge, shared by the great illuminating disk in the 'eavens behind us. We had indeed entered upon a barren land, which even the dwellers of its own world renounced.

• • • • • • • • • •

XX.

Nearly a day had passed since we first entered this great sterile, superheated plain, and notwithstanding our speed, the end was nowhere in sight, even at the expiration of eleven hours. The temperature had become so oppressive that we had no appetite, and sat fanning ourselves with wet cloths and moistening our heads and faces and wrists, in a vain effort to keep cool. At this time the thermometer registered one hundred and ten degrees, and was steadily rising. We had tried various elevations, but could not perceive that it was more tolerable at a height of five hundred than one hundred feet from the ground. In fact it was the same everywhere, and upon every side of us—above, below, before, behind. We had discussed the advisability of returning, but pushed ahead with the conviction that a change for the better must soon come. We dreaded to retrace our steps with the possibility of being lost, and were loath to miss the strange sights that might be in store for us in the regions of the antarctic opening. There could be no question that the heat was subterranean, and indeed when we had last landed the sand was so hot that we could scarcely bear our feet in it.

I was searching the horizon ahead, while Torrence was examining the sky for electrical phenomena, when a sight met my eyes that filled me with unspeakable horror. We were rushing upon a sea of liquid fire, which extended in the distance as far as eye could reach, and from east to west without apparent limit. It was an awful picture. There was no escaping it, unless by retreat. I shouted to Torrence, who turned immediately from the sky, to the fearful horizon ahead.

"There is nothing to be done," I cried, "but return!"

The atmosphere was quivering like a glowing oven, and from the fiery sea to the sky above the waves of vapor rose and fell like the spirits of the flames themselves. As we drifted on, the heat grew more intense, and the vital principle of the atmosphere was gone. The sea was rushing upon us with awful speed, and with each minute of advance the air became more stifling. Torrence's hand was upon the lever, but not to slacken speed. Was he mad? Had the fellow become insane? I asked him the question, for although rising to a tremendous height, he had pushed the air ship up to her highest speed, and it would be but a few minutes before we should be launched directly over that awful hell of fire.

"Have you lost your mind?" I shouted; "what are you about?"

"Gurt, brace yourself for a strain; we can stand it!"

"Stand what?"

"Go below! Get some buckets of water and sponges. I am going to cross that sea!"

"Stop!" I cried, grasping his arm, "are you going to kill us?"

He shook me off.

"Get the water," he said, "and be quick about it."

Still I was immovable, while the air ship seemed to leap through the air at the rate of a mile a minute. I could scarcely breathe. The fiery world ahead was not a mile away. Our lungs would be consumed in that horrible incandescent vapor. No living creature could stand it. I continued to hesitate.

"Damn you!" roared Torrence; "if you don't get the water you can stand where you are and be burned. I would cross that sea if it were a thousand times hotter than hell. But I tell you I do not believe it is wide, and we shall be safely over in an hour, if you will trust me. Don't stop to talk, for I am determined, and will drag both our skeletons through to the bitter end, sooner than turn back now!"

I ran below as fast as possible after the water, for I saw that argument was useless, and my fears for Torrence's sanity were also aroused.

On reaching deck the sea was beneath, and the incandescent atmosphere around us. I saw Torrence through a yellow haze, holding fast to the lever, and cramming his handkerchief into his mouth. I staggered toward him with the bucket, and pressed a wet sponge upon his head; doing the same immediately for myself. The water saturated us, and enabled us to get our breath, which came in gasps. I plied the sponges constantly and regularly, at the same time watching the horizon for a change, with the deepest anxiety; but the sea was dazzling and the volatile gases which ascended both blinding and stifling. As far as the eye could reach, before, behind, and upon either side, great lurid flames leaped up from the ground, and beyond the limit of their powers this deadly vapor surrounded and penetrated every tissue of our being. At each breath, these poisonous gases burned and scorched their way into our lungs, shriveling our lips and throats like the fumes of sulphur. Again and again I rushed below for water, and again staggered on deck scarcely able to support my load. But it was not until the sixth or seventh trip, when the hair on our heads was positively singeing, and the skin or my brother's face looked like parchment, that I made the fearful discovery that the water was *nearly out!* I was drawing upon the last cask. What was to be done? It would be useless to talk to Torrence; he would drive the air ship into hell before he would turn back, as he had already said. Should I endeavor to overpower him, seize the lever myself, and retreat, if indeed it were yet possible to do so? or should I die in furthering his insane determination? I crawled on deck with the last bucket of water, still undecided.

"*The water is out!*" I yelled through the roaring of the flames. "Do you still persist?"

Torrence did not answer, but pointed below, and in an agony of horror I saw what he meant. Our end was at hand; for the vessel was sinking into the fiery mass beneath.

"It's the heat!" he said hoarsely. "It's too late to talk about returning. The fire has damaged the vibrator. We can't keep her afloat an hour to save our souls; and the end may be nearer ahead than behind us!"

He then stood quietly watching our gradual descent into the pestilential fumes with an indifference that amazed me. I should not say that he was indifferent, but that he had every appearance of it. We sank upon the deck, side by side, mopping ourselves with the last spongeful of water and wondering how soon the end would come. Suddenly Torrence jumped up and staggered to the rail.

"It is cooler!" he shouted; "I feel it. We are still high above the fire. If we can keep afloat for ten minutes longer we are saved!"

"How do you propose to do it?" I gasped.

"Throw out the gold! Throw out the gold!" he roared.

We were unable to stand erect, but stumbled, and

THE SECRET OF THE EARTH. 217

crawled, and staggered into the saloon Alas! we were too weak to lift the metal in the original packages, but took out huge chunks from the sacks, throwing them overboard through the windows.

"Be quick, for God's sake, called Torrence, as a great yellow flame leaped into the air higher than the others. We were heaving out the yellow metal as fast as possible, and bag after bag had been disposed of, when we both became sensible of a marked change in the atmosphere.

"It is cooler!" I said, taking time to rest for a second.

Torrence implored me not to stop, so I resumed the work, and together we had thrown out half the gold, when we sank down thoroughly exhausted. For several minutes neither of us had strength to move, not really caring much whether we were burned alive or not. But at last there came a change, and we crawled to port and looked overboard. We had passed the fiery sea, and were hovering over a sandy desert, similar to the one already crossed.

"We are saved!" exclaimed Torrence, pressing his hand against his parched cheek; "this desert evidently surrounds the crater."

"Strange name for an ocean of fire!" I remarked.

"Perhaps you would rather say the fountain head of the crater," he replied; "for I believe that this sea of burning bitumen is the foundation for one or more of the volcanoes in our own world. Does it not seem strange that the story of a fiery hell, situated beneath the earth, should have such a striking exemplification in fact?"

I admitted that it was extraordinary. and then crawled to the upper deck, and looked about. The sea of fire was still visible in the distance, and despite the fact that half our gold was gone, we were falling rapidly earthward. The self-registering thermometer showed that we had passed through a temperature of one hundred and thirty-five degrees, which seemed incredible; a heat which no human creature could have stood, were it not for the entire absence of moisture, and, paradoxical as it may appear, for the constant application of the wet sponge. Of course this water was cool by comparison with the air, otherwise it would have scalded us. As it was, its constant evaporation preserved our lives. Even now the thermometer recorded one hundred and fifteen degrees, but this was cool and comfortable.

Much as we regretted the loss of the gold we were impelled to throw over still more, being anxious to reach water, and a better climate before undertaking repairs upon the vessel; and so we probably threw over the trifle of a hundred thousand dollars in additional ore in the effort to restore our buoyancy. Fortunately we were not obliged to part with our jewels, wherein lay our principal wealth.

The vessel was now pushed to her full capacity, which was not more than twenty miles an hour, and constantly decreasing, together with an alarming tendency to drop earthward. We had just come through such horrors that nothing could seriously disconcert us, and I felt, moreover, every confidence in my brother's ability to repair and readjust the vibrator as soon as we had reached a suitable place for the work.

About half a bucket of water was left, obliging us to use it with the greatest economy, and as the heat was still intense, our thirst continued to be quite painful. We kept our places on deck, scanning the horizon for indications of water or vegetation, but the burning red sand usurped the earth in every direction. We felt,

THE SECRET OF THE EARTH. 219

however, that there was reason to hope for relief, on account of the increased humidity and the gradual falling of the temperature. However slight this may have been, it indicated that we were going in the right direction, if we could only hold out long enough.

Steadily our speed fell off, and slowly, but steadily, we sank earthward. At last, when an indescribable apathy was stealing over us, we discovered a sight which filled our hearts with hope. It was a range of sharp, precipitous mountains, silhoueted against the southern sky.

It seems proper in this connection to explain the use of a word which might appear paradoxical in our peculiar situation. The word I refer to is "horizon." To an outsider the expression might seem only applicable to conditions of the external globe, but when it is borne in mind that our range of vision rarely exceeded twenty miles, it will be seen that the concavity of the earth was not any more apparent than the convexity would be with us, in a similar panorama. Beyond this, the state of the atmosphere afforded as true a horizon as any upon our exterior plane. To be sure it was not always so clear cut as our own upon certain occasions, the land blending with the sky, as on a cloudy day with us, but there is nothing in that respect which is not thoroughly agreeable and natural. No one could have guessed, from the simple appearance of earth or sky line that he was not a dweller of the outer world. The sights which amazed us were those already described, and perhaps of these the most astounding was the great disk of light in the heavens.

The mountain range, which had been gradually looming up before us, now gave us fresh courage, for surely where there are mountains there must be water. Help was ahead, but we must reach it before the air ship collapsed. The poor thing which had been so buoyant, so fleet and powerful hitherto, was now a miserable cripple, requiring constant care to keep it afloat. Every bulky or weighty object that we could possibly spare was thrown over, but there came a time when we saw that she must sink to the ground within a mile. Our speed had also been greatly decreased, so that during the last hour we could have walked very nearly as far as we had sailed. At last we settled gently upon the red, burning sand like a feather undecided whether to fall or rise. We scrambled over the side, and for the first time since leaving London felt the poverty of man's power of locomotion.

"And is this to be the end of all our efforts?" I inquired despondingly, throwing myself on the hot sand beside Torrence.

"Undoubtedly, if we lie here more than five minutes!" he answered, wiping his face with the damp sponge.

"And what do you propose doing?" I inquired.

"We must get to those hills, dead or alive," he replied; "and we must be about it directly."

"Do you intend walking?"

"Yes, if we can't patch up the machine."

"We are a helpless couple, as it is," I remarked, rising, for the sand was burning me.

"It's a long way from home," observed Torrence with a sickly smile.

I grinned.

"Yes, and how magnificently we were talking about sailing through the South Pole; treating the earth as if it were a mere ball to be jumped about in at our pleasure. I feel as if I had suddenly fallen from the powers of a god to those of a paralyzed caterpillar!"

But Torrence was up.

"I am dying of thirst," he said; "we must get to the

THE SECRET OF THE EARTH. 221

hills or perish in the sand. Do you know we shall be raving maniacs if we remain in this temperature without water? Let us get to work and see what we can do. I have brought all kinds of tools and materials, perhaps we can get her afloat again."

And so we crawled back into the big machine and down into the lowest compartment, where the great vibrators and delicate mechanism were located. We worked hard for hours, under the most trying conditions, where heat and thirst were maddening, and feeling that every moment's delay brought us nearer the end of what we could stand. At last we effected what Torrence believed would be a temporary adjustment of the parts, for it was all we could do under the circumstances.

"With water and a cooler atmosphere I could make a perfect job," he declared; "but I am exhausted, and this must answer for the present."

We climbed up on deck again and touched the button and shoved over the lever. The glory of the next minute eclipsed every sensation of exultant joy, for the air ship rose like a Phœnix from the ashes and sailed. We dared not rise too high until better work should be done, but at fifty feet above the ground we again pressed ahead at twenty miles an hour. How long this would last we trembled to think, but more than forty minutes had elapsed before we observed any lessening of the speed; and then our hearts sank in proportion as we slowed down and dipped earthward.

The temperature had materially fallen, but there was still no water in sight, and our thirst was becoming unbearable, and at last the horrid thud, as we again touched the earth sickened us.

"Can we not patch her up again?" I asked.

"As a matter of fact, we can," said Torrence, "but the

bearings won't hold as long as before, for the simple reason that I have not the physical strength to adjust them properly."

"Let us try it at all events, and for God's sake be quick about it." I felt that my thirst was overcoming me.

At the end of an hour we rose again, but this time not so high, nor could we go so fast, and at the expiration of twenty minutes we were again upon the ground.

And so all day long we repeated these terrible heartbreaking experiments, each time rising a little less, and falling a little sooner. I use the word day as a mere measure of time, as, of course, there was no darkness; and all day long the blue mountains hung like a painting against the sky, and seemed to get no nearer. Our resources were nearly exhausted. We could not speak above a whisper. My throat ached, and the skin about my neck and cheeks felt like paper. But our salvation lay in the air ship; by no other possible means could we hope to escape the awful fate which threatened us.

. . . .

XXI.

DESPERATE men will sometimes develop superhuman power, and I think when Torrence next went to work upon the nerve-trying mechanism of the vibrator, he must have made an abnormal effort. However this may have been, the ship arose with renewed energy, and darted through the air with a speed that astonished us both. This sudden accession of power lasted for quite two hours, and when she sunk again to earth the rugged hills were wonderfully near. Again he tried his hand upon the splendid structure, but at last it was evident that neither nature nor art would respond. He was too weak to adjust the vibrator, and without the vibrator the vessel would not rise. We strained every nerve, and made every shift imaginable, but she would not budge. Torrence was lying upon the deck, unable to move after the terrific struggle below, for the adjustment of the parts required not only physical force, but the exercise of nearly every sense as well. The hearing, the sight, the touch, must all be in perfect condition, and the strain of bringing these up to par, when so far below their normal state, was terrible, and now quite beyond his ability to achieve.

"How far are the hills?" he asked in a hoarse whisper.

"Hills," I answered, "my dear boy, they are towering cliffs of sheer rock."

"And do you see no vegetation among them?"

"None. Indeed, so far as I can tell there is not a shovelful of soil in the range!"

"But there must be water," he insisted, although I could see no sign of any from where I stood, nor could I admit to myself that the prospect was against it.

"There may be," was all I could answer.

"Gurt, old man, it is our only chance. You must go afoot."

"Alone?"

"Yes, alone, for I am not able to move. Do you think you can reach it?"

"I will try; but do not get out of heart. If there is any water to be had I will find it. Yes, and I will bring it to you, dear boy. Don't give up. I promise."

"God bless you. If I could go I would, but I can't!" was all he said.

I then staggered down the ladder and wandered off, hardly knowing how or where, in search of water, for one drink of which I would have sacrificed the entire wealth of our cargo.

Keeping the dark cliffs in view, I bent my steps toward them with a strange misgiving.

The sand lay hot and deep in ridges, undulations, and depressions, like the swell of the ocean; characteristics which had not been so pronounced until I found myself crossing them afoot, and walking over waves into which I sank shoe deep at every step. Full of pain, and exhausted I plunged ahead, dazed and bewildered, conscious only that I was making the last effort for our salvation. On and on I trudged toward those terrible precipitous rocks ahead, at a rate which could not have carried me more than a couple of miles in a single hour; and at last I sank down exhausted to rest.

I looked about me. Where was the air ship? The

vessel was nowhere in sight, and I wondered if I had come farther than I thought. It was impossible that the distance between us had made it invisible. The machine had simply disappeared from the face of the earth, suddenly and inexplicably.

In every direction the desert stretched, and above was the sky. It was impossible that Torrence could have repaired the damage without me, and sailed. I was bewildered, horrified. I felt that I was lost forever and irredeemably, for even my footsteps had been obliterated by the creeping of the sand, doubtless the effect of subterranean heat. I was crushed; and as I sat there, burning and aching in every inch of my body, and in mental agony as well, I cried.

Then I remembered the undulations of the plain, and was convinced that the air ship was lying in one of the hollows between them, just out of sight. Although this thought was comforting in one sense, it was not so in another, inasmuch as it did not relieve the situation. The vessel was as hopelessly lost as if she had sailed away without me. At least so I felt about it. I shouted as loud as possible, but at best could not have been heard a hundred yards, for my throat was parched and painful, and its power gone. Death seemed close at hand, and closer, perhaps, from a certain apathy which was stealing over me.

Stretching out at full length upon the sand, the cliffs beyond had an ominous look. There was no appearance of life, neither was there tree or bush to indicate the presence of water. Sheer cliffs, of unscalable form, towered above me. Like the ruin of some vast Titanic home the rocks were piled in huge masses, uncouth blocks and pinnacles, from the sandy depths beneath to the vapory heights above. The wind whispered through dark alleys and deserted passages, and at open casements; at least these sounds appeared to reach me in that awful solitude, and I was overpowered with the sense of a breathing, intelligent world around me.

As I lay there staring stupidly up at the rugged forms of tower and pinnacle surmounting this strange wall, I was struck with the appearance of dark spots in the face of the cliff near the summit, which had a peculiar regularity, as if they might be windows, cut or blasted out by human hands. This interested and set me to examining the place more carefully, when I became astounded at what I could no longer doubt was an artificial design extending along the top of the precipice. Could it be possible that this great natural wall was crowned with a castellated structure built by men, and so closely resembling the cliff itself as to be indistinguishable from it?

I raised my head and examined the place with growing curiosity. Yes, there could be no question about it, the whole top of the wall was built up artificially. Perhaps it was some great fortress, or decaying monastery; for the singular blending of art and nature made it seem as if the two had grown together through vast periods of time.

As I lay there, dreading the effort of rising, and indeed almost too weak to proceed, there came a strange sound through the air, which grew louder, and more inexplicable each minute. I listened, wondering if it could be in my own ears, as signal of approaching death, and almost wished it might be. Was it a rushing wind creeping down from the heights above, or the portent of subterranean upheaval? It grew, and while vaguely surmising the cause, I became suddenly aware of a fearful object, hovering above. I started to my feet, staggered and fell, for directly over me was one of those gigantic birds. It swooped earthward, and I crouched in horror, as I saw that it was making directly for me.

The end was at hand. I should be pecked to pieces before I was dead, and my flesh be consumed like carrion by this damnable, awe-inspiring monster. Even had I the strength to resist, a dozen men could not have coped with such a creature. I lay quietly waiting to feel that awful beak pecking at my heart, my eyes, my brains, and suffered the agony of a thousand deaths. Down it came; it was close above, and the stench upon the air was overpowering. I could not move, for the paralysis of a consuming fear devoured me. I looked straight up into those baleful eyes, and my attention was attracted by a strange thing, for around the bird's neck was suspended a gilded barrel of peculiar form. Now was I alive, or was I dead? for at that moment a sight presented itself which might well have made me doubt. When close above the ground, and within fifty feet, the bird stopped and by some dextrous movement of beak and claw, disengaged the barrel, which dropped quietly upon the ground, leaving the animal free to fly away as quietly and mysteriously as it had come. It disappeared among the rocks near the summit of the cliff.

Crawling toward the cask I examined it, and discovered to my unspeakable joy that it was divided into two compartments, in one of which was about five gallons of cold water, while in the other was a quantity of fruit. Had this strange creature been sent from heaven? but I could not stop to think until after I had drunk and eaten, and then falling down upon my knees thanked God for his deliverance, for even here in this awful desert I was watched and cared for.

I was a new man, but the thought of my brother dying in the air ship came upon me with renewed force. Could

I ever hope to find him? The heights above offered the only chance of doing so, for there I could overlook the inequalities of the sand hills, discover his position, and with carefully established bearings reach the spot. It was a frightful undertaking, but my only hope.

Hanging the cask with its remains of food and water across my back by the cords attached, I again pushed forward, and after an hour's patient trudging was relieved to find the sand less tenacious, and far more shallow; in fact, the walking had become comparatively easy, but the climb had not commenced. When it did I discovered what appeared to be a natural rocky way leading above. Up this dangerous path I directed my steps, and although the work was steep and laborious, it was a relief to have solid ground once more beneath my feet.

At the end of two hours I had ascended to a great elevation, but to my amazement the air ship was not yet visible. The atmosphere over the plain was quivering with heat, and its dense gaseous condition may have obscured the vessel, but I was greatly distressed that it had not come in view. Another hour's climb and still the noble craft was hidden from my sight.

It was growing cooler, but neither watercourse nor vegetation had been encountered, yet the black, towering rocks closed in upon me on every side. Whither was the path leading, and what would be the end? It would be useless to return, to be lost in the drift. There was but one object to steer by, and but one hope to which I could cling, and that was the great barren rock that supported me. If once my back was turned upon this single landmark, there was absolutely nothing to look to. And so with aching heart, and the gravest misgivings, I struggled on, stopping constantly to search the plain below.

So far the path had been narrow and tortuous, a mere rut, twisting in and out among the irregularities of the wall, but suddenly I found myself standing upon a horizontal ledge, like a natural piazza overlooking the plain. On my right, at the back of this landing, the cliff continued to rise in a sheer ascent of perhaps a hundred feet, and here I again observed those dark openings, which I had seen from below. It was a remarkable formation, and I walked along it with an uncanny dread lest here was the abode of some unknown being which might resent my intrusion.

The farther end of this extraordinary promenade was blocked by a mass of rock, but upon examination I found a narrow alley which led to the rear, and communicated with a vast internal passage, dimly illuminated with an amber light coming from above, and falling about the walls in strange scintillations of green, purple, blue, crimson and gold. I stood for a moment staring in surprise, and then, overcome with curiosity, walked into the interior. The corridor in which I found myself was at a right angle to the esplanade, and ran directly into the mountain. It was of vast height, although the peculiar configuration prevented my gaining any accurate knowledge of its altitude, as the light filtered through semi-transparent masses above, whose distance from the floor was irregular and difficult to estimate.

The gloom of twilight reigned about me, but the coloring was of a splendor indescribable. Above, below, around were these spark-like points of illumination, shifting and changing like the twinkling of stars, or the flash of precious stones, and of every conceivable color and tone. I wandered on in stupid amazement, wondering whither it would lead. The passage seemed interminable, and of ever increasing splendor. The illumination from above would change from amber to erubescence, and then it would fall upon my path in sudden rifts of green or gold, and then return to its original amber tint again.

At last I came to what was undoubtedly an indication of life, and of human life, too, for here at the end of the corridor was a door. Not a common door, but a great cumbersome stone portal, which was made to swing in a socket at the end. I stopped before this emblem of humanity in awe. What was beyond it? I listened, but no sound came from within. A massive chain of gold was hung from the point where with us a lock or latch is affixed, and I could not doubt that it was intended as a handle to pull upon. My curiosity was wrought to the highest pitch, and I longed to grasp that chain and swing open the aperture. Twice my hand was upon it, and twice I drew it away in terror; but at last, trembling with excitement, and overcome with an unholy desire to solve the mystery within, I seized it and pulled with all my might. The door swung open, and I stood face to face with an extraordinary sight.

An apartment of magnificent proportions was before me. In size I should say that it approximated a cube of a hundred feet. It was lighted from above through a ceiling of transparent mosaics, arranged in superb designs, apparently emblematic of historical events. The walls had been carved out of the solid rock in pictorial cameos. These pictures surrounded the room. They were perfect in delineation, and of unparalleled workmanship. The floor was laid in rich mosaics, also arranged in pictorial form, and the light from above was just strong enough to add a mystery to the scene. Never had I dreamed of anything so wonderful. In all this vast apartment, above, below, and upon every hand, there was

THE SECRET OF THE EARTH. 231

such lavish decoration that the eye was bewildered; it was impossible to take it in.

As I stood there, marveling, gazing, I seemed to be the only living creature in this great silent hall, and by degrees, as I gained courage, I wandered on toward the center of the floor, trying to take in and understand the marvelous scene, but as I have said, it was impossible to comprehend it at a glance, or even to perceive the details of more than a small part of what actually existed.

I had reached a point about halfway across the floor, my head strained at every angle in reviewing the marvels around me, when suddenly I was startled by a sight that made my heart give one great leap. Upon a slightly raised dais, surrounding the room, I had observed not less than a hundred richly decorated chairs. These were carved, gilded, bejeweled and caparisoned in a manner that made it difficult to tell exactly what they were, but I had decided that they were seats, and intended to examine them a little later. Imagine, therefore, my horror to discover that upon each chair sat a human being, so strange, so mysterious, and of so awful an aspect, with gilded and painted faces, that I had not recognized them before. Indeed these creatures were so richly robed, and in that respect so closely resembled their surroundings that it was only when one of them moved that I discovered my mistake. I had been watched then from the moment of entering the room. There was nothing to do but apologize for my intrusion; explain my errand, and retreat as gracefully as possible.

I prostrated myself before this grave assembly; told how I was in search of aid for my brother, who was perishing from thirst on the plain. I asked if they would appoint a delegation to assist me in carrying water and finding him. I said that he was exhausted with the heat, and that I feared he would perish if not relieved immediately. Of course all this I might as well have said in Choctaw; but what else could I do? Yes, there was one other thing which I did. I pointed to the barrel of water on my back, made a motion as if drinking, and then pointed out at the plain, signifying that another was there who needed their aid. But these strange, gaunt men neither smiled nor answered me. They sat silently looking on with their dark, wonderful eyes, and did not even so much as glance at one another. Had I been one of their own number I would, apparently, have created as much surprise. Filled with chagrin and horror at the extraordinary situation in which I found myself, I began slowly to retreat, keeping my eyes fixed upon these unearthly beings, and their environment. Indeed their recognition had been so sudden and unexpected that I half looked for other developments in what had appeared fixtures of the apartment. In doing this I observed that the spaces between the pictorial cameos on the walls were filled from floor to ceiling with what appeared to be stacks of metallic tablets. It seemed possible that the place was a vast library, or depository of historic records, some of the scenes of which were depicted upon the walls. Could it be that these men composed a guard for their preservation?

Slowly I retreated toward the door by which I had entered, stepping backward, and never relaxing my eyes from a close and careful scrutiny of the scene. Glancing at the farther end of the room, I was suddenly electrified by one of the mural decorations I had not before observed. It was a representation of a man and woman being driven through a great natural gateway; but that was not all, for the portal through which they were passing was an accurate delineation of **Mount Horror and Mount Gurthrie.**

THE SECRET OF THE EARTH. 233

For a moment I stopped, and then overcome with the significance of the picture and the horrible mystery of my surroundings, turned, and fled toward the door. Seizing the chain which hung within I flung it open and rushed out; but, alas, I had mistaken the entrance. There were other doors, and I had taken the wrong one.

I was in a dark, narrow passage, with the door behind me closed, and as I soon discovered with no chain to reopen it, nor would it yield to my pressure. With my hand against the wall I groped forward, feeling carefully with my feet at the same time. The passage was not straight, and as it turned from side to side I realized that I was wandering through a crevice in the earth.

On and on I crept, until at last, overcome with terror at the thought of my position, and the probable fate which awaited me, I sank down upon the floor, almost wishing that I had perished in the plain below. As I sat there brooding over our misfortunes, a strange odor was wafted through the passage, which I recognized at once as belonging to those gigantic birds of the desert.

XXII.

The peculiar odor alluded to grew more intense, until it became almost insupportable. I got up and stumbled on, hoping to escape it, and find an outlet to the open air, wondering at the same time if the alley led to a nest, or general rendezvous of these extraordinary creatures. The passage I was following was not only crooked, but in places it inclined upward, leading me to look for an opening above. The darkness was intense, and perhaps I felt it the more from the fact that there had been no night since the last great headland of Europe had faded from our view.

I could form no idea of the distance I had groveled along this black, noisome rift, when a flickering light greeted my eyes ahead which filled me with joy, although it was evidently not the light of day; still it relieved the awful sensation of having been trapped alive in a tomb of solid rock. The light approached slowly; evidently it was a long way off when first observed, and the reflection on the walls was all I was able to see for quite a time, but at last I heard approaching footsteps. There was a sharp angle ahead, and upon turning it, I found myself face to face with a human being bearing a torch. We stood for a second staring at each other. The man, if man it were, was tall, gaunt, with copper-colored skin, painted and gilded in geometrical designs, and with white hair that fell about his face and neck. He wore a crimson paletot which hung from his shoulders without belt or girdle. He was nearly a head the taller, and as I stood watching him in the flickering light of the flambeau, I was chilled, subdued, humbled, realizing that I was in the presence of a being whose powers I could not fathom. Without a word he turned, and with majestic wave of firebrand, motioned me to follow. I did as I was bid, knowing nothing else, and together we threaded the subterranean passage in its upward trend.

We struggled on up the incline, which ended in a vaulted chamber, where were standing vessels of water, and a quantity of peculiar-looking food upon a marble slab. In a corner was a pile of mats, doubtless intended for a bed. The walls were rough as if blasted from the living rock. About forty feet above my head was an opening through which the blessed daylight entered. My attendant left without a word, closing the heavy stone portal behind him.

Finding myself alone, I began to investigate the surroundings with a view of escape. It would have been useless to return as I had come, for even had my chamber door been open, the other end of the passage was closed against me; but the man had fastened the great stone portal after him; it was immovable in its stone socket. I was sealed up alive in a vault whose only opening was far above my head. How to reach that outlet was now what most concerned me.

Here I again observed the peculiar odor of those gigantic birds; if it became much stronger I thought it would stifle me. Examining the walls of my prison I found them in many places rough enough to afford a lodgment, huge blocks, projecting into the apartment; but the height was great, and I dared not attempt climbing to the opening above unless sure of finding a passable way to the top. The outlet was not directly in the apex of the roof, but upon one side, near the spring of the arch. The light was dim, and it was some time before I had fully mastered the bearings, but after a careful search I discovered in a remote corner a regular ledge of projecting rock, which appeared to go all the way to the ceiling. Indeed it looked as if it might have been used as a stairway to communicate with the roof. I lost no time in trying this, feeling uncertain as to what fate awaited me. And so, with the little barrel still upon my back, commenced the ascent immediately. As I had thought, it led without difficulty to the aperture, and I begun to congratulate myself with the thought that there was no intention of making me a prisoner after all, when so easy a way had been provided for my escape.

But this idea was quickly dispelled on finding myself upon the top of this lofty formation, which fell away upon every side in great chasms, and awful rifts, impossible to cross or descend with any means at my disposal. It was clear enough why there had been no effort to prevent my emerging here.

Far out over the desert the atmosphere still quivered in the dreadful heat, but even at this tremendous elevation I could see nothing of the air ship. Was it too small an object to be recognized so far away, or was it hid by the undulations of the sand; or, could it be possible, no, I could not believe it was possible, but still the thought would come to me, that Torrence had repaired the damage, and sailed away alone to continue the exploration by himself? I am sure such a conception would never have entered my mind were it not for the awful strain I had been subjected to.

Wandering across my prison roof I looked down into one of the great abysses beneath, a kind of natural courtyard, and beheld there a scene that interested me, and explained the presence of the odor, so often observed. Half a dozen of these gigantic birds were stalking about in this inclosure, and while I looked a man came among them bearing a barrel, the counterpart of the one I possessed. Going to the nearest, he fastened the vessel about its neck, and immediately after it flew up directly past where I stood, and out over the desert. Suddenly it flashed upon me that I might have fallen upon some strange monastery, where the *Fathers* dispatched birds instead of dogs to rescue those lost upon the plain below. It was merely a thought; I had no way of proving it, and give it for what it is worth. But even the thought was a comfort to my harried soul.

Fortunately I had water and food with me, and had no desire to return to the chamber, although momentarily dreading to be summoned before some august power to account for myself. I spent hours in searching the walls below, endeavoring to discover some rift or ledge by which I might descend; but there was not the shadow of a chance upon any side. Exhausted I lay down and slept, but my sleep was troubled, and I soon found myself tramping the hard ground again. I could see nothing but starvation ahead, and imagined the indwellers of the glittering cave beneath quietly awaiting my end; although for what purpose I could not guess.

I have not the slightest idea how long I remained upon this barren mountain top, but after hours of mental torture I suddenly caught sight of the air ship flying toward me high above the desert plain. My heart gave one great leap of joy, and then I relapsed into a dreadful fear lest Torrence should not see me. In an instant I had pulled off my shirt and was waving it frantically. I watched for an answer, but no, he was not on the lookout; still I would not relax my efforts until every hope had passed. I shouted, I roared, I waved my shirt and coat frantically. I ran as fast as possible about the rock to attract his attention. I took off one of my boots and beat upon the water barrel; but still he did not signal in reply. I was beside myself with horror at the thought of being left alone in this mysterious world. Surely though, even if he passed he would return to look for me.

On and on came the air ship, as magnificently as ever. He had managed then without me to repair the damage, for never had she sailed more splendidly, more superbly than now. Nearer and nearer she came. What if the terrible noise I was making should arouse my captors below, and they should seize and carry me down to their own mysterious regions again? The thought sickened me, yet I dared not cease my bellowing and shouting for a single instant. So near the mountain, and yet no signal. Oh, horror! was he going to leave me? He had reached a point directly above my head; and now he could not see me if he were on deck. It was my last hope.

"Torrence! Torrrence!" I cried, as if my heart would break.

Oh God! The agony of that minute as I saw the vessel quickly drift away upon her course, leaving me lost and alone or in the companionsip of men whose methods of life were inscrutable. Once more I yelled. It was my last and greatest effort—and—what did I see——? Yes, it had borne fruit. The great machine paused in its flight, and Torrence looked over the rail. I waved my shirt frantically. He saw me—he heard me. The motion was reversed; and then, like some majestic bird, she settled earthward.

It would be useless to attempt a description of my feelings at that moment. I cannot even realize them myself. I only know that when the huge **monster** touched the mountain top I sprang upon her side like a madman, and clutched wildly at the footboard before the ladder was dropped. In a minute I was aboard; the rail snapped to behind me, and we were sailing tranquilly away from the horrible scenes that had so beset us. But before a hundred yards had been placed between us and those awful cliffs, a body of men had ranged themselves in line to witness our departure. I do not pretend to account for what I saw in those rock-bound halls; if this were fiction I would doubtless do so; but as it is, I can only offer the suggestions already made, be they worth what they may.

We now flew rapidly away over rough and interminable ranges of mountains. Pure chaotic masses of stone, without a trace of vegetation in sight. Indeed there was no soil to support tree, bush, or herbage. We crossed frightful chasms, hundreds of feet deep, we scaled terrific heights, and looked down from the top of precipices into darkened valleys. Crags were heaped upon crags. Dreadful gorges yawned beneath us. Nothing in our own world can compare with this region, and when it is remembered that not a drop of water, or shovelful of soil is to be found, the terror of the place may be faintly pictured.

At intervals we caught sight of those gigantic birds, which resembled the fabled roc, and which were apparently hatched in these desolations, for they were at home here where no other creature could support life, and what they found to live upon it was impossible to guess. They came swooping up from out the black chasms beneath, and after circling about us in curiosity, would descend again into the awful gulches from which they sprang.

We were days in crossing these rugged ranges, which

we called "the mountains of death," and we feel sure that the distance across them was more than a thousand miles. The heat throughout was intense, although nowhere did it compare with what we had already experienced.

Torrence told me that one of those gigantic birds had come to his aid with water, just as it had to me, and the remains of his cask and mine furnished all our drink until we reached the Crystal River, a stream we found and named from its clearness; but this was not until we had put "the mountains of death" entirely behind us. The strange castellated structure upon which I had fallen was the only human habitation we discovered throughout our passage across these rugged ranges, and it remains a mystery to both of us where the inhabitants procured their food supplies, or even the water they drank and furnished to others. How that extraordinry edifice was ever constructed, or how its inmates communicated with the world beyond is likely to remain an unsolved mystery to the end of time.

The air ship had behaved beautifully after leaving the "castle of the dead hills," as we called it, and Torrence told me that he had succeeded in making a perfect adjustment after getting the water, and that he believed the vibrator would not trouble us again. It was fortunate it had not, while crossing "the mountains of death," as there were long stretches where it would have been difficult to have found enough level land for a resting place, and any misbehavior on the vessel's part might have precipitated us into subterranean depths from which we could never have risen.

Having decided to push through the opening at the South Pole, and desirous of reaching our own world as early as possible, we put the vessel to a high rate of speed, after having filled our water casks at the Crystal

River, and bathed in its cool, delicious current. The
land beneath us had again become green and beautiful,
and the atmosphere of a temperature which left nothing
to be desired. Our haste was not because we would reach
the south polar regions at any pleasanter season, but
from terror lest the air ship should collapse. It was a
kind of homesickness, growing apace; a terror of pending
disaster and ultimate inability to reach the land of our
birth.

For days after this we traveled at a rapid rate, over a
varying country. We crossed great forests, flowering
plains of unparalleled beauty, and trees whose fruits we
stopped occasionally to test. And here we saw animals,
nearly as large as our elephants, but with heads like the
wild boar. We passed over thickly settled districts,
where the inhabitants rode upon animals of great speed
and delicacy of build, although but slightly resembling
our horses. We hovered over magnificent cities densely
populated, and with temples and monuments of passing
splendor; but we did not stop at any of these, from our
utter inability to communicate with the inhabitants.
There were rivers teeming with ships, and loaded with
passengers, but upon every hand was the evidence of
rest and recreation. No work; no commerce; no effort
to live. But wherever we were seen the ubiquitous trumpet announced our approach and departure in an anthem
of wonderful beauty.

At last my dread that we were approaching a great
internal ocean was realized, for we came to a halt on the
summit of a lofty cliff, with a splendid vision of the sea
beyond. There was something in the appearance of the
water that made us both believe it was more than a mere
inland lake. The surf which rolled in upon the shore,
the distant white caps, and the raw, saline smell in the

air, suggested a watery waste of vast extent. It was a rugged coast, and we decided to overhaul our machinery before venturing into the unknown beyond.

On this headland we cooked our dinner, just as we had done upon the North Cape, indeed there was something so similar in the appearance of the two places that we were reminded of our adventure there, and took care that there should be no repetition of it.

A careful examination of the vibrator showed that Torrence had repaired it perfectly, and there seemed no possibility of further trouble, but to make assurance doubly sure, we applied extra bolts to secure the damaged parts, and were then, as Torrence declared, in a better position than when we left London.

The great light disk in the heavens had been slowly ascending toward the zenith, with our advance upon the equator, and as it now stood about ninety degrees from the vertical meridian, or halfway between the horizon and overhead, we imagined we must be somewhere nearly under the tropics of our own world. There had been no falling off in the light, it being disseminated throughout the interior with equal purity and force; and as Torrence explained, when the northern summer waned, with the passage of the sun across the line, the south polar opening would gradually supplant the deficiencies of the north. I wish we could have remained in our new world long enough to have witnessed this change, but we could not make up our minds to so long a stay.

"It does seem astounding," I said to Torrence, as we sat sipping our coffee, "that the people of this world should never have discovered their close proximity to our own outer sphere, which is indeed equivalent to another planet!"

"No more astounding," he answered, "than that we,

who so continually boast of our superior powers, should through all these ages have failed to even suspect their existence. We search the heavens for indications of life upon our sister planets, and neglect this world beneath our feet. That to me is more astounding than the other!"

The outlook ahead was melancholy; possibly due to the uncertainty of when we should again see land. We continued our meal in silence, and then with a final look at the machinery, re-embarked to cross this unexplored sea.

The cliffs rapidly faded away in the distance, while the sky above, and the water beneath, alone remained to us. We felt like the tenants of some meteor traversing the regions of interplanetary space.

We now flew onward with tremendous velocity, for there were no pitfalls, no mountains to avoid, and nothing of interest to see. Moreover, Torrence had come to the conclusion that a rapid rate of transit was less inclined to disorder the machinery than the reverse.

Hour after hour we swept ahead through this realm of mystery, constantly scanning the horizon for speck, or sail, or life upon the sluggish waves, and wondering if human eyes had ever looked upon the picture flowing beneath us.

"I feel quite sure," said Torrence, "that this sea will not extend to the Antarctic Ocean. For various scientific reasons I am convinced that land predominates upon the interior, and we are much too far from the southern opening to make it at all probable that no more land will be met. This body of water may be a thousand miles across, or even more, and there may be channels communicating with the South Pacific, although this is mere conjecture; but land we shall have!"

As the geography of the interior was quite as familiar as that of the opposite side of the moon, it seemed absurd to form any opinion concerning it, but Torrence had decided views upon every subject.

About four hundred miles out upon this mysterious ocean we were astonished by the sight of a ship. She was rigged and bedecked in the same extraordinary style that the river boats had been; and it was certainly in evidence of an equable climate, that these gaudily attired vessels dared venture so far to seaward. She was moving diagonally across our path, with her stern toward us. In the distance her singular sails flashed in the light, and as we approached we saw a similar crowd of gayly attired passengers upon her deck. We took them quite by surprise, and as we hovered across their mastheads, a tremendous shout, followed by the blare of trumpets, greeted us. Although wondering whence they came, and to what distant shores they were bound, we knew it would be useless to tarry, in the hope of gaining any information, and after extending our blessing hurried on.

Strange thoughts crowded into our minds at the sight of this vessel, and questions that could never be answered forced themselves upon us. Was there any commerce in this mysterious world; and if so, how, and where was it conducted? Through all the territory we had traversed there had been no indication of trade. The people simply lived without effort or want. But what had these vessels to do with their lives? Surely pleasure excursions would hardly venture so far in such frail, ornate contrivances, resembling the gilded craft of fairyland. Might not many of our nursery rhymes have originated in old traditions, having their fountain head in this forgotten land of our inner world? It was a curious thought, and there were constant sights suggesting it.

Within twenty-four hours of our embarking upon this unfamiliar ocean a hazy purple line appeared across the horizon, which indicated land. We had come about twelve hundred miles over the water, but for aught we knew might simply have crossed an arm of the sea itself, whose size, of course, we were unable to estimate. We first reached land over a promontory, upon either side of which the water trended in deep bays. Far down upon the western coast we thought we caught the outline of a gilded city, whose minarets and towers stood faintly against the misty sky. But the world we had discovered was so vast we could not hope to do more than gain the merest superficial suggestions of what it contained.

Again the dry land was beneath us, picturesque and greener than ever. Similar fruits and trees greeted us here as upon the other continent. Indeed the climatic conditions appeared so equable throughout the interior, with the exception of the desert and the country contiguous to it, that there seemed no reason why the same food supplies should not be raised throughout.

But we were rapidly approaching the southern gateway of this newly discovered Eden, and I looked forward with horror to the darkness and cold which were soon to envelope us. Beyond that, I had the most pleasurable anticipations of returning to our paradise after acquainting the outer world with the results of the voyage.

XXIII.

It took more than a week of rapid traveling to cross this last continent, during which time we ate and slept alternately, one of us constantly remaining on watch above. Many cities were passed of a splendor exceeding anything known upon our side of the globe, and during the transit we witnessed what we could not doubt were different nationalities, if not different civilizations. These changes were, however, not easy to estimate, from the fact that all we saw was so strangely, so utterly foreign that differentiations which would be marked and strongly apparent to a denizen of the inner sphere, were only slightly in evidence to us. It was as if a native of darkest Africa should journey abroad through Europe; it is not likely that he would perceive much dissimilarity between German, French, English or Russian citizens.

We halted only at long intervals, and generally in thinly settled districts, to overhaul our machinery, or stretch our legs upon the ground. The amount of territory covered during that week was vast, the air ship being kept at her highest speed. We crossed rivers, great lakes, or inland seas. We saw sights well worth recording, and marvels which we longed to investigate, and would indeed have done so were it not for our utter inability to communicate with the people; and perhaps some day, even if we should not return, it will be worth while to write a fuller description of all the wonders we encountered in that strange inner world; that world which, since the dawn of creation, has been so close at hand, and yet whose existence we have never suspected.

Far to the south we crossed a body of water so closely studded with mountain islets, that many were connected by bridges, and nowhere could there have been a thousand yards between them, and this for a distance of five hundred miles. And yet here were evidences of a past civilization, in the deserted old castles, and rock carvings which abounded among them. We hovered close above some of the largest of these relics, without eliciting a response from a human being. Manifestly they had been deserted for untold ages. The golden trumpet had vanished from these desolate halls, neither was there any sign of life within.

A change was coming over the air. There was a chill and the light was fading from the sky.

"We must prepare for cold weather ahead!" said Torrence.

And then we went down into the cabin and made everything as taut and snug as possible. The hatching to the upper deck was closed, and every crevice carefully chinked. Our portholes were fastened and screwed down. Our ventilators arranged, so that the outer air could only reach us through coils of heated pipe; and if the air ship did not fail us, it seemed impossible that we should suffer in our rapid flight across the frozen sea of the Antarctic regions.

Gradually our disk of heavenly light receded toward the north; and it was clear that we were rapidly approaching the south polar opening. At last it sank entirely out of sight, leaving us in a chill, rapidly closing twilight.

By the time our preparations were completed, it became necessary to start the heaters, put on warmer clothing, and confine ourselves to the cabin. We had bade a final adieu to the summer land, and the rigor of the south polar regions was ahead. Darkness was coming down upon us, as well as the cold, and occasional masses of floating ice were seen from time to time.

At last the stars became visible, the first we had seen in more than a month, and then there shot up into the sky a great pink light—the *aurora australis*—to remind us of the bright and happy land behind. At that minute I felt a yearning to return; for there was the world of dreams, of poetry, rest, beauty and contentment.

"Torrence," I said, shuddering at the thought of what lay ahead, "how long will it take us to cross this horrible sea of ice and darkness?"

"If we press her, we can do a thousand miles a day. You can figure for yourself. But this region of cold and starlight need not disturb you, for we can dash through it like a meteor. Indeed, were it not for the danger of unlooked for eminences, we might sleep until reaching the land of the sun. But that, of course, cannot be, as a constant lookout through the forward port will be necessary."

The vessel had been furnished with a powerful headlight, which cast a dazzling illumination among the mirror-like surfaces beneath; and as we sat staring into the trembling path, constantly stretching away before us, we felt indeed, as Torrence had suggested, like the parasites of an earth-bound meteor, traversing these regions of ice and darkness in a single night

Our cabin lamp was lit, and we were stationed at the forward lookout. Torrence glanced at the speed indicator.

"Seventy miles an hour!"

I was startled. A mishap at such an awful rate of transit would smash us into a thousand atoms, and the news of our discovery be lost to the earth. But my brother was calm and unconcerned; he had no misgiving while one or the other of us remained on watch.

"It beats the Erebus and the Terror," I answered nervously, peering into the marvelous vista ahead, and the rapidly extending pathway dancing and flickering in the wonderful headlight.

Fresh panoramas were constantly unrolled in the glimmering distance. There were scenes that were strange and alarming. Pinnacles and ridges of ice—antochthonous—awful—would compel us to rise to sudden and terrible heights, to clear them. It was like a steeple chase on a gigantic scale. We were leaping fences, and clearing ditches; only the fences were ice masses hundreds of feet in height, and the ditches horrible chasms whose depths could not be guessed. On and on we flew, through these regions of mystery, which the most daring explorer had never even approached, and without a flying machine it seemed likely he would never penetrate. We did not suffer from the cold, wrapped up in our cozy cabin, although our spirit thermometer, which was placed directly outside one of the windows, where we could see it, marked a temperature as low as—eighty degrees. It was an atmosphere of death, and fortunately we were hermetically sealed against it.

"I propose," said Torrence, "that our next voyage into the interior of our planet be made through the south polar opening at midsummer, about January, to enable us to see what kind of country we are passing through!"

"That is easy enough to see now," I answered; "ice mountains, ice oceans, ice continents, icebergs, ice valleys of death; surely no living creature could exist in such icy solitudes, in such unutterable cold!"

"But you must remember this ice belt is probably not nearly so wide during the summer months. There is doubtless a change."

"Remember the Palæocrystic Sea!" I suggested.

"True," he answered, "but remember it was narrow, and that we have never seen it in the winter."

"Of all our experiences," I observed reflectively, "the present situation strikes me as the most remarkable, skurrying through these frozen regions like a comet, and spying out the land by the light of a candle. It is surely not the method most in vogue among pioneers!"

"It has certainly not been done frequently before," he answered; "but now that we know the way, a trip to the interior by either of the poles may become a desirable pleasure excursion; in fact it may grow into a fashionable fad, who can tell, and the future may develop——!"

He stopped suddenly, and we both became transfixed with horror at the sight that confronted us.

Directly below, but standing on the very pinnacle of one of the ice hummocks, was a human being, revealed by our headlight. The man was facing us, and waving his arms furiously. Could anything be more blood-curdling than such a sight in such a place? No ship or sled, nor indication of life was visible, save this solitary, deserted creature. The region was impenetrable to human beings; we knew it; it seemed incredible, and yet there it was, a living man, and alone, in this untraversed, and untraversable wilderness of ice.

Such solitude, such isolation, such an impossible fact, was like a sudden vision of the supernatural.

We had been moving at tremendous speed, but before we had quite passed this weird object Torrence had slowed down the air ship and a minute later had brought it to a halt.

We quickly wrapped ourselves in the heaviest eider-down and fur garments we possessed, not daring to open a window for communication until thoroughly protected, as, of course, we intended taking the poor creature aboard, and to save his life, were it possible to do so. When every precaution had been taken, we backed the vessel, and lowered ourselves to a level with the ice. When the headlight had been brought to shine against the ice mass, a great white bear lowered himself down the side and leisurely walked away. He had been alarmed, and his curiosity aroused at the sight of our light, hence the mistake! We had a roaring laugh over the absurdity of our error, and then proceeded upon our journey at the former rate of speed.

We passed three ranges of lofty mountains, which looked as if they must forever bar the entrance to these regions of cold and darkness; for they were flanked with terrible glaciers and precipices, thousands of feet high, and sheathed in great ridges of glittering ice.

We rose to fearful altitudes in crossing the summits of these sublime and awful crags, and wondered if there was no gap or opening at sea level between them. Doubtless there must have been, but our shortest course lay directly over their highest elevations, not being inclined to take the time to explore their topography. By the light of day the view from these heights must have been grand beyond description, but at the time of year in which we crossed there was little to be seen. It is worthy of record that at an altitude of eleven thousand two hundred and eighty feet we encountered a temperature of ninety-one degrees below zero Fahrenheit. I cannot conceive that there is a colder spot on earth.

Dawn at last gladdened our eyes, and then the glorious sun became visible, though not until we had passed far beyond these unknown regions of Antarctic ice, but then our own world was about us, and we watched the growing day with intense interest. As we sped northward over the great Pacific, the air grew warmer, and life again became possible on deck.

Opening the hatchway we went above, and aired ourselves in the pure breeze of heaven, which blew gently across our bow, and was warm and grateful.

Then on we flew for days at a more moderate rate, following a direct line north over the South Pacific. We intended to make port in San Francisco, and then cross the continent in easy stages to New York. But man proposes and God disposes.

One afternoon, while smoking our cigars on deck, and enjoying the balmy air of the tropics, Torrence was surprised in looking over the rail to discover that we were much nearer the water than he had supposed. Going down immediately to the lower controlling board, he examined the apparatus and readjusted his screws and buttons, and tested the lever, but the vessel did not respond as she ought to have done. We were gradually sinking toward the surface of the water, and nothing we could do would check the descent.

"I can't understand it," said Torrence in dismay, "unless the vibrators have become deranged again, through exposure to the intense cold, and the ensuing heat. Contraction and expansion must be the cause. It is impossible to remedy it while in the air. We must seek some island immediately. Even then I am afraid, before we shall be able to proceed, that it will be necessary to duplicate some of her parts, which may require the aid of a machine shop. But for the present we must look out for our lives!"

We took an examination of the sun, and investigated

THE SECRET OF THE EARTH.

our charts. We were south of the tropic of Capricorn, and far removed from those island groups that lay to the north and west of us. Indeed we were in a very ticklish place, for to the best of our knowledge there was no land anywhere in our vicinity. After so long and marvelous a voyage, after having encountered such perils of air, water, fire, ice, and land, it did seem doubly hard to perish in our own world, before even the news of our discovery could be given to that world.

There were two things which it seemed important to do without delay; the first was to throw overboard the rest of our gold quartz, and every weighty object; the second was to seal up this record as quickly as possible in some water-tight vessel, in the hope that it might be picked up, and the result of our remarkable journey become known. I rushed down into the galley to find a suitable cask for the purpose, but before I had secured what I wanted, I heard Torrence calling me above. He had discovered a blue line on the horizon which he believed was land. A careful examination convinced me that he was right, and our efforts were immediately directed to reaching it, and to saving our treasure as well. Having a direct goal in sight we now put on all speed, and flew over the water at the rate of seventy miles an hour, a thing we should have hardly dared to do except under the circumstances, but our lives, our news, and our cargo were at stake.

Lower and lower we sank toward the waves, but nearer and nearer came the island. Would we reach it in time? It was a wild, frantic race between distance and elevation. The air ship was screwed down to her utmost capacity in speed, but she was also falling at a rate which made the outcome doubtful. Having come so far with our treasure we naturally felt averse to parting with it. Enough gold quartz to have had any material effect upon the buoyancy of the vessel would probably have been worth more than a million dollars, and with salvation so near ahead, we were inclined to make every effort to save it all. Our jewels were inestimable, and no serious burden, and would, of course, either be saved entirely, or go to the bottom with us.

On we flew, now skimming so close against the waves that we could hear the spray as it dashed against the bottom, but we were rushing upon the island with terrific speed. We could see now that it was well clothed with foliage, and that a clean, flat beach lay before us, where we could land without difficulty, if we could only reach it. On and on we swept, but each dash of the waves was more ominous. At last a great white swell raised us bodily; would we sink with it? No, we were still a few feet above the sea, but the water had retarded our progress, and the vessel trembled violently in recovering herself. On again; but now every wave was slamming against our bottom, and throwing us up and down with a violence that seemed as if it must destroy us, if continued for more than a minute. Slam, bang, crash, as we bounded from wave to wave, and steadily settling between them, and yet how far away the island looked. We were clinging to the rail for dear life, not daring to go below for fear of being drowned, and holding on above lest we be knocked overboard. Suddenly Torrence left me, and rushed down the ladder at the risk of his life.

"Let's pour a barrel of oil over the water!" he shouted.

I was with him in a minute, and together we emptied the remains of our oil cask over the water. The effect was instantaneous. The waves subsided at once, and we found ourselves floating a few feet above the surface. It now seemed possible to reach the shore. Another minute decided the question, as we checked speed suddenly, and then dropped gently upon the beach. We had conquered, but where had we landed at last?

Examining our charts, with which we were amply provided, we discovered that the island to which we had escaped was not mentioned among them. It does not belong to any of the archipelagoes in this part of the world, and is situated hundreds of miles from its nearest neighbor, in a region clear out of the track of vessels, being in long. 113.40 west—lat. 26.30 south. It is uninhabited, and surrounded by a reef of rocks, and exceedingly dangerous to approach by vessels.

We made a thorough examination of the machinery, and our fears were confirmed. While the air ship is intact in every part save one, that one is just beyond our power to repair. In a mechanical laboratory this article could be replaced in a couple of hours, but here, alas, we have not the necessary conditions.

"It is a trifle," said Torrence, "and I should have brought a duplicate, but it is a trifle which has quite undone us!"

His words were ominous; more so than I appreciated at first, but as time continues to pass without bringing relief, their real significance is forced upon me.

We have been here now for more than a year, having landed upon the 8th of August, 1894, while it is now the 20th of September, 1895. Fortunately our island is well supplied with fruits and fish, or we should be in even sadder plight than we are. It seems incredible that we should have traversed so great a portion of the earth's surface, and skimmed her interior from pole to pole, to find ourselves at last stranded upon this lonely shore, where the sight of a sail has never relieved the monotony of our solitude. It does indeed look as though Providence guarded the knowledge of our wonderful secret from the world at large, else why should we not have been permitted to carry it a little further.

I have written this record of our adventures, and shall now seal it up carefully in a cask and consign it to the waters when the wind blows off shore, in the hope that it will be carried out to the track of vessels, and picked up by some passing craft, and so be the means of bringing us aid, and of conveying the news of our wonderful discovery to the world.

All day the wind has been blowing hard off shore, and the time has come to start the cask upon its doubtful voyage. Everything is ready; and in less than an hour earth's greatest secret will be cast upon the waters. May it bring us relief.

TORRENCE ATTLEBRIDGE,
GURTHRIE ATTLEBRIDGE.

THE END.

SCIENCE FICTION

An Arno Press Collection

FICTION

About, Edmond. **The Man with the Broken Ear.** 1872

Allen, Grant. **The British Barbarians:** A Hill-Top Novel. 1895

Arnold, Edwin L. **Lieut. Gullivar Jones:** His Vacation. 1905

Ash, Fenton. **A Trip to Mars.** 1909

Aubrey, Frank. **A Queen of Atlantis.** 1899

Bargone, Charles (Claude Farrere, pseud.). **Useless Hands.** [1926]

Beale, Charles Willing. **The Secret of the Earth.** 1899

Bell, Eric Temple (John Taine, pseud.). **Before the Dawn.** 1934

Benson, Robert Hugh. **Lord of the World.** 1908

Beresford, J. D. **The Hampdenshire Wonder.** 1911

Bradshaw, William R. **The Goddess of Atvatabar.** 1892

Capek, Karel. **Krakatit.** 1925

Chambers, Robert W. **The Gay Rebellion.** 1913

Colomb, P. et al. **The Great War of 189—.** 1893

Cook, William Wallace. **Adrift in the Unknown.** n.d.

Cummings, Ray. **The Man Who Mastered Time.** 1929

[DeMille, James]. **A Strange Manuscript Found in a Copper Cylinder.** 1888

Dixon, Thomas. **The Fall of a Nation:** A Sequel to the Birth of a Nation. 1916

England, George Allan. **The Golden Blight.** 1916

Fawcett, E. Douglas. **Hartmann the Anarchist.** 1893

Flammarion, Camille. **Omega:** The Last Days of the World. 1894

Grant, Robert et al. **The King's Men:** A Tale of To-Morrow. 1884

Grautoff, Ferdinand Heinrich (Parabellum, pseud.). **Banzai!** 1909

Graves, C. L. and E. V. Lucas. **The War of the Wenuses.** 1898

Greer, Tom. **A Modern Daedalus.** [1887]

Griffith, George. **A Honeymoon in Space.** 1901
Grousset, Paschal (A. Laurie, pseud.). **The Conquest of the Moon.** 1894
Haggard, H. Rider. **When the World Shook.** 1919
Hernaman-Johnson, F. **The Polyphemes.** 1906
Hyne, C. J. Cutcliffe. **Empire of the World.** [1910]
In The Future. [1875]
Jane, Fred T. **The Violet Flame.** 1899
Jefferies, Richard. **After London; Or, Wild England.** 1885
Le Queux, William. **The Great White Queen.** [1896]
London, Jack. **The Scarlet Plague.** 1915
Mitchell, John Ames. **Drowsy.** 1917
Morris, Ralph. **The Life and Astonishing Adventures of John Daniel.** 1751
Newcomb, Simon. **His Wisdom The Defender:** A Story. 1900
Paine, Albert Bigelow. **The Great White Way.** 1901
Pendray, Edward (Gawain Edwards, pseud.). **The Earth-Tube.** 1929
Reginald, R. and Douglas Menville. **Ancestral Voices:** An Anthology of Early Science Fiction. 1974
Russell, W. Clark. **The Frozen Pirate.** 2 vols. in 1. 1887
Shiel, M. P. **The Lord of the Sea.** 1901
Symmes, John Cleaves (Captain Adam Seaborn, pseud.). **Symzonia.** 1820
Train, Arthur and Robert W. Wood. **The Man Who Rocked the Earth.** 1915
Waterloo, Stanley. **The Story of Ab:** A Tale of the Time of the Cave Man. 1903
White, Stewart E. and Samuel H. Adams. **The Mystery.** 1907
Wicks, Mark. **To Mars Via the Moon.** 1911
Wright, Sydney Fowler. **Deluge: A Romance** and **Dawn.** 2 vols. in 1. 1928/1929

SCIENCE FICTION

NON-FICTION
Including Bibliographies, Checklists and Literary Criticism

Aldiss, Brian and Harry Harrison. **SF Horizons.** 2 vols. in 1. 1964/1965

Amis, Kingsley. **New Maps of Hell.** 1960

Barnes, Myra. **Linguistics and Languages in Science Fiction-Fantasy.** 1974

Cockcroft, T. G. L. **Index to the Weird Fiction Magazines.** 2 vols. in 1 1962/1964

Cole, W. R. **A Checklist of Science-Fiction Anthologies.** 1964

Crawford, Joseph H. et al. **"333": A Bibliography of the Science-Fantasy Novel.** 1953

Day, Bradford M. **The Checklist of Fantastic Literature in Paperbound Books.** 1965

Day, Bradford M. **The Supplemental Checklist of Fantastic Literature.** 1963

Gove, Philip Babcock. **The Imaginary Voyage in Prose Fiction.** 1941

Green, Roger Lancelyn. **Into Other Worlds:** Space-Flight in Fiction, From Lucian to Lewis. 1958

Menville, Douglas. **A Historical and Critical Survey of the Science Fiction Film.** 1974

Reginald, R. **Contemporary Science Fiction Authors,** First Edition. 1970

Samuelson, David. **Visions of Tomorrow:** Six Journeys from Outer to Inner Space. 1974